Books by Kaitlyn Dunnett

KILT DEAD

SCONE COLD DEAD

A WEE CHRISTMAS HOMICIDE

THE CORPSE WORE TARTAN

SCOTCHED

BAGPIPES, BRIDES, AND HOMICIDES

VAMPIRES, BONES, AND TREACLE SCONES

Published by Kensington Publishing Corporation

BAGPIPES, BRIDES, AND HOMICIDES

KAITLYN DUNNETT

KENSINGTON BOOKS
www.kensingtonbooks.com

KENSINGTON BOOKS are published by

Kensington Publishing Corp.
119 West 40th Street
New York, NY 10018

All Kensington titles, imprints, and distributed lines are available at special quantity discounts for bulk purchases for sales promotion, premiums, fund-raising, educational or institutional use. Special book excerpts or customized printings can also be created to fit specific needs. For details, write or phone the office of the Kensington Special Sales Manager: Kensington Publishing Corp., 119 West 40th Street, New York, NY, 10018. Attn. Special Sales Department. Phone: 1-800-221-2647.

Kensington and the K logo Reg. U.S. Pat. & TM Off.

ISBN-13: 978-0-7582-7266-9
ISBN-10: 0-7582-7266-9
First Kensington Hardcover Printing: August 2012
First Kensington Mass Market Printing: July 2013

eISBN-13: 978-0-7582-8900-1
eISBN-10: 0-7582-8900-6
First Kensington Electronic Edition: August 2012

10 9 8 7 6 5 4 3 2 1

Printed in the United States of America

For Scotti Smith

who already knows that Henry Sinclair
discovered America

Chapter One

Liss MacCrimmon's mother's idea of "helping out in the shop" consisted of rearranging every bit of merchandise sold at Moosetookalook Scottish Emporium. True, Violet MacCrimmon dusted as she went, but the overall result was chaos. By the end of the first week of her parents' visit, Liss no longer knew where anything was. If an entire rack of ready-made kilts could disappear—she'd finally located it tucked away behind a large display case—Liss feared that the search for any of the hundreds of smaller Scottish-themed gift items she kept in stock might last hours, even days.

"Mother, please!" Liss exclaimed, fighting the urge to pull at her hair in the best cartoon-character tradition. "I know you're trying to be helpful, but I like that section of the shop the way it is."

"Nonsense," Vi said. "Nothing is ever so perfect that it can't be improved."

She disappeared behind one of the bookcases that gave the illusion of privacy to the shop's "cozy corner," an area furnished with two overstuffed chairs and a coffee table. There customers could make themselves comfortable while they examined Liss's offering of novels set in Scotland or featuring characters of Scottish descent and volumes of nonfiction with a Scottish theme. There were a few histories and biographies, but for the most part Liss stocked cookbooks, instruction manuals, and coffee table books full of pictures. The how-to books covered everything from dancing the highland fling to preparing your own haggis.

The lemony scent of furniture polish wafted across the showroom, making Liss's nose twitch even as her hackles rose. Vi MacCrimmon was accustomed to getting her own way. She'd only recently retired after teaching world history to junior high school students for thirty-five years. Nothing fazed her, least of all objections from her only child. There was no stopping her, short of seizing her bodily and shoving her out the door.

For a brief moment, Liss toyed with the idea of doing just that. Vi was five inches shorter than she was and proportionately petite. But Liss reassessed the idea as one of those comfortable, overstuffed, *heavy* chairs shot out from behind a bookcase and traveled a good two feet beyond. Vi kept her figure with ruthless workouts at a local gym. For a woman of fifty-eight, she was in great shape.

And you *are almost thirty years old,* Liss reminded herself, *not thirteen.* It was absurd to revert to the behavior of her childhood simply because her mother hadn't changed one iota in all the years they'd lived apart. Besides, there was something more important at stake here than the arrangement of displays in her place of business. Liss's parents had returned to Moosetookalook because she was about to get married. Unchecked, Vi's meddling wouldn't stop with the Emporium. She'd already talked her daughter into making major changes in the wedding plans. Liss had no doubt but that Vi had other "improvements" in mind.

Grimly determined to reclaim control of the situation, Liss marched across the shop and flattened her palms against the soft fabric of the easy chair. Putting her back into it, she shoved. A loud scraping sound made her wince and fear for the state of her hardwood floor, but she didn't stop until she'd returned the cumbersome piece of furniture to its original location.

Vi turned from one of the bookcases, a dust cloth in one hand and a spray bottle of furniture polish in the other. Her frown was a formidable weapon and she knew how to use it. Liss had to squash the impulse to back away, apologizing with every step. She held her ground, but it was a near thing.

Her mother's eyes were pale blue behind stylish glasses and her hair was still the same dark brown as Liss's. At first glance, Vi looked a good ten years younger than she was. Liss reminded herself that Vi's hair needed help to stay that color. Then she looked closer, homing in on the lines inscribed in her mother's face. They were deeper than she remembered.

Liss faltered. Both her parents were getting older. One day, perhaps sooner than she expected, given that all four of her grandparents had all died before they reached the age of seventy, she wouldn't have her mother to complain about anymore.

Vi frowned. "Is something wrong, honey?"

"Sit down, Mom." Liss sank into the chair she'd just manhandled and pointed to the other. Giving direct orders rarely worked on either mothers or cats, but that had never stopped Liss from trying. This time, she lucked out.

Vi hesitated for a moment, then shrugged and sat.

She placed the polish and the dust rag on the coffee table with exaggerated care before she folded her hands in her lap. The pose put Liss in mind of the deceptively prim heroines of Regency romances. In common with those dauntless females, Vi attempted to appear demure but the expression in her eyes shattered the illusion.

Fixed on Liss, Vi's steely stare sent her daughter straight back into adolescence. It might be irrational, but Liss felt exactly as she had the time she'd been caught sneaking back into the house at three in the morning. She'd been fifteen and determined to attend the midnight showing of a movie her girlfriends had been raving about. All these years later, she couldn't remember the title of the film, but she'd never forget how devastated she'd been by her mother's disappointment in her.

She cleared her throat. "The shop looks lovely, Mom. It hasn't been this clean in months. But I don't want to change the cozy corner. It's always been kept just this way."

If there was one thing Vi MacCrimmon understood, it was tradition. Throughout Liss's childhood, Vi had been the one who'd drummed her Scottish heritage into her head, all the while encouraging her to take up traditional Scottish crafts and skills. Because of Vi, Liss had won prizes for dancing at Scottish festivals all over New England during her youth and had gone on, after two years of college, to pursue a career as a professional Scottish dancer.

The curious thing was that Vi didn't have a single drop of Scottish blood in her veins. When she'd become Mrs. Donald MacCrimmon, however, she'd wholeheartedly adopted her new husband's family background. She'd become more Scottish than any native-born Scot.

That was hardly surprising, Liss supposed. At the time of their marriage, he'd owned and operated Moose-tookalook Scottish Emporium in partnership with his sister. The store had been opened thirty years before that by Liss's grandparents.

"I was just trying to help." Vi sounded more reproachful than apologetic.

Liss read the subtext with the effortlessness of long practice. It was: *Do you kick puppies, too?* She squirmed in her chair. What was it with mothers and guilt? She felt like the worst kind of bully when all she'd done was ask Vi to cease and desist.

Stop rearranging my shop, she thought. *Stop trying to take over my life!*

Aloud, she said none of that. She kept her voice as soothing and conciliatory as she could manage. "I know you mean well, Mom. And I appreciate all you've done here. But you didn't come back to Maine to clean the cobwebs out of my shop. Look outside. It's a beautiful day. You and Dad should go for a drive. Maybe visit old friends."

"Well, I suppose there are one or two people I'd like to see," Vi mused, "and there are some wedding details that need attention."

Alarm bells sounded in Liss's head. Loud ones. "Everything is right on schedule, Mom. I've checked off nearly every item on all my to-do lists." Liss was a champion list maker.

"But you haven't taken care of the most important item. Here it is the end of May, with your wedding scheduled for the twenty-fifth of July, and you still haven't found a wedding dress." Vi leaned forward, her expression earnest and concerned. She took Liss's right hand in hers.

"I'm thinking about it." Put on the defensive, Liss felt her muscles tense. She willed herself to relax. This was *her* wedding. She had to stick to her guns.

"You said you liked my suggestion of a Renaissance-style gown." Vi gave Liss's hand a squeeze, then released it.

"I did. I do." Liss had the feeling that she was digging herself deeper into a pit with every word. Agreeing with her mother was always risky. "I just haven't decided which one I like best. I've narrowed it down to two choices, both pictured in that magazine you sent me." It had arrived in the mail shortly before Vi herself had turned up on Liss's doorstep.

"Well, then, I have the perfect solution. I know a wonderful seamstress who can *make* your dress. She can incorporate whatever elements you want."

There had to be a catch, Liss thought, but she couldn't find one. "That's a wonderful idea, Mom, but are you sure she'll be able to take on a commission like that on short notice?" Liss regularly dealt with kilt makers and they always needed eight to ten weeks to deliver the finished product. Her wedding was exactly eight weeks and one day away. That was cutting it very close.

"Oh, yes." Vi's face wore a smug smile. "I've already talked to Melly about it on the phone. That's her name: Melly Baynard. If you really like the idea, I'll drive down to Three Cities this afternoon and discuss the dress with her face to face."

Three Cities, actually only one city, wasn't very far away, perhaps an hour and a half by car, but Vi sounded much too willing to take on the chore. "Maybe I should be the one to go talk to her," Liss suggested.

"Oh, I don't mind. It's been years since I've seen Melly. We went to college together. Back in the dark ages," Vi added with a self-deprecating chuckle. "I've been dying to spend some time with her and catch up on what she's been doing. The only things I know for certain are that she's currently the wardrobe mistress and costume designer for the theater department at our old alma mater, and that, since it's summer semester now, she isn't as busy as she would be during the school year."

Translated, that meant Liss's mother had *already* made arrangements for Melly Baynard to make the wedding gown. Liss's first instinct was to balk at the idea. Then she remembered that old adage about not cutting off your nose to spite your face. She didn't have a better idea, and in her mind's eye she could envision the perfect dress. Her mother was right. It needed to be custom made.

Decision reached, she stood. "Okay, Mom. Go talk to her. I'll give you the pictures from the magazine and write notes right on the pages to make sure there's no confusion about what I like and don't like."

That, she reasoned, would keep her mother's contributions to the design at a minimum. It was too much to hope that she'd entirely keep her fingers out of the dress pie.

Beaming, Vi bounded up from her chair and leaned across the coffee table to give Liss a quick hug. For a moment, Liss was engulfed in the scent of violets, Vi's signature perfume. A peck on the cheek followed.

"This is all that's wonderful, darling. I promise that you won't be sorry."

As she watched Vi waltz out of the Emporium, humming cheerfully to herself, Liss wasn't so sure about that.

* * *

Ten days later, Liss had almost all of the contents of Moosetookalook Scottish Emporium back where they belonged. The pieces of her life were another matter.

She got up early on that Tuesday morning, slipped into workout clothes, and trotted three doors down the street to a newly opened business called Dance Central. Before she got started on the exercise program that had once been a daily part of her routine, she executed a spin and a few moves from a Scottish step-dance in front of the floor-to-ceiling mirrors.

The reflective surface extended the length of one wall and gave her a clear view of every flaw in her out-of-practice performance. The body in the skintight, long-sleeved black leotard was still good—five-feet nine-inches tall, lithe, and slender, if a few pounds heavier than it had been during her pro career—but the knees would never be the same. The long scar across one showed plainly in the glass.

Liss shifted her focus upward, meeting blue green eyes framed by pale skin and shoulder-length dark brown hair. She made a face at her reflection and turned her back on it. The rosin she'd stepped in with her dance shoes, to prevent sliding on the wooden floor, made a faint whooshing noise as she walked.

Sandy and Zara Kalishnakof, old and dear friends from the days when she'd made her living as part of a Scottish dance troupe, had moved to Liss's hometown, Moosetookalook, Maine, after the company disbanded. They'd bought a building on the town square, settled into the upstairs apartment for living quarters, and turned the storefront into a dance studio. The first classes had begun just a bit more than a week earlier, on the first day of June.

Sandy and Zara gave lessons to both children and adults in a variety of disciplines, everything from ballet to competitive ballroom to break dancing. All the offerings had attracted a satisfying number of pupils. It had helped that there were no other dance teachers nearby. And that dance competitions had recently become so popular on TV.

Even before Dance Central officially opened, Zara had been urging Liss to join her private workouts, both for the exercise and for the companionship. Liss hoped to make it a habit, but so far she'd been lucky to manage three days out of seven.

"So how are the wedding plans coming?" Zara asked.

"The idea of eloping is starting to sound better and better," Liss said as she headed for the barre set into the wall opposite the mirrors.

"Wedding jitters?" Zara was a slender, green-eyed redhead of the carrot-top variety. She sat on the floor, bent double over long legs encased in hot pink tights. They were stretched out straight in front of her. Since her forehead was now resting on her knees, her voice was muffled. "I had them right before Sandy and I tied the knot. But I'm glad we went through with our small family wedding. It wouldn't have been the same without his folks there."

"I could handle a small family wedding." Liss extended one of her own legs along the barre and bent at the waist, reaching for her toes.

It had been just over two years since her knee had given out on her during a performance, ending her career as a professional dancer at the age of twenty-seven. She'd regained her mobility but she'd never again be quite as agile as she'd once been. Her left leg would always be a little weaker than the right. If she tried to go back to dancing to earn a living, she'd have been like a football player who insisted on playing after he'd had a knee or ankle replaced.

Athletes who kept going too long paid a terrible price when they finally retired—more surgery and lots of pain. Liss hadn't seen the point in either when both could be avoided. She'd come back home, joined her Aunt Margaret in the family business, and settled down to start a new life.

She hadn't expected it to include love and marriage, although she had no complaints about that aspect of things. Her fiancé, Dan Ruskin, was just about perfect. What flaws he had, she could live with. Her only complaint was that actually *getting* married seemed to be so darned complicated!

At times, eloping *did* seem very appealing. Back in February, on Valentine's Day, their good friends Sherri Willett and Pete Campbell had done just that. Rather than cope with her divorced parents and his controlling mother, they'd taken Liss and Dan along for witnesses and gone to a local justice of the peace. The only other person invited to the ceremony had been Sherri's seven-year-old son, Adam.

"Why does planning a wedding have to be such a hassle?" Liss mumbled into her knee.

"Now, Liss—surely the worst hurdles are past. You're all set on the venue, right?"

Liss gave a short bark of laughter, switched legs, and resumed stretching. "Some venue! We're getting married at the Western Maine Highland Games instead of in a church because my mother decided it was fate that the date Dan and I picked and the weekend of the Scottish festival were the same."

"You *agreed,*" Zara reminded her.

"I had no idea what I was getting into. I was a little distracted at the time. And ever since my folks got here—*weeks* ahead of time—my mother has been slowly but surely taking over *every*thing. First it was the dress, then the cake. Now she's gotten it into her head that Dan and I should jump the broom!"

"It is a fine old Scottish tradition," Zara teased her.

Liss groaned. "I should never have let her talk me into a historical theme for the wedding in the first place. When she first suggested it, it sounded romantic, like something out of a fairy tale. I was always a sucker for Disney's *Cinderella* when I was a kid." She sighed. "Even after I realized that Mom had something more medieval in mind, I thought I'd be fine with it. The modern versions of the gowns are gorgeous, and I liked the idea of a circlet of flowers instead of a veil. But now—Mom doesn't just want the broom in the ceremony, she wants the sword *and* the anvil. It's too much."

Changing positions, Liss began a series of pliés.

"What Mom has in mind is a complete revamping of the wedding ceremony to include the medieval Scottish tradition of handfasting. Along with anvil, sword, and broom, it involves—literally!—tying the hands of the bride and groom together with silken cords or ribbons."

"I get the anvil," Zara said, "because in the old days a blacksmith could perform the wedding ceremony. And I know the bride and groom jumping over a broom is supposed to bring good luck to the marriage. But what's with the sword?"

"According to some sample ceremony Mom found online, the groom is supposed to drop to his knees and offer the wedding ring to the bride on the tip of his sword."

Zara giggled.

"Get your mind out of the gutter! The sword is supposed to symbolize his promise to protect her."

"A real sword?"

"A real sword. I'd be lucky not to cut off a fingertip trying to get the ring off the blade."

A bemused look on her face, Zara paused in her routine. "Then what? Do you put the ring on your finger yourself?"

"Oh, no. There's far more to it than that." Liss's pliés began to more closely resemble deep knee bends than a graceful ballet exercise. Just thinking about the details Vi had dropped on her ratcheted up her tension level. "The bride just holds on to the ring while she takes the sword. Then she makes like the queen of England conferring a knighthood. You know—touch the blade to the left shoulder, then the right shoulder, then the top of the head."

"I don't think the queen does the top of the head."

"Whatever!" Liss scowled as she realized she'd lost count of how many pliés she'd done. "Anyway, then the bride returns the sword to the groom and gives the ring back to him, too, so he can put it on her finger."

"Still on his knees?"

"Probably. Mom didn't say."

"How about his ring?"

"The bride presents it to him inside a chalice. The groom takes the ring out and hangs on to it while he pours wine into the chalice, which the bride is holding for him. Then he drinks a toast to her before he hands the chalice back to her. Then he returns the ring so she can put it on his finger."

"While balancing the chalice?"

"Apparently."

"Just a tad chauvinistic, don't you think?"

"That's the least of the reasons why I'm not doing it. Tradition is all well and good, and I'm sure some couples would find all the trappings of a medieval wedding romantic, but my Cinderella fantasy stopped at the dress. Besides—kneeling in front of me with a sword?

There's no way Dan would ever agree to that! I had trouble enough convincing him to wear a kilt."

Zara stifled another giggle. "Chill," she advised. "You'll work it out. Compromise with your mother. And don't worry about Dan. He's crazy in love with you. He'll go along with whatever you decide *you* want to do."

"On some things, sure. Like agreeing not to wear earplugs when the bagpiper plays." Dan was not a fan of Scottish music. "And he did manage to convince his brother to get with the program. Sam didn't think the best man should have to wear a kilt just because the groom was going to."

"What was Sam's problem?" Zara asked between stretches. "Bowlegged?"

Liss had to smile at that as she left the barre. "Trust me, *all* the Ruskin men have excellent legs."

She settled herself on the floor and began another series of bends from a sitting position. Zara was right, she admitted to herself after the first set. Dan had been more agreeable than she'd expected. She knew he'd have felt far more comfortable wearing a tux. She might have been persuaded to let him if he'd made an issue of it, but it was too late to change their minds now.

The kilts would arrive at the shop sometime this week. She hoped Dan would wear his a bit around the house, so he'd get used to the feel of it. It would help that the Black Watch tartan was very dignified. It had a nicely macho military connection, too, since the Black Watch was an infantry battalion in the British Army, a part of the Royal Regiment of Scotland.

Zara scooted closer and curled her legs beneath her, tailor-fashion. Liss envied her ease of motion. Once upon a time, she'd been able to move just as smoothly. Now her knee made an annoying crackling sound when she bent it at too much of an angle, and it started to ache if she stayed in one position for very long.

"You fuss too much, Liss. Everything is going to be just fine. And after the wedding, you and Dan will be married. Trust me when I say that makes it all worthwhile."

"Yeah, but I have to survive till then. I just hope Mom doesn't come up with any more inspired ideas."

For the rest of the exercise session, Liss made a concerted effort to shake off her gloomy mood and stop grumbling. By the time she returned home, in spite of the steady drizzle of rain that greeted her the minute she stepped outside Dance Central, she felt much more cheerful. A quick shower, another cup of coffee, and a few minutes of playing with her two cats, Lumpkin and Glenora, completed the cure. She was about to slip out the back way, cross the narrow strip of lawn and the driveway that separated her house from Moosetookalook Scottish Emporium, and enter the shop through the stockroom door when her mother burst into the kitchen.

"Everything is ruined!" Vi MacCrimmon wailed.

Liss stared at her in bewilderment. It wasn't like Vi to lose her composure. "What happened?" she asked, catching her mother by the arm and steering her toward the kitchen table.

Once there, Vi sat, propped her elbows on the placemat, and buried her head in her hands. "Disaster," she moaned.

"Mom!" Concern had Liss speaking more sharply than she'd intended. "Snap out of it. Tell me what's wrong."

Vi reared up, eyes flashing. "Those idiots at the fairgrounds have cancelled their contract with the highland games!"

Liss blinked at her in surprise. "Can they do that?"

"They *say* there's a conflict—some other group with

a prior claim to that weekend. Oh, what does it matter how or why? If there are no Western Maine Highland Games, then there is no Medieval Scottish Conclave, and if there is no Medieval Scottish Conclave, then your beautiful wedding will be *ruined*." Once again her voice rose to a wail.

"Oh."

" 'Oh'? Is that all you have to say?"

"It's not a disaster, Mom. Dan and I can always be married in the church." For her mother's sake, Liss tried to sound disappointed, but inside her head she started doing a happy dance.

"Absolutely not! I won't see all my plans ruined!" Vi got to her feet and starting pacing.

"Now, Mom, be reasonable. If the games are cancelled, what choice do we have?"

It was the wrong question to ask. Liss knew it the moment the words left her mouth.

A determined expression came into her mother's eyes. Her jaw hardened. She stiffened her backbone and squared her shoulders. Then she glanced at her watch. "You'd better be off to work, Liss. You don't want to be late opening the shop."

"There's no rush." That was the advantage of being her own boss. "What are you up to, Mom?"

"Nothing, dear. I just have some phone calls to make." Vi continued to pace, wearing a path in the floor from the table to the stove and back again. "I need to talk to Joe Ruskin. We'll have to make some changes in your wedding plans. What a pity you already mailed the invitations. We'll have to let everyone who's coming know there's a new location."

"I suppose so."

Liss wasn't particularly concerned about that aspect of things. The wedding was still weeks away and almost everyone who was coming could be reached by e-mail. What did trouble her was the determined look in her mother's eyes. She felt uneasy about leaving Vi to her own devices, but what choice did she have? She knew from past experience that nothing she said or did right now would slow down the force of nature that was her mother. She'd have to wait until Hurricane Vi blew herself out and then try to repair whatever damage she might have done.

Chapter Two

At a little past two o'clock that afternoon, through the plate glass front window of Moosetookalook Scottish Emporium, Liss watched Sherri Campbell cross the town square and head in her direction. The square was the center of their small village of just over a thousand souls. It was a pretty little park, even in the rain, and contained decorative trees and flower beds, a gazebo, a small playground, and paved walkways that wound through the whole of it. And, of course, as in most small Maine towns, there was also a memorial to the Civil War dead.

The houses that surrounded the square were uniformly faced with white clapboard and dated from the late nineteenth and early twentieth centuries. Most of them had businesses on the first floor and living quarters on the second. There was one structure, however, that had been built of red brick. The municipal building housed the town's office, firehouse, library, and police station. Sherri, Liss assumed, had just finished her six-to-two shift for the day. She'd changed from her pale blue Moosetookalook police uniform into khaki slacks and a loose sweatshirt. She hadn't bothered with an umbrella.

Abandoning a halfhearted effort to keep ahead of the dust bunnies that had accumulated since her mother's cleaning spree, Liss went behind the sales counter to put away the rag and the spray bottle. The bell over the door tinkled cheerfully as Sherri opened it and breezed in on a wave of humid air. She was a petite blonde who looked more like an ex-cheerleader than a serious officer of the law, but that appearance was deceiving.

"I can't stay long," she announced as she made her way past a rack of tartan skirts and the shelves that displayed imported Scottish foodstuffs—everything from canned haggis to shortbread. "I need to go home and rescue Adam from my mother."

Liss made a sympathetic noise. Compared to Ida Willett, Vi MacCrimmon was a joy to deal with. Ida had opinions about everything, especially child rearing, and she wasn't shy about letting her daughter in on them. Above all, she didn't think Sherri should continue to work now that she'd managed to snare a husband.

"What's up?" Liss asked.

"Have you talked to your mother lately?"

"Not since this morning. Why?" Liss felt behind her for the high, three-legged stool Dan had made for her. She had a feeling she should be sitting down for whatever Sherri had to tell her.

"Vi has been busy. From what Pete just told me, it's thanks to her that the Western Maine Highland Games have been saved."

"Seriously? She convinced the folks who run the fairgrounds to change their minds?"

That would be good news for all the competitors, including Sherri's husband, Pete. He regularly won prizes in the stone of strength and the hammer throw. A lot of people would have been disappointed if the games had been canceled—not just athletes, dancers, bagpipers, vendors and the like, but all the folks who came, year after year, to enjoy the annual celebration of their Scottish heritage.

"Not exactly," Sherri said. "She came up with an alternate venue. The organizers of the games have been invited to use the grounds at The Spruces."

Liss didn't know why she was surprised. It made perfect sense that Vi would try to persuade Joe Ruskin, Dan's father, to open the hotel grounds to the highland games and medieval conclave. Why not, she'd have argued, when The Spruces was already hosting Liss and Dan's wedding reception and providing lodging for both out-of-town wedding guests and tourists who planned to attend the games?

"Joe can use the windfall," Liss mused. Her future father-in-law had completely renovated the hotel, which was more than a century old. The Spruces had reopened the previous Fourth of July. Business was steadily improving, but Joe couldn't afford to turn his back on any chance to make a profit.

"The games do attract hordes of tourists," Sherri agreed, leaning her elbows on the counter, "but I'm not sure that's a good thing."

"Why not?"

"This year they added the Medieval Scottish Conclave to the mix."

"And?" Liss made a "hurry up and get to the point" motion with her hands. It had been the addition of the conclave, a loose organization that included such diverse elements as a reenactment group, a Celtic harpist, and a falconer, that had inspired Vi MacCrimmon to suggest the historical theme for Liss's wedding.

"Because of the reenactment planned for the conclave," Sherri said. "At least three groups intended to picket the event. That's why the Carrabassett County Agricultural Society suddenly discovered that they'd double-booked the fairgrounds. They didn't want the hassle."

Liss nearly toppled off her perch. "Picket lines? What on earth is there to protest? And how could there have been demonstrations in the works without my hearing a word about it until now?"

Sherri sent her an incredulous look. "Maybe because you've been a tad preoccupied with wedding plans? Not to mention spending time with Dan and entertaining your parents." Vi and Mac MacCrimmon had turned up nearly two months earlier than expected to move into Liss's guest room for the duration.

"Okay. Point taken. But I still don't understand why anyone would object to a few women in long dresses and a knight or two."

"Apparently there's more to it than that. The SO was already getting worried and now that the whole shebang is moving to The Spruces, Moosetookalook PD gets to panic, especially since both Pete and I are in the wedding party and off duty that day." While Sherri worked for the local police department, Pete was a deputy with the Carrabassett County Sheriff's Office.

"*What* more? Details, Sherri. I'm not coming up with any logical reason for an organized protest."

"Okay, here's the thing. There's this guy named Palsgrave—he's a college professor—who is a leading light in the Medieval Scottish Conclave. He put a group together to reenact a battle that he claims took place between a bunch of early Scottish explorers and a band of Indians. The Indians apparently killed one of the Scots. Then the Scots massacred the entire tribe in retribution."

Liss was more confused than ever. She couldn't remember any battle between Scots and Indians. All the famous battles that sprang to mind had been between the Scots and the English, and the Scots had lost most of them. "So?"

Sherri held up one finger in preparation for enumerating which groups were ticked off. "A Native American organization is upset because they're being portrayed as bloodthirsty savages." A second finger joined the first. "Some folks who are descendants of this Scot—did I mention that Palsgrave claims he discovered America about a hundred years before Columbus?—they don't like the idea that Palsgrave holds their ancestor responsible for murdering innocent women and children. There's also an outfit called Columbus First. They're planning to picket because they don't want anyone else to get credit for finding this continent. And just now, when I was talking to Pete on the phone, he said he'd heard a rumor that some church group was also considering getting involved. I don't have a clue what has them riled up."

"Sheesh! Next you'll be telling me the Irish plan to demonstrate because Saint Brendan got here even earlier than Henry Sinclair."

Now it was Sherri's turn to look confused. "Sinclair? Like the hotel over in Waycross Springs?"

"Yes, and like the Scottish explorer you were just talking about. And that's pretty much everything I know of the story." Vi was the history buff in the family. Liss had never shared her mother's fascination with the past.

"Well," Sherri continued, "the upshot is that a lot of folks were threatening to raise a ruckus at the fairgrounds if Palsgrave's group did their reenactment thing at the highland games. When the powers that be in the agricultural society got wind of it, they wimped out. The

official story is that they discovered a scheduling conflict—that another group had contracted for the use of
the fairgrounds first. But it was really the threat of demonstrations that had them looking for a loophole in the
contract."

"I suppose suing the fairgrounds wouldn't settle anything fast enough to be of use," Liss said.

"You'd be lucky to get a court date this century."

"So now the games move to The Spruces and so do
the picket lines." She sighed. "I'll bet Mom didn't bother
to warn Joe about that little detail."

"Would it have made a difference?" Sherri asked.

"I honestly don't know, but I think I'd better find out."

Sherri glanced at her watch. "I've got to run. Do me a
favor and keep me in the loop."

"Sure," Liss promised.

Distracted by her own thoughts, she barely heard the
bell jangle when Sherri left the shop. She slid off the
stool and headed for the cozy corner. It took her only a
moment to find the book she was looking for. The trade
paperback bore the title *Pre-Columbian Scottish Explo-
ration and Settlement in the New World.* It had been
written by one A. Leon Palsgrave.

Margaret MacCrimmon Boyd, Liss's aunt, had insisted they order the book, Liss recalled, not only
because of the Scottish connection, but also because
Palsgrave was a Maine author. That had been shortly before Margaret sold her share of the Emporium to her
niece.

Liss glanced back at the shelf. They had ordered six
copies and hadn't sold a single one. A peek at the price
told her why. The book was absurdly expensive for a
paperback. She checked the copyright page next, expecting to find that it had been self-published. To her

surprise, it had been issued by a reputable university press.

The blurb on the cover confirmed Sherri's story. Palsgrave claimed that a Scot, Henry Sinclair, had reached North America in the 1390s, making landfall at various points along the northeast coast. Liss had heard mention of Sinclair before, but she had never been interested enough to delve into details of the story . . . until now.

She settled into one of the easy chairs. A quick peek at an author photo showed her a dark-eyed man with a shock of white hair and strong facial features. Then she began to read.

After she closed the shop that afternoon, Liss drove out to The Spruces. It didn't take long to get there. The hotel was only a couple of miles from the center of town. The trip would have been even shorter if the road hadn't twisted and turned and gone up and down enough hills to qualify as a roller coaster.

From below, villagers could look up and see the highest rooftops of The Spruces standing out against a scenic backdrop of tree-covered mountains. Up close, the hotel revealed itself as a gleaming white three-story building with octagonal towers at each corner. They rose to four stories while the central tower had five floors and was topped by a cupola. The present structure had first opened for business in 1910, although there had been a hotel in this location for some twenty years before that.

Liss parked in the staff lot but she didn't go inside right away. Instead she took a moment to enjoy the view. Even on an overcast day heavy with mist, it was impressive. The grounds contained a pretty gazebo at the center of the back lawn. It was the twin of the one in the town square. A blanket of green extended for more than the length of a football field, ending in a wooded area that stretched for a considerable distance before merging with civilization. Expanses of manicured lawn, unbroken save for the occasional flower bed, bench, or piece of decorative statuary, spread out from the other three sides of the hotel. Unquestionably, the grounds were more than adequate to accommodate the highland games.

But if space wasn't a problem, surely there were others. Aside from the threat of demonstrations, there was the damage heavy foot traffic would do to the grass. And what about those colorful flower beds, wooden benches, and bits of fanciful statuary that dotted the landscape? The thought of turning a large crowd of people loose in this pristine setting brought the words "bull" and "china shop" to mind.

Liss tried to visualize all the booths and stages that would have to be set up. Each one would leave its mark, no matter how careful the organizers were to fill in any holes made by tent poles, stakes, and the like. Some of the events, like tossing of the caber and the stone of strength, would also leave marks. The lawns at The Spruces would never be the same.

Liss shook her head and with the movement realized that the mist had turned back into a steady drizzle. It was past time she stopped procrastinating and went inside.

When she'd finger-combed the worst of the moisture from her hair, she made her way to Joe Ruskin's office. Unlike the rest of the hotel, which screamed luxury, he kept his work space plain and utilitarian. She found him sitting behind his desk and scowling at a computer screen.

"Got a minute?" she asked, poking her head into the small, cramped space. Besides the desk, there were several file cabinets and two visitors' chairs.

Like his son, Joe was over six feet tall with the kind of muscular build that came from hard physical labor. On Joe, Dan's sandy brown hair had acquired a hint of gray at the temples—very distinguished, Liss thought—and Joe's molasses-brown eyes and mobile lips were set off by a series of laugh lines.

Examine the father to see what the son will look like in forty years, Liss thought, smiling to herself. The smile faded when she remembered the corollary to that old saw: *check out the mother to see what the daughter will become*. Liss was certain she was *nothing* like her mother and she hoped she never would be.

"Problem?" Joe asked.

"Maybe." She sat, her hands twisted in her lap. "I hear my mother conned you into hosting the games."

He chuckled. "It didn't take much persuasion, Liss. I could see the advantages right away."

"I'm not sure she told you the whole story."

He leaned back in his chair, studying her through eyes disconcertingly like his son's. "She told me the one thing that matters—that she wants your wedding to be perfect. So do I."

"Joe, the ceremony isn't officially part of the Medieval Scottish Conclave. We were just going to use the site . . . for the ambiance," she added, quoting her mother with a self-conscious little smile.

"I get that, Liss. But it would be a shame to have to cancel the whole shebang. The Western Maine Highland Games have been held in Carrabassett County for decades. I just can't understand what the fairgrounds folks were thinking to make such a stupid mistake with the scheduling."

Liss drew in a deep breath. As she'd feared, her mother hadn't given Joe the whole story. In a rush, wanting to get it over with, she told him everything she'd learned from Sherri, along with what little more she'd been able to gather from other sources in the course of the last few hours. Then she threw in her observations about the kind of property damage that would inevitably occur, given the events the games included and the size of the crowd they'd draw.

"Even if the organizers do their best to clean up after themselves," she concluded, "you may be looking at more expenses than you bargained for."

"What is it you Scots say, Liss—*dinna fash yersel*?"

"Don't worry," Liss translated, and had to smile at his pronunciation. "Yes, but—"

"Believe me, I've taken all that into consideration. I admit I didn't know about the possibility of a picket line till you told me just now, but I've got the rest of it covered. The deal I made with the highland games people includes compensation for damages and extra funds for security. In addition, they've paid me a healthy fee up front for our use of the grounds."

She'd been right, Liss thought. Joe had needed the cash. "What about the media? Demonstrations will undoubtedly have the news vultures circling."

He shrugged off her concern. "That will be annoying, as the protests will be, but this is private property. We can keep both picketers and the press off the grounds. And on the plus side, any television coverage should show The Spruces in the background of every shot. That's free publicity, Liss. Can't beat that."

"It will come at a cost."

"A negligible one. Look on the bright side—this change in venue will be good for the other businesses in Moosetookalook, too. The Emporium should do especially well, what with all the fans of things Scottish in town."

"Except that the store won't be open."

Moosetookalook Scottish Emporium was always closed during the highland games. They had a booth at the fairgrounds instead. Although it was always profitable, this year she'd planned to give it a pass. After all, she was getting married on the Saturday of the games and would be on her way to Scotland on the Sunday. Her mother had talked her into changing her mind.

Liss frowned. The current agenda called for hiring a couple of people to man the booth on Saturday, then turning it over to Vi and Mac on Sunday. Liss had duly recruited two employees of The Spruces for the Saturday shift. Now, they'd be needed for their day jobs. She wouldn't feel right depriving Joe of their services. He didn't have a huge staff to begin with. Usually family members filled in as needed, but on Saturday they'd all be involved with the wedding.

"I'm glad you're all right with this," she told Joe as she stood, "but just thinking about the logistics is giving me a headache."

"Then leave that end of things to me and your Aunt Margaret," he suggested.

Liss readily agreed. These days, Margaret MacCrimmon Boyd was events coordinator at The Spruces and she was very good at her job.

"And to your mother, of course," Joe added. "You can bet I jumped at the offer when Vi volunteered to serve as our liaison with the organizers of the games."

* * *

By the time Liss got home, her mother already had an early supper prepared. Over the meal, Liss broached the subject of the change in venue. Before she could say more than a few words, her mother rushed into speech.

"Don't you worry about a thing," she said. "It's all under control."

"Even the demonstrators? You didn't mention them to Joe."

"She didn't mention *any* of this to me," her father said. "Fill me in."

Liss's father looked like exactly what he was, a sixty-three-year-old successful businessman, now retired. He had a full head of salt-and-pepper hair and eyes the same blue green Liss had inherited. Early-onset osteo-arthritis had prompted him to move to Arizona twelve years earlier, but he was still able to play the bagpipes. As Liss explained about Professor Palsgrave's theory, the reenactment, and the various reasons people objected, the ready smile that was a big part of his personality flattened into a grim line.

"Violet, what have you done?"

Liss glanced at her mother. Vi was the picture of innocence. "I have saved your daughter's wedding."

"Don't you think you and I should have discussed the situation before you suckered Joe into offering the hotel?" he asked.

"There was no time to waste." Vi bent to lift Lumpkin, Liss's oversized yellow Maine coon cat, into her lap. Lumpkin immediately stretched out a paw, attempting to snag a sliver of leftover chicken.

"The wedding is still several weeks away. A couple of hours wouldn't have made any difference."

Liss didn't understand why her father was so upset.

She wondered if it was the rain that was making him so grumpy. Dampness did make his arthritic joints ache. That had to be it, she decided. Unfortunately, the weather did not explain the thundercloud over her mother's head.

"Stick to meddling in our daughter's wedding," Mac said, "if you *have* to interfere in something."

"Oh, for heaven's sake!" Vi shot to her feet, dislodging Lumpkin. In retaliation, he tried to bite her foot. Vi was too quick for him. She was already halfway across the room. "This *all* has to do with Liss's big day. I don't want it to be spoiled by *any*thing. Not picket lines. Not—"

"Neither do I." Liss's father reached down to stroke Glenora, the small black cat busily stropping his ankles in the hope of cadging some of the chicken for herself. "That being the case, perhaps Joe should ask the nutty professor to cancel his part of the program."

"If Dr. Palsgrave wouldn't back down so the games could stay at the fairgrounds," Vi said, "he won't pull out now."

"It couldn't hurt to ask," Liss interjected. This whole debate was making her uneasy. She wasn't accustomed to hearing her parents quarrel. Ordinarily, they got along extremely well. Her father simply agreed to go along with whatever her mother wanted. She fixed Vi with a pointed stare. "Since Joe tells me you're the contact person, you should be the one to talk to him."

From the doorway, where she stood poised for a dramatic exit, Vi expelled a theatrical sigh. "If you insist. I'll set up a meeting."

"Take my sister with you," Mac suggested in a disgruntled tone of voice. The expression on his face was grim. "Better yet, deal with Palsgrave in a phone call and save yourself the long drive."

Vi didn't answer. She just flounced off down the hall.

Liss turned to her father. "What's going on?"

"Nothing you need to worry about, sweetheart." He glanced at his watch. "Weren't you going to go over to Dan's this evening?"

Literally throwing her hands in the air, Liss left.

Plucking a whoopie pie out of the bakery bag she'd brought with her, Liss settled in beside Dan on the sofa in his living room. Her fiancé sent a tired smile her way and slung an arm around her shoulders. She knew he'd barely had time to take a shower and grab a sandwich before she arrived, even with the detour she'd made to Patsy's Coffee House to pick up dessert.

Dan had been working long days in the family construction business, hoping to finish up several ongoing projects before their wedding so that he could take three weeks off for their honeymoon with a clear conscience. In spite of today's rain, he'd put in ten hours straight.

Liss fed him a bite of the rich snack, smiling as some of the marshmallow fluff filling oozed out from between layers of chocolate to end up just under his nose. "White mustache," she whispered as she wiped it away, then licked her fingers clean.

"Mmmm," he agreed.

She peered into his dark brown eyes, expecting to see a spark, but he was too worn out to muster up a smile, let alone a smoldering look. She poked him in the ribs. "Stay awake. I need to give you an update on our wedding."

"I'm fine with whatever you want," he mumbled sleepily.

Eyelids at half mast, Dan rested his head against the

back of the sofa. Liss suspected he would drift off at any moment. She talked fast, filling him in on the day's developments.

He surprised her by speaking when she finally ran down. "Do I still have to wear a kilt?"

"Yes."

"Still bagpipes?"

"Yup."

"So, the only change is that we're going to exchange our vows at the hotel instead of at the fairgrounds, right?"

It sounded much less complicated when he put it that way. "Right."

"Sounds good to me."

Liss had to wonder if he'd missed the part about the picket lines, but she decided not to ask. "I was thinking we could hold the ceremony in the gazebo."

"Works for me." He yawned hugely. "Are we done with wedding talk?"

"I guess so."

"Want to fool around?"

She laughed. "I might, if I thought you could stay awake long enough. As it is, I think you should toddle off to bed—alone—before you fall asleep where you sit."

"I will be so glad when home is the same place for both of us." With another jaw-cracking yawn, he stumbled to his feet to walk her to the front door. His house was the next one beyond Dance Central. It would take Liss less than two minutes to get home.

"Soon," Liss promised when she'd given him a tender good night kiss.

"Definitely," he agreed. "Picket lines or no picket lines."

"So you were listening."

"Heard every word. But I also know something else. Come hell or high water, never mind picket lines, you and I start our life together as man and wife on the twenty-fifth of July."

Chapter Three

Liss's mother and her Aunt Margaret duly met with Professor Palsgrave. It was not a productive session. He refused to cancel the battle.

A few days after that meeting, the man Mac MacCrimmon had dubbed "the nutty professor" walked into Moosetookalook Scottish Emporium. He was better looking in person than in his author photo, a tall, white-haired gentleman with intense dark eyes, a prominent nose, clearly defined cheekbones, and a square jaw.

"Good morning," said A. Leon Palsgrave. He spoke in a cultured voice that had probably been wowing young female students for decades. Charisma oozed out of his smile.

Although Liss immediately understood the impact Palsgrave had on most people, she herself remained completely unaffected by it. She supposed being in love and about to get married gave her immunity to the charms of any man other than her fiancé.

"May I help you?" She had the fleeting thought that she ought to ask him to autograph the six copies of his book currently taking up space on her shelves. Then she decided that he didn't need the ego boost. Better to let him think she hadn't even recognized him.

"We are looking for Violet MacCrimmon."

Belatedly, Liss realized that Palsgrave hadn't been the only person to enter Moosetookalook Scottish Emporium. Two women had trailed in after him.

Physically, they could not have been more different from each other. The older of the two appeared to be in her midforties and if she topped the five-foot mark, Liss would have been surprised. Loose, bulky clothing made her look almost as round as she was tall. She had short, curly, ash-blond hair and eyes of such a bright blue that Liss suspected they were colored contact lenses.

The second woman was much younger than the first, making Liss think she might be a college student. She was also a walking contradiction. Her muddy brown hair, downcast eyes—Liss couldn't even tell what color they were—and poor posture were at odds with lush feminine curves displayed in tight jeans and a black T-shirt emblazoned in white with the slogan "Drink Coffee: Do Stupid Things Faster With More Energy."

Palsgrave did not introduce either of his companions. There was more than a trace of impatience in his voice when he addressed Liss the second time. "Do you know where we can find Violet MacCrimmon? It was my understanding that she lives in one of the houses on the town square."

Liss gestured in the proper direction. "You'll find her right next door."

"Excellent." The charm was back. "Thank you so much for your help."

Ignoring the wares Liss offered for sale, he headed straight for the exit, but the plump woman who'd come in with him, and who had been studying a display of

Celtic jewelry, stopped his retreat by the simple expedient of catching hold of his arm as he went past.

"This is beautiful stuff," she said, sending a sweet smile Liss's way. "You have good taste."

"Thank you. I—"

Palsgrave's irritated voice cut her off in midsentence. "We're in a hurry, Caroline. You can shop later."

Caroline's expression hardened. "This store specializes in Scottish items," she said with tightly leashed annoyance. "We're interested in publicizing the Medieval Scottish Conclave. I'd call that a match made in heaven."

Palsgrave continued to look peeved, but he studied his surroundings with more care. Survey complete, he addressed his colleague in a more conciliatory manner. "What did you have in mind?"

Caroline turned to Liss and produced a card that identified her as Caroline Halladay, professor of medieval studies at the same small, private college where Palsgrave taught history. "Would you be willing to put a display in your front window to help us publicize the Medieval Scottish Conclave?"

"What kind of display?" Liss was wary of committing herself. On the other hand, good public relations with members of the conclave might translate into more sales at the Emporium's booth at the highland games.

"Well, since we're doing a reenactment of a medieval battle, I envision an assortment of reproduction weapons— a hand-and-a-half broadsword, a claymore, perhaps a dirk."

"Weapons?" Liss let the other woman hear the reluctance in her voice. "I don't really think that—"

"Why not? You have an assortment of skean dhus in your display case. They're weapons, too, even if they are small. If you're willing to sell them, you can hardly object to simply displaying others."

There wasn't much Liss could object to in that statement. She knew firsthand how deadly the decorative little knives she carried could be. She searched for an alternate reason to refuse the request. "These reproduction weapons—aren't they valuable?"

"Not particularly. I'd guess they cost no more than two hundred dollars apiece." She glanced at Palsgrave for confirmation and received his nod of agreement. "The whole collection probably wouldn't be valued at more than a thousand. I'm sure your insurance covers that much."

"You said these are reproductions. Are any of them sharp enough to cut someone, say, a curious customer who decides to pick one up for a closer look?"

"The blades come ready for an edge, but they aren't presharpened. Perfectly harmless." She shrugged. "Still, if it will calm your worries, I'm sure we can construct some sort of backdrop that will discourage patrons from reaching into the display window. If people can't get at the swords, they can't get hurt."

In spite of these reassurances, Liss was on the verge of rejecting the idea when her mother emerged without warning from the stockroom. It was instantly obvious to Liss that Vi had come in through the back door, and that she had been listening to the discussion for some time—certainly long enough to have a good idea of what was going on. With a breezy wave of greeting to the others, she joined Liss behind the sales counter and leaned over to whisper in her ear.

"It's an excellent idea, Liss. Don't blow it."

"Mother, I—"

She broke off as Vi reached across the counter to shake Caroline Halladay's hand and seal the deal. Further protest on Liss's part would have been much too little and far too late.

"When can you bring the swords?" Vi asked the professor.

Caroline glanced toward the other woman. "What is my schedule like tomorrow, Willa?"

"You have no morning appointments, Professor Halladay."

"Tomorrow, then," Caroline told Vi. "Before ten in the morning. The sooner the better for publicity purposes."

"Wonderful." Vi's approving smile was blindingly bright. "Now, if you three will accompany me next door, I have coffee and cookies waiting."

"This isn't a social call," Palsgrave snapped. "We're here on business."

"Don't worry. I'll be wearing my hotel liaison hat while we eat." Apparently unaffected by his surly attitude, a smiling Vi led all three representatives of the Medieval Scottish Conclave away, no doubt to try, once again, to talk them out of staging their reenactment.

"Well," Liss muttered to herself once the front door of the shop had closed behind them, "*that* was interesting."

The next day, Willa and Caroline came back with the weapons. Liss was fascinated in spite of herself by the enormous two-handed Scottish claymore. The blade alone was more than three feet long and looked as if it would be awkward to handle. It probably weighed a ton, too.

"How on earth did they lift one of those, let alone wield it in battle?" she asked.

Willa grinned at her, showing a mouthful of very white teeth. The contrast made the freckles across her sun-browned skin stand out. Her eyes, Liss saw, were the color of agates.

"I read somewhere that you'd have to be able to benchpress two hundred and fifty pounds before you could swing one, but just picking it up and running somebody through with it wouldn't be so hard." She suited action to words, pantomiming the skewering part. "It only weighs about four pounds," she added as she placed the sword in Liss's display window atop a bed of black velvet.

"You seem to know a lot about the subject. Are you a history major?"

"My star pupil," Caroline boasted, before Willa could answer for herself.

Willa flushed with pleasure at the praise. "My father says it's in the genes," she confided. "My great-great-grandmother was an archaeologist."

"Grand*mother*? She must have been among the earliest women in the field."

"She was. Back then women didn't even have the vote yet."

"We're here to work, not talk, Willa," Caroline interrupted when her assistant drew breath to expand on what was a decidedly nonmedieval topic. "Boast about your heritage on your own time. Right now we need to finish up here and hustle back if we're to reach Three Cities again in time for the start of battle practice."

Liss retreated and stayed out of their way until they'd finished arranging the contents of the window. An hour later, she stood on the sidewalk in front of the Emporium to study the result. She had to admit that Caroline and Willa had produced an eye-catching display. The swords gleamed in the sunlight. So did the hilt of one of the dirks. It was decorated with acrylic "jewels," much like the ones Dan used on the "magic wands" he made in his woodworking shop and sold in various gift shops around the state.

Another sword, this one double edged and used, according to Willa, for both thrusting and slashing, had a decorative "basket" hilt. There were three dirks and five swords in all. One of them, despite appearances, was so lightweight that even Liss would have been able to swing it one handed.

Off to one side, Caroline had placed a small, tasteful poster advertising the Medieval Scottish Conclave and the "reenactment of a famous battle" that would be staged at it. The final touch had been the curtain of black velvet she'd hung across the back. As promised, it was designed to discourage customers from handling the merchandise.

Unfortunately, it also restricted Liss's field of vision. From inside the store, she could no longer see the contents of her display window. And instead of having a pleasing view of almost the entire town square, now she would barely be able to catch a glimpse of the street beyond the plate glass. Through the narrow strip of window that did remain visible, all she could make out of anyone passing by was a disembodied head.

The next three weeks passed quickly and quietly. The Fourth of July came and went. On the sixth, Liss was pulled out of the stockroom, where she'd been filling online orders, by the repeated jangle of the bell over the front door of the shop, a signal that more than one customer had come in. By the time she emerged, two men were leaning over the velvet backdrop that hid the swords and the younger of the two was reaching into the display window.

"Please don't touch the swords!" she cried.

Both men, startled, turned to stare at her as she approached them. The younger one, who appeared to be in his early twenties, was built like a nose tackle, but any threat Liss might have felt because of his size vanished the moment she got a good look at his boyishly freckled face and shock of red hair. He'd withdrawn his arms from the display and now lifted one hand in a little wave of greeting. He thrust the other into the pocket of his baggy cutoffs.

The older man looked to be at least eighty. He was bald as a cue ball and his eyes had the bulgy look of someone with cataracts. In spite of his frail appearance, he was the one wearing a formidable scowl.

"Are you the proprietor?" he demanded, jabbing his cane in Liss's direction so forcefully that he teetered and had to steady himself by placing one hand against the nearest wall.

"I am. How may I help you?" She stopped several feet short of where the two men stood.

"You can remove that abomination from your window."

"One of the swords?"

"The swords are fine." He snorted and leaned a little more heavily on the cane. "Give credit where credit's due, they've included a hand-and-a-half broadsword just like the one punched into the rock at Westford. But you've got no call to promote blasphemy. Take down the poster."

"Blasphemy?" Liss repeated, taken aback by his word choice. "Isn't that a little strong?"

"Granddad worships his ancestors," the redheaded giant said in a surprisingly musical voice. The sound was accompanied by a rhythmic jingling—the keys in his pocket. "We're kin to the Westford Knight."

The old man gave a curt nod in Liss's direction. "Alistair Gunn at your service, miss. Descended from both the Gunn and Sinclair families."

Liss needed a moment to make sense of these statements. Her careful reading of Professor Palsgrave's book paid off as she recalled the essentials of the Henry Sinclair legend. According to the account allegedly left behind in the early fifteenth century by the admiral of Sinclair's fleet of ships, a man named Antonio Zeno, Sinclair had followed directions he'd acquired from a fisherman who'd been shipwrecked on the North American continent years before. The Scottish nobleman, who also held a title from the kingdom of Norway, had eventually made landfall in present day Nova Scotia. Sinclair had sent Admiral Zeno back to Scotland but had himself wintered in the New World. In the spring, he'd sailed south, ending up in what later became Westford, Massachusetts. There, it was said, one of his knights, a member of the Gunn family, had died. The cause of death was unknown. Had he been killed by hostile Indians? Or had it been a disease or an accident that had taken his life? No one really knew.

The so-called "Westford Knight" was a shape inscribed on a rock ledge, supposedly created by Gunn's comrades as a memorial. There was certainly *something* there, but whether it was the result of natural weathering, or the shape of a hand-and-a-half broadsword, or the entire figure of a medieval knight in effigy depended on which "expert" was giving an opinion.

Liss moved a little closer to the two men by the window. "I'm Liss MacCrimmon. I gave the Medieval Scottish Conclave permission to put up that display. I'm sorry if you find the poster offensive, but it stays where it is." The whole point had been to publicize the event. Without the sign, all she'd have left would be a collection of medieval weaponry.

"Henry Sinclair no more slaughtered innocent savages than I did."

The old man's harsh tone of voice and belligerent stance halted Liss's forward progress, although she told herself she wasn't afraid of him. In spite of the cane, she doubted he posed any physical threat to her, not at his age. But she had a hunch that he was an old pro at skewering his opponents with words. Given a choice, she'd prefer not to cross verbal swords with him.

She held both hands up in front of her, palms out. "I don't want to get into an argument on that score or any other, but this display simply promotes activities at the upcoming highland games."

"No one can remain neutral," Gunn stated.

His grandson rolled his eyes. "Come on, Granddad. You asked the lady to remove the sign and she turned you down. That's the end of it. Time to go home."

Liss sent a grateful smile the young man's way.

"You haven't heard the last of this," Gunn muttered as his grandson led him out of the Emporium. "I can walk by myself, Gabe! I'm not so feeble that I need your arm to lean on!"

Liss breathed a sigh of relief as she went back to the stockroom. Then she grinned, suddenly picturing an army of little old men carrying picket signs. If Alistair Gunn was typical of those who were protesting Dr. Palsgrave's reenactment, then at least the highland games wouldn't need to worry about the demonstrations turning violent.

On Thursday, July 9, sixteen days before her wedding, Liss closed the Emporium and drove to Three Cities for the final fitting of her wedding gown. Sherri, Zara, and Vi rode with her, the first two because Melly

Baynard had ended up making their dresses, too, and Vi because there was no way to avoid taking her along.

Melly had a small house on a narrow side street but the room she used for dressmaking was large and sunlit. She had Liss out of her street clothes, into her gown, and up on a stool within five minutes of their arrival.

Ordered to stand still with her arms out to her sides, Liss felt a sense of unreality creep over her. She was completely surrounded by wedding paraphernalia. An assortment of wreaths and circlets had been spread out on a worktable. Clear plastic boxes contained bits and bobs of lace, ornate buttons, faux jewels, and other decorative accessories. Even the chairs had become display racks for ribbons and silk cords in various colors. Her eyes narrowed when she realized why they were there. Obviously Vi had not yet given up on the idea of a handfasting ceremony.

Light, feminine fragrances teased the air, from Vi's familiar Eau de Violets to the mild and pleasing scent originating from a vase filled with roses. In the background, an air conditioner hummed quietly, barely audible over the rise and fall of female voices.

The only one not talking was Melly Baynard, aside from the occasional command to stop squirming, mumbled around a half dozen or so straight pins held between pursed lips. It amazed Liss that she was able to say anything without accidentally pricking herself or, worse, swallowing one of the pins whole.

Equally amazing was Melly's genius with a needle. The gown she'd made for Liss was exquisite. The long, fitted sleeves were "slashed and puffed" at the shoulders in the best Renaissance tradition. The bodice hugged Liss's bosom and the neckline had metallic lace trim designed to match the elaborate "girdle"—really a decorated fabric belt shaped to a V in the front—that separated it from a beautifully draped, floor-length skirt. Liss did not plan to wear any jewelry, only the wreath of flowers, and she'd leave her hair loose beneath it.

"Stop squirming," Melly mumbled again.

Although the dress already looked flawless to Liss, Melly was a perfectionist. She'd been tugging and tucking, pulling and pinning, for a good quarter hour. Liss tried to hold herself rigid and tamp down on her impatience to see the final result. She was no stranger to fittings for costumes, having been a performer for so many years, but this felt different. This time it wasn't make-believe.

The awe in Sherri's voice echoed Liss's sentiments. "This is so gorgeous!" The petite blonde turned this way and that in front of a three-sided mirror, admiring her matron-of-honor gown. It was similar in style to the one Liss wore, minus the trim, and had been made of cotton velveteen rather than silk. The color, a muted shade of dusky rose, was perfect for Sherri's fair coloring.

"Pete's going to be speechless when he sees you," Liss predicted. Although Dan's brother, Sam, was his best man, Sherri's husband was also in the wedding party.

"You know," Vi said, "we still have time to have authentic medieval clothing made for the groom and groomsmen. Black Watch kilts are all well and good but that tartan didn't exist in medieval times."

"And, of course, what I'm wearing is *so* authentic," Liss said under her breath.

In spite of her general lack of interest in history, she knew a bit about historical costumes. Her old dance troupe, Strathspey, had regularly performed pieces set in Scotland's past. A middle-class, medieval bride would have worn plain brown wool to her wedding, perhaps accessorized with a ploddan cloak—one woven in three colors in a checkerwork pattern.

"Give it up, Mom," she said in a slightly louder voice. "It was hard enough getting Dan and Sam to agree to wear modern kilts."

She heard a muffled snort from Zara's direction and turned that way. Her second bridal attendant wore the same gown Sherri did, only in moss green.

"Like it?" Zara asked, fluffing her bright red hair.

"Wonderful. Now remind Mom what men wore in the good old days." Zara hadn't been with Strathspey as many years as Liss had, but she was just as familiar with the costuming.

"Scottish dress for a man during the Middle Ages and until as late as the mid-sixteenth century," Zara said, taking the stock pose of an actor declaiming lines, "consisted of a *léine*, a full, pleated, saffron-yellow linen shirt that hangs to the knees; an *ionar*, or short red jacket worn over the shirt; and a *breacán brat*, which is a long rectangular piece of striped wool—purple and blue in the example I know of—flung atop the jacket like a cloak and fastened with a large brooch at the shoulder. The gentleman's legs and feet were, invariably, bare, which was why the English called Scots warriors 'redshanks.' And, of course, to make the outfit complete, a man wore a gigantic broadsword slung across his chest."

"It wouldn't kill you to try for a tiny bit more medieval flavor." Vi sounded sulky.

Liss ignored her. Zara's recitation hadn't hurt her mother's feelings. Violet MacCrimmon had skin as thick as an armadillo. She was also unrelenting when she lobbied for something she wanted.

"You're missing a golden opportunity to make your big day unique and memorable. Handfasting is a beautiful ceremony, no matter what that Brownie says."

Liss closed her eyes and prayed for fortitude. "You talked about this to Reverend Browne?"

"Well, of course I did." Vi picked up a pair of scarlet ribbons and idly wound them around her own wrists. "I've known Brownie for years. Your father and I attended his church when we lived in Moosetookalook. I honestly thought he'd be more reasonable about the whole thing, especially since he'd already agreed to perform the ceremony at the highland games. That just goes to show how closed-minded some people can be."

"Doesn't it just," Liss muttered. "What, exactly, did you say to him?"

"I told him you'd like to substitute a handfasting ceremony for the traditional wedding vows."

"And he said? Ouch!" The yelp was involuntary. One of Melly's straight pins had stabbed her.

"I told you to stay still," the seamstress mumbled, and tugged one last fold of cloth into place.

"Brownie said it was a pagan rite and he wanted no part of it. Foolish man." Vi let the ribbons fall back onto the seat of the chair. "What's the difference, I asked him, whether you use the time-honored words of the hand-fasting ceremony or let the bride and groom write their own vows?"

Liss's gaze remained fixed on the discarded ribbons and the nearby silken cords. No, Vi hadn't given up. And she still had time to dream up more embellishments. Next she might decide that having Liss arrive at the ceremony in a horse-drawn carriage was a good idea. Or maybe she'd propose that her daughter be carried to the altar in an ornately decorated litter balanced on the shoulders of a half dozen liveried servants. Liss wouldn't put either suggestion past her.

When the grandfather clock in the corner began to

strike twelve, Liss seized on the excuse to change the subject. "Turn on the television, will you, Mom? I'd like to catch the news at noon."

Vi looked disgruntled, but she complied with Liss's request. She was a bit of a news junkie herself. She wandered back to the display of ribbons and cords while the first two stories ran. Neither was of earth-shaking importance, but they served Liss's purpose. Slowly, she began to relax.

"And now we have a breaking news story to report," the anchorwoman said in the super-serious tone that usually meant a fire, a shooting, or a five-car pileup. "Details are still sketchy, but our sources at Three Cities Police Department tell us that a man has been found dead under suspicious circumstances. The state police have been called in to investigate."

Eyes narrowed, Sherri took a step closer to the screen. She looked every inch the police professional, even in her Renaissance gown. "If the local authorities have asked for help, you can bet the guy was murdered."

It was a pity someone had died, Liss thought, but at least the killing had not taken place in Carrabassett County. The victim wouldn't be anyone she knew, and thank goodness for that! She'd had enough contact with dead bodies during the past couple of years to last her a lifetime.

The scene on the television shifted to a reporter standing some distance from a large brick building. Crime scene tape fluttered in a light breeze and off to one side a uniformed officer was turning away a couple of gawkers.

"I'm here on the campus of Anisetab College," the reporter announced. "Behind me is Lincoln Hall, the classroom building where the body was found only a short time ago. No official identification has been made by police, pending notification of next of kin, but witnesses tell us the victim was the head of the history department here at Anisetab."

Liss felt Melly's hand clench on the fabric of the wedding gown. She looked down at the other woman in time to see pins scatter to the floor as Melly's lips went slack. The seamstress's skin had gone as colorless as ice.

At almost the same instant, Liss heard her mother gasp. Heedless of the ribbons she was crushing beneath her, Vi collapsed into the chair. Her hands began to shake so badly that she had to clasp them in her lap to keep them still. Her face was as ashen as Melly's.

"Oh, my God," Vi whispered. "Lee."

Chapter Four

Liss hopped down from her stool. Ignoring the pins poking into her side, she knelt beside her mother. "Mom? What is it? Do you know the man that reporter is talking about?"

"It has to be Lee," Vi whispered. She looked at Melly for confirmation.

"Has to be," Melly echoed. "He's the department head."

Like Liss, Melly Baynard had dropped to her knees, but she'd done so to collect the fallen straight pins. "Get up, Liss," she hissed as she retrieved them. "You're going to ruin your skirt."

"Oh! Your wedding dress!" Stricken, Vi tried to hurry her daughter to her feet by pushing at her elbows. "Stand up, for goodness' sake!"

Liss stood, but she kept her gaze on her mother.

"Come away from that window," Melly fussed, "unless you want to give the neighbors a free show." She started to unbutton the back of the gown.

"The sun's wrong." Liss moved, but slowly, still puzzling over Vi's reaction to the news story. "No one can see in."

Although she wasn't concerned about peeping Toms, she allowed herself to be herded back to the middle of the room. As soon as Melly had removed the wedding gown and carried it out of the room to be safely hung away, Liss stripped off her silky slip and snatched up the blouse and slacks she'd worn for the drive to Three Cities.

Something strange was going on here. Liss had never seen her mother so rattled. The signs of Vi's distress were unmistakable. Her chin trembled. Her eyes were unfocused and brimming with unshed tears.

Sherri came back into the room. Liss hadn't been aware that her friend had left, but now she saw that Sherri had changed out of the rose-colored gown. Apparently, she'd also made a phone call. She was just tucking her cell back into the pocket of her jeans.

"The dispatcher at Three Cities PD is a friend of mine from my days at the sheriff's department," Sherri announced. "She says there's no question about the identity of the victim. It was Alfred Leon Palsgrave."

Leon, Liss thought. But that wasn't the name her mother had whispered. She'd said *Lee*, as if she'd known the late Professor Palsgrave rather better than she'd let on. Liss brooded over the implications of that all the way through their farewells to Melly and their departure for home.

"So, was Lee Professor Palsgrave's nickname?" she asked her mother once they were in the car and on their way back to Moosetookalook.

"What? No." Vi's vehement denial had Liss clenching her hands on the wheel. "You must have misheard. And I'd hardly refer to the professor by his first name in any case."

"Mom." Liss injected a note of warning into her voice.

"Oh, all right!" Vi exclaimed, annoyed. "Dr. Palsgrave was my faculty advisor when I was a student at Anisetab College. But I hadn't seen him in years. Not until the other day when Margaret and I went to talk to him."

"To discuss the Medieval Scottish Conclave?"

"Yes. Oh, dear. I suppose this means the reenactment will have to be cancelled."

"No 'the show must go on'?" Zara asked, sotto voce, from the backseat.

Liss rolled her eyes but didn't make any of the sarcastic comments that sprang to mind.

"The participants are all amateurs," Vi said, taking Zara's remark seriously. "Many of them are students looking for a good grade. But Professor Palsgrave was the driving force behind the enterprise. Without him, it will likely fall apart."

Sherri spoke up. "I'd count that as a blessing. If there's no battle, then there won't be any picket lines, either. The demonstrators won't have anything to protest, and that will be one less thing for all of us to worry about on Liss's wedding day."

"One *should* always look for the bright side," Vi agreed, but her voice had a brittle edge to it that made Liss nervous.

Abruptly, Vi changed the subject, asking Sherri and Zara what they thought of their gowns. The conversation remained firmly fixed on wedding plans for the remainder of the drive.

Liss kept silent, her eyes on the road. Both hands clutched the wheel a bit too tightly, until a pins-and-needles sensation in her fingers forced her to loosen her grip. She couldn't stop thinking about her mother's odd behavior or the stricken expression on Vi's face when she'd first heard that it was Palsgrave who was dead. She *had* called him Lee. Liss was sure of it. So why had she been so anxious to deny it?

Her question was still unanswered at six that evening when she cut across the square to have supper with Dan. By then, in time for the early news broadcast, the police had admitted that the death was a homicide, although they still hadn't confirmed the victim's ID.

Liss had to admit that she was curious about what had happened to Professor Palsgrave. The man had made an impression on her. As she headed up Dan's driveway toward the separate building that housed his workshop, however, she cautioned herself to avoid any mention of the murder. If she told Dan about Vi's strange response to it, his knee-jerk reaction would be to warn her not to start snooping. That would be irritating, since she had no intention of doing so. Why would she? This time around, she had only the most casual connection to the case.

Dan didn't notice her at first. He was using his table sander to "carve" magic wands for the gift shop at The Spruces. Each one was made by gluing and pressing together strips of several varieties of wood, then shaping the result by taking away, as Dan put it, "anything that doesn't look like a wand." The results of this process, in various lengths—some curved, some straight, and some with acrylic "jewels" attached to their points—sold very well to tourists.

Although he worked full time for his family's firm, Ruskin Construction, Dan had slowly been making a name for himself as a custom woodworker. Just as the hotel was Joe's passion, creating beautiful things out of wood was Dan's. Eventually, he hoped to open a shop where he could sell the assortment of items he most enjoyed making—everything from jigsaw puzzle tables to decorative boxes to cradles.

One of the things on Liss's checklist for the evening was a discussion of which of their houses they were going to live in after the wedding. They'd been debating the issue for weeks now without coming to a decision. They had to pick one soon. The other house would then be converted into display rooms downstairs and a rental unit on the upper floor.

Dan glanced up from his work, spotted Liss, and turned off the machine. "What do you think?" he asked, holding up the wand.

"Yum," she said, but her gaze was on the rangy, six-foot-two craftsman, not the craft.

One of Dan's eyebrows quirked upward under her scrutiny and he laughed. "Stop looking at me like I'm a three-course meal. I'm trying to get a serious critique here. I haven't used this particular combination of woods before. This is cocobolo." He pointed to what appeared to be one of several different colored stripes running along the length of the quirkily curved wand. He identified each of the others in turn: "Butternut, black walnut, cherry-wood, and bird's-eye maple."

"Very pretty." Liss hoisted herself onto a high, three-legged stool similar to the one she had in the Emporium, except that Dan had made this one very early in his woodworking career. It teetered alarmingly every time she shifted position.

Dan set aside the magic wand, leaned back against one of the worktables, and folded his arms across his chest. "So? Any word on who killed the nutty professor?"

She shook her head. It figured Dan would have heard about the murder. He drove with the radio on in his truck and the story would have been headline news all afternoon. As for Palsgrave's ID, he'd undoubtedly talked to Pete Campbell, Sherri's deputy sheriff husband.

"Can we talk about something else? Anything else!"

"My pleasure." He offered a hand. "I vote for a discussion of houses. Come on. I've got stew bubbling in the slow cooker and I picked up a fresh loaf of garlic bread at Patsy's on my way home. We can debate while we eat."

"You make it sound as if we're deciding between roast beef and pork chops," Liss complained as they crossed the backyard and entered Dan's kitchen. The room was long and narrow and she could see all the way down the hallway to the front door. "We're talking about where we're going to live for the rest of our lives."

They had an embarrassment of riches when it came to houses. Liss had inherited the house next door to Moosetookalook Scottish Emporium shortly after returning to Maine. Dan had bought the one they were in now several years earlier. Both houses faced the town square. Both were old and gracious, spacious, and had been upgraded to be energy efficient. Liss was fond of her place, the first home she'd ever owned. But she had an attachment to Dan's house, as well. It was the one she'd grown up in. The previous owner had bought it from her parents when they'd left town to move to Arizona.

"I tried making a list," Liss admitted when they were settled in the dining room with steaming bowls of stew and crusty slices of buttered bread in front of them. "It didn't help."

When Dan held out a hand, she fished in her pocket for a folded piece of lined yellow paper and dropped it on his outstretched palm. She'd listed all the pros and cons she could think of. He read while they ate and was frowning when he set the page aside.

"It's a dead heat," he said.

"Unfortunately. Your place has three baths while

mine only has two, but I have that big bay window over-looking the town square." The former owner had en-joyed keeping a watchful eye on the activities of her neighbors.

"That window would work well for displaying my stock."

"But this house is more open downstairs—better for the flow of customer traffic." She gestured toward the living room. Instead of a door between the two rooms, there was a wide archway. Hidden pocket doors could be pulled closed, but almost never were.

"Your place could easily be gutted to achieve the same effect," Dan said. "And it's located on a side of the square that already has two storefronts."

Liss ate another forkful of her stew, chewed on a bite of bread, and pondered. Dan was right about that. Stu's Ski Shop was situated on the other side of the Empo-rium. This house, on the other hand, sat between Sandy and Zara's dance studio and the home of John Farley, an accountant. Farley only used one room of his residence for business. Based solely on location, it did make better sense to turn her house into a storefront and live in Dan's house.

"I have an upstairs balcony," she reminded him.

"And I'm sure whoever ends up renting the apartment we put in will be delighted with it. Especially if Sherri and Pete are our tenants."

"Do you know something I don't?"

"Not a thing. But the place they're in now, above the post office, is awfully small."

When Liss closed her eyes, she could clearly envision how the open area at the back of her house, combining kitchen and dinette, could be divided to provide an of-fice, storage space, and a much smaller kitchen to use as a break room. Then, once they opened up the walls between what was now her living room and her library, Dan would be left with a display area of excellent proportions for the products he created from wood.

"What about my books?" Liss asked, thinking of the hundreds of volumes now housed in the library/office off her living room. "I'm not getting rid of a single one."

He grinned at her. "Well, we could put them in one of the guest rooms upstairs . . . or we could convert the entire attic into your new library."

Her eyes went wide with surprise and delight. "What a perfect solution!"

"I thought so. Finish your supper and we'll go up and take some measurements."

He sounded entirely too smug. Liss attempted a scowl and discovered that her lips wouldn't cooperate. She ended up smiling, but she wasn't quite ready to let him off the hook.

"I can see where it's going to be very convenient to be married to a building contractor," she remarked as she speared the last chunk of stew meat in her bowl, "but I still have one problem with living here."

"Oh?"

"It will be *so* much farther for me to walk to work every morning. Instead of living right next door to the shop, I'll have to pass Dance Central, turn the corner, and go all the way past the ski shop to reach the Emporium. What if there's a snowstorm?" She batted her eyelashes at him in a deliberate caricature of the helpless female.

Dan knew perfectly well that she was teasing him, but he went along with the game. "In that case," he drawled, "I guess I'll have to take care of you, little lady. I'll drive you to work in bad weather. I've got chains on my truck, you know." He made that sound like a wonder of modern technology. Then his grin widened. "Or I could carry you from here to the Emporium—right through the middle of the town square."

"I'm too heavy!" she protested with a laugh.

"Want to bet?" Before she could even think of objecting, he'd swept her out of her chair and into his arms. They were both laughing like loons by the time he'd lugged her up two flights of stairs to the attic.

It was nearly midnight before Liss walked back across the square and let herself in to the foyer. She bent down to pet Lumpkin, who had appeared out of nowhere to bump his head against her leg. She froze in that position at the sound of shouting from above.

Voices drifted down from the second floor. The words were indistinguishable but the tone was clear. Her parents were arguing. The very idea shocked her. She could count on the fingers of one hand the number of times she'd heard them raise their voices to each other when she was growing up.

Liss moved quickly through the downstairs to the kitchen, away from the sounds of the quarrel. She set out cat food and refilled water dishes by rote, helped herself to a glass of water, and waited. She did not want to go upstairs to bed, not when her room was right next to the one her parents had occupied since May. Only a closet separated them and the walls were thin.

But she'd forgotten that the guest room was directly over the kitchen. When her mother's voice rose to a screech, Liss couldn't help but hear her words.

"What have you *done*?" Vi shouted.

"I haven't *done* anything!" Mac yelled back at her. "What do you take me for?"

An abrupt silence fell. Just like that, the quarrel was over.

Liss realized she'd been holding her breath. Slowly, she let it out. If her parents had more to say to each other, they were doing it very quietly.

She had a sudden vivid flash of memory. She'd been around eight and had thrown a temper tantrum over something or other. Vi had made a shushing noise and demanded, in an exasperated tone of voice, "Do you want the neighbors to hear?"

At that age, Liss could have cared less who overheard her outburst, but her mother had been appalled at the possibility they were airing their dirty laundry in public. Vi was a great believer in keeping private matters private. How extraordinary that she'd so far forgotten herself as to shout at her husband!

When five long minutes passed with no further outbursts, Liss decided that her mother was probably giving her father the silent treatment. She'd used that tactic a few times during Liss's youth, on both husband and daughter. Most of the time, though, 4 Birch Street had been a happy house.

Liss's parents had been devoted to each other and to her, their only child. She'd been pampered. No. To be honest, she'd been spoiled. And she'd been taken along, even as a baby, to the Scottish games and festivals her parents enjoyed so much. Mac had entered bagpipe competitions on a regular basis. Now and then, he'd even brought home a trophy or a ribbon.

When she'd graduated from high school, Liss's parents had made the decision to move to Arizona, where the climate was supposed to be kinder to arthritis sufferers. Liss had assumed they'd been happy there. Vi certainly hadn't had any difficulty finding another teaching job and Mac had done spectacularly well with his investments, beating the odds even in a difficult economy. The possibility that all had not been as well between them as she'd supposed left Liss feeling shaken and uncertain.

She stayed put for another ten minutes before finally leaving the kitchen and wending her way upstairs to her room. Every couple had disagreements, she told herself. She was making a mountain out of a molehill. But she was glad of it when both Lumpkin and Glenora joined her in the big bed. Since she didn't yet have a husband's arms to comfort and cosset her when she was troubled, the soothing effects of stroking two cats would have to suffice.

Liss was just about to leave the house for work the next morning when her doorbell rang. She frowned, glancing at the kitchen clock. Not many Moosetookalook people went visiting at this hour and those who did knew to come around to the back entrance. A few—Dan, Sherri, and Zara came to mind—would simply walk in through the unlocked kitchen door and call out her name after they stepped inside.

"Doorbell's ringing," her father said in a sleepy voice. He'd poured himself a mug of coffee and was trying to decide whether he felt like cooking breakfast or could make do with a bowl of cold cornflakes.

Feeling unaccountably nervous, Liss hurried out into the narrow hallway. It ran between the downstairs bath and a closet on her left and the side wall of the library on her right, coming to an abrupt end when it opened out to become part of Liss's living room. Straight ahead was the door leading to her small foyer, an enclosed space that served as a buffer against the cold outside on blustery winter days. The foyer had its own closet for heavy coats and boots and also gave access to the stairwell that led to the second floor of the house.

The man waiting on the front porch was not in uniform, but everything about him screamed "cop," from his sturdy build and short-cropped hair to his stone-faced expression. He held out a leather folder containing his badge and ID. Liss glanced at them only long enough to discern his rank.

"How can I help you, Detective?"

"Ms. MacCrimmon?"

"Yes. I'm Liss MacCrimmon." She remained in the doorway, blocking his entrance. In spite of the official-looking state police identification, he made her uneasy. She knew the officer responsible for this area. In fact, she'd dated him for a while. Where was Gordon Tandy? And who was this stranger? And what did he want?

"Is Donald MacCrimmon at home? I understand he's staying here for the summer."

The soft shuffle of a slipper-clad foot on the stair riser and a faint whiff of violets warned Liss that her mother was lurking just out of sight around the bend in the stair. It surprised her that Vi didn't reveal herself. Her mother sneaking around? The world was even more out of whack this morning than she'd supposed.

Liss hesitated a moment longer. She wanted to ask questions, but she knew from experience that a representative of the state police was not going to answer them. State cops collected information. They didn't share. Resigned, she opened the door wider and gestured for him to come in. "This way."

Her father had decided on cereal. He sat with his bowl, a glass of orange juice, and his oversized mug of coffee at the small, wooden, drop-leaf table Liss used for all her meals. Lumpkin and Glenora, feline expressions hopeful, had arranged themselves at his feet, ready to pounce on any morsel that happened to fall to the floor. They didn't budge when Liss returned to the kitchen, even though she'd brought a stranger with her.

Barefoot, clad in sweatpants and a T-shirt, his hair still tousled from sleep, Donald MacCrimmon appeared to be no more alarmed than the cats were. "Company so early?" he asked.

"Not exactly," Liss said.

The detective showed his badge again and introduced himself as Stanley Franklin.

"Call me Mac," Liss's father invited. "Everyone does. Folks call you Stan?" He dipped his spoon into the cornflakes, carried it to his mouth, and chewed as if he didn't have a care in the world.

"Let's stick to Detective Franklin for the present." He pulled out a chair for himself and sat.

"You go along to work, Liss," her father said. "I know what the detective here wants and it's nothing that needs to concern you." He made a shooing motion.

Franklin scooted his chair a little closer to the table and produced a small, spiral-bound notebook from the inside pocket of his suit jacket.

Normally, Liss would have exited through the back door, since it was closest to the entrance to the Emporium's stockroom. Instead, she retraced her steps into the hall and stopped as soon as she was out of sight of the table. She was still well within eavesdropping distance.

There was no reason why she should rush in to work. It wasn't likely she had customers lined up around the block. If, by some miracle, she did, then they'd just have to wait until she got there to let them in. Something strange was going on with her father. Something vaguely ominous. She didn't intend to leave the house until she knew exactly what it was.

Liss closed her eyes, the better to concentrate on the

low murmur of voices in the kitchen. She nearly jumped out of her skin when a hand reached out through the door of the tiny downstairs bathroom and pulled her inside.

"What does he want with your father?" Vi's fingers tightened painfully around Liss's forearm.

"He didn't say. What do *you* think he wants?"

Instead of answering, Vi released Liss and started toward the kitchen. Liss hauled her back into the minuscule space between sink and toilet.

"What is this about, Mom? You're starting to scare me."

With a violent jerk, Vi freed herself from Liss's grasp and bolted. Liss followed, entering the kitchen just in time to see Detective Franklin finish fingerprinting her father.

"What are you *doing*!" Vi screeched.

"Relax, Vi," Mac said. "It's just for purposes of elimination. Nothing to worry about." He stood and walked casually over to the sink to wash up. "Are we done now, Detective?"

"For the present." Franklin rose, nodded to Vi and Liss, and let himself out through the back door.

"Daddy? What's going on?"

"Nothing to worry your pretty little head about," Mac said. But he concentrated on scrubbing his fingertips and wouldn't meet her eyes.

Vi made an exasperated sound.

"Nothing," he repeated.

Vi looked from her husband to her daughter, threw her hands up in the air, and stormed out of the room. Her slippers made a loud flapping noise with every rapid step and when she passed through the foyer door, she slammed it behind her. Liss winced.

"Hadn't you better get to work?" Her father's voice sounded as mild and unconcerned as ever.

"Are you sure you don't want to tell me—?"

"I'm positive. Run along, sweet pea. And trust me—there's nothing for you to worry about."

Liss wasn't convinced, but she knew her father well enough to be sure he didn't intend to satisfy her curiosity. By the time she unlocked the back door to the Emporium, she was already toying with the idea of phoning Gordon Tandy and asking him for information. She decided against it only because she suspected Gordon would be just as stubborn as her father when it came to revealing anything useful. He'd get on his high horse and tell her it was police business and none of hers.

That was exactly what worried her—that the police had business with her father. Why on earth did the police want Donald MacCrimmon's fingerprints?

Liss tried to ignore the sense of impending doom that hung over her and concentrate on business as usual, but it wasn't easy. She had only one walk-in customer that morning, and there weren't many orders waiting to be filled from the online shop. At eleven, she put the BACK IN FIFTEEN MINUTES sign on the door, locked up, and walked over to the post office to collect her mail. That took all of five minutes.

Rather than go straight back to the Emporium, she circled the town square to Patsy's Coffee House and bought a fresh-baked sticky bun and a newspaper, selecting the one published in Three Cities rather than Portland, Lewiston, or Waterville. It wasn't her usual choice. She wasn't even consciously aware that she'd had a reason to pick that particular newspaper to read, not until she was back in the Emporium and looked below the fold.

A recent picture of Alfred Leon Palsgrave took up an eighth of the page. It was a good, clear photograph showing his head and shoulders. Liss skimmed the article on the murder that had taken place at Anisetab College the previous day.

"Huh," she said under her breath. Details were still sketchy. No murder weapon was mentioned. No cause of death. No suspect's name. It just stated that the police were "continuing their investigation" and that autopsy results were expected sometime in the next week.

Her mother's voice shouting "What have you *done*?" echoed in Liss's mind. It was quickly followed by an image of her father, head bowed and washing ink off his fingers.

You're leaping to conclusions, she warned herself. There was absolutely no reason to think either of her parents had any connection to Professor Palsgrave's murder.

Except that her mother had obviously known him well enough to call him Lee.

Liss tried to remember what she had been told about her parents in their younger days. They'd dated in high school and, after Vi graduated from college, they'd married. But what had happened during those four years away from Moosetookalook? With a snap, a pencil Liss hadn't realized she'd been fiddling with broke in two. She dropped the halves as if they'd burned her fingers.

She considered closing the store and going home. Instead she stayed behind the sales counter with the newspaper and reread every word of the article about the murder. It didn't tell her much that she didn't already know. The victim had been sixty-five, a tenured professor of history, and unmarried. His next of kin was apparently a sister in Cleveland. Sixty-five, she mused. That meant he'd been a very young professor at the time Vi was a student.

Liss booted up her laptop. Once online, she typed Palsgrave's name into the search engine. It wasn't difficult to find information on the late professor. The hard part was choosing what to read first. Two hours later, when Liss finally logged out, she had a splitting headache.

She'd found more than she'd bargained for. Way more. To say Palsgrave was controversial—within his small academic circle, at any rate—was putting it mildly. He'd had an excellent reputation as a scholar. That book he'd written, the one Liss stocked in the Emporium, had been the latest of several, although it was apparently the one that marked the beginning of his obsession with Henry Sinclair.

Other scholars believed Sinclair might have reached the shores of North America at the very end of the fourteenth century. They agreed that one of Sinclair's knights, a man named Gunn, had probably died near Westford, Massachusetts. The late professor, however, appeared to be unique in his interpretation of what had happened afterward. Palsgrave had been convinced that Sinclair massacred the "savages" who'd killed his friend—a brutal act of revenge. That was the event he'd intended to reenact at the Western Maine Highland Games.

Had he been murdered to stop the reenactment? The idea seemed far-fetched, but Liss knew from experience that violence could be triggered by the most trivial of motives.

The state police were looking into Palsgrave's death, she reminded herself. His murder was not her concern. With a firm hand, she closed the laptop . . . and let out a yelp when her mother burst into the shop.

The bell over the door jangled madly when Vi shoved it closed behind her. Her eyes were wild and her expression stricken.

"Mother, what's wrong?" Liss shot out from behind the counter, her stomach clenching in fear.

"The police are back." Vi's voice was anguished and so shrill it hurt Liss's ears. "They have a search warrant. They think your father killed Lee Palsgrave!"

Chapter Five

They weren't allowed inside the house.

With her mother, Liss stood on her own sidewalk, annoyed and frustrated, watching shadows move past her windows and wondering what on earth all those big, burly state troopers thought they were going to find.

A tug on her sleeve had her looking down to meet the curious gaze of her ten-year-old neighbor, Beth Hogencamp. "What's going on?" the girl asked.

"I wish I knew. Beth, honey, will you do me a big favor?" At her nod, Liss sent the girl to the police station in the municipal building. "If Sherri Campbell is there, tell her she's needed right away, okay?"

Beth's coltish legs ate up the distance as she shot across the town square, long, wavy brown hair streaming behind her like a banner. The daughter of the owner of Angie's Books, another downtown Moosetookalook business, Beth had started learning Scottish dances from Liss almost two years earlier and had more recently become Zara's star pupil.

Vi's attention remained fixed on Liss's front porch.

"This is ridiculous," she muttered. "They've no cause to tear your house apart."

"It isn't as if I own any priceless antiques. And I'm sure they're being very careful."

She lied. She wasn't certain of any such thing. She'd never had her possessions searched before, although she had once been obliged to clean up a mess in the Emporium—the result of fingerprint powder. She hoped she'd never have to repeat that experience.

"Are you sure they didn't say what they were looking for?" she asked her mother.

"You mean, is it bigger than a bread box?" Vi's sarcasm verged close to bitterness as she strode determinedly toward the porch, leaving Liss to stare after her in consternation.

Vi's entrance was blocked by a uniformed officer. Turned away at the door, she did not return to her daughter's side. Instead, she went back to the Emporium and sat down on the porch steps.

Sherri gave a low whistle as she came up beside Liss. "What's going on?"

"Darned if I know. Mom says Detective Franklin and his men showed up with a search warrant, but you know the state police. They never tell anyone anything."

Sherri, even in uniform, had no better luck than Vi had experienced. While Liss watched from her post on the grass just inside the town square, her friend was politely but firmly denied access. "He says I'll have to talk to Detective Franklin," Sherri reported, "but that Franklin is too busy to speak with me right now."

"I'll just bet he is. Probably going through my underwear drawer."

Sherri's eyebrows shot up.

"Sorry. I'm a little upset over this."

"No kidding. I would be, too. Any idea what they're looking for?"

"Well, at a guess, I'd say a murder weapon, but since they haven't released any information on how A. Leon Palsgrave was killed, I have no idea what that weapon might be."

"Hmmm," Sherri said, looking thoughtful.

"What have you heard?"

"Rumors." She shrugged. "Nothing worth repeating."

"But Palsgrave *was* murdered?"

"Oh, yes. The state police may not be talking, but the student who found the body was overheard when she came tearing out of Lincoln Hall. Apparently, there was blood all over the place."

"I guess he wasn't poisoned, then."

Sherri acknowledged the dark humor with a fleeting smile. "Could have been shot, bludgeoned, or stabbed, but what I heard suggests the murder weapon was a knife."

"I can't see it," Liss said.

"See what?"

"My father stabbing someone. Anyone, let alone a guy he didn't even know."

"Whoa. Start over. I think I missed a beat. What does your father have to do with this?"

"Franklin took his fingerprints this morning, the first time he was here. It doesn't take a genius to guess that he thinks my father had something to do with the murder."

"Are you saying that Mac was in the victim's classroom?"

"I don't know! Dad refused to talk about it."

"This is not good." Sherri sounded as worried as Liss felt.

Liss looked around for her mother and found Vi still

sitting on the steps. She had her elbows propped on her knees and her face buried in her hands. If Liss hadn't known Vi better, she'd have thought her mother was crying. That, of course, was impossible. Vi *never* cried.

"Don't look now," Sherri whispered, "but we're drawing a crowd."

Liss didn't have to turn to know that half the town was probably collecting on the square behind them. News spread fast in small, rural communities. That was a good thing in an emergency, when volunteers were needed to put out a fire or search for a missing child, but just this once Liss wished the grapevine wasn't quite so efficient.

Dan's sister Mary tapped Liss on the shoulder. She might have been visiting the playground section of the square with two-year-old Jason—it boasted a jungle gym, slide, swings, and a small merry-go-round—but Liss thought it more likely she'd gotten a phone call from someone and come out to investigate. Two-month-old Katie was strapped into a baby sling across Mary's chest.

"Are you okay?" Mary asked. "You aren't in any kind of trouble, are you?"

She shook her head. "Don't worry. There's no contraband on the premises."

"Is there anything I can do to help?" Mary's molasses brown eyes were so like Dan's that Liss nearly confided in her, but there was no point in burdening her future sister-in-law with her worries.

"I'm fine. Really. Everything will be . . . fine. They aren't going to find anything incriminating."

As if to prove the truth of her words, three state troopers filed out of her house, followed closely by Detective Stanley Franklin. They were all empty handed.

Liss's father appeared in the doorway behind them. She could see Mac clearly. He was not in handcuffs. She breathed a sigh of relief.

Then Detective Franklin crossed the sidewalk in front of the house and stopped beside Mac's car. "Search it," he ordered.

"Now wait just a minute," Liss objected. "This has gone far enough. You have no right to harass innocent people."

"What about the not-so-innocent?" Franklin's expression remained both bland and uncompromising.

"It's okay, Liss," her father called from the porch, just as she was about to go toe-to-toe with the detective. "I gave them permission to look in the car. I've got nothing to hide."

"It's the principle of the thing," Liss muttered.

Mac came slowly down the porch steps, careful to hold on to the railing—a sure sign his knees were bothering him. The smile he meant to reassure her with was a trifle shaky but quite genuine.

Behind her, she heard the trunk of her father's car creak open. Because her gaze remained on his face, she saw his eyes go wide with shock.

"What the—?"

By the time Liss turned, broad male backs blocked her view of the inside of the trunk. "What is it?" she hissed at her father. "What's in there?"

"It looked like—" He shook his head in disbelief. "No, it couldn't be."

"What?"

"A sword." His skin had turned a sickly shade of green. "Good God."

Vi materialized at her husband's side and grabbed hold of his arm. As she led him back to the Emporium and urged him to sit down before he fell down, Liss's gaze shifted to her display window. She wasn't really surprised by what she saw.

Or rather, by what she didn't see.

One of the reproduction weapons was missing. Where the hand-and-a-half broadsword had been, there was now only a long, empty stretch of black velvet cloth.

The state police evidence technicians took their time going over the display window. When they were done, Liss would have an unholy mess to clean up. Fingerprint powder stuck to everything.

"All that black velvet may as well go straight into the nearest trash bin," she grumbled under her breath.

"Settle down," Sherri warned in a whisper. She'd stuck with Liss, accompanying her back into the Emporium, hanging out the CLOSED sign, and brewing a fresh pot of coffee in the stockroom.

"I wish I could." And she wished she knew what was happening next door, where Detective Franklin had taken her father for more questioning. At least Franklin hadn't arrested him on the spot, but she didn't know how long that situation would last.

"We'll sort things out," Sherri insisted. "Obviously, someone's trying to make Mac look guilty. It was a pretty clumsy attempt at a frame-up."

Liss squeezed her friend's hand. "Thanks for the vote of confidence."

She was grateful that Sherri didn't automatically assume the worst. She wished she could be sure the same held true for her mother. Vi was acting as if she believed her husband *had* killed "Lee" Palsgrave.

Of its own volition, Liss's gaze shifted to the ceiling.

Once Vi had realized that, for the time being, she wouldn't be allowed to go back inside Liss's house, she had taken refuge in Aunt Margaret's apartment. Although Liss was now sole proprietor of the Emporium, the building still belonged to her aunt. Liss paid a modest rent to continue to operate on the premises.

Liss expected that the police would want to question her mother. She wondered what Vi would say. As upset as she was, her comments might do her husband more harm than good.

"There's so much I don't understand," Liss whispered.

"Just tell Franklin what you do know," Sherri advised as they watched the detective mount the front steps and open the door to the Emporium. "Everything, even if you don't think it's important. And even if you think it makes your parents look bad. There's no point in keeping secrets. In any investigation, everything always comes out in the end, and it always makes things worse if it turns out that you held back information."

"I know." She sent Sherri a wry smile. "Sadly, as you are well aware, this is not my first encounter with murder." But it was the first time her father had been nominated as prime suspect.

A uniformed officer had already taken Liss's statement about the missing sword. Now Detective Franklin informed her that he wanted to go over every detail of that deposition again. After he sent Sherri away, he pointed to the window.

"Show me where this—what's it called? A broadsword? Show me exactly where it was in your display."

She walked him to the window. "Right there. Dead center." She winced at her unfortunate choice of words. "It was the largest weapon in the display. And I'd just like to point out that my father has arthritis in his hands, his wrists, and his neck, as well as in his knees and ankles. It would be extremely difficult for him to lift such a weapon, let alone use it effectively."

"What gives you the idea that the sword was used in a crime?"

"I'm not stupid." Exasperated all over again, Liss glared at him. "A moron could put two and two together and guess that you think the missing sword was used to kill Professor Palsgrave."

Franklin neither confirmed nor denied her statement, but Liss's excellent imagination was quick to paint the crime scene in gruesome detail. Blood everywhere, Sherri had said. That would certainly have been the case if Palsgrave had been slashed with the hand-and-a-half broadsword. Or hacked to death. Liss swallowed convulsively.

"If my father had wanted to use a sword at all, and I can't imagine why he would have, then it would have made far more sense for him to borrow one of the lightweight weapons, like that thirty-inch tapered blade arming sword."

Although the state police detective spent a few more minutes examining the contents of the display window, he kept his thoughts private. "Is that coffee I smell?" he asked when he'd finished his inspection.

Play nice, Liss reminded herself, and directed him toward the cozy corner and the coffee pot and mugs Sherri had set out. Her friend was right. She had to cooperate with the police. She just hoped Franklin didn't ask her too many questions about her mother. Quite honestly, Liss did not know how to answer him if he wanted details of Vi's relationship with Professor Palsgrave.

"I understand this was a display of reproduction weapons, rather than the real thing," Franklin said when he'd doctored his coffee with cream and sugar and taken the first swallow. "What's the difference?"

"Value. If those swords had been made in medieval times, they'd be worth a fortune. And weight. The real ones are much heavier."

"Those look pretty real to me."

"They're supposed to look real, but they weren't made to slay enemy soldiers in battle. Most of the people who use weapons like those in reenactments keep the blades dull or blunted. I'm not an expert on the subject, but I'd think that, even in the interest of authenticity, most people would prefer not to risk being maimed or killed while engaging in what is, essentially, a hobby. Are you planning to arrest my father?"

Franklin ignored her question. "Were these blades sharp?"

She managed not to glare at him. She took a moment to make sure she wouldn't sound testy, then answered honestly. "I don't know. I didn't exactly run my fingers over any of them to find out. I didn't even handle most of them. I don't see why it matters. Anyone with a kitchen knife sharpener could turn a dull blade into one that could kill." At his raised eyebrow, she added, "I read a lot of murder mysteries."

"Who set up the display?"

"Professor Caroline Halladay and her assistant. Willa somebody. A student."

"Willa Somener?" Franklin asked.

"That sounds right." Liss was surprised that he knew the name, but she supposed he'd encountered her at the college. "I only met her twice, both times with Dr. Halladay."

Franklin scribbled something in his notebook. "When did you last see the missing sword?"

"I don't remember. I know it was there on Monday, but I can't be certain after that. The cloth draped across the back of the display keeps me from seeing into the window from the store side, and I had no reason to stop and stare at it from outdoors. In fact, I'm not sure I've even walked past that window during the last few days. I go the other way to get to the post office and I come in and go out through the back door most of the rest of the time."

"Why did you notice on Monday?" Franklin persisted.

Liss shrugged and told him about the visit from old Alistair Gunn and his grandson. Franklin made more scribbles. She tried to read his handwriting, but couldn't decipher it. When he flipped back a few pages to consult earlier notes that looked more like hen scratches than words, she decided he probably used some kind of cop shorthand.

"You were closed from five in the afternoon on Wednesday the eighth until ten this morning, the tenth. Is that right?"

She nodded. "Yesterday I had a fitting for my wedding gown. I was out of town most of the day."

"Congratulations." He sounded as if he meant it.

Liss mellowed slightly. "Thank you."

"You were late opening this morning."

Any lessening of the antagonism she felt toward him evaporated. "We had an unexpected early morning visitor. I was held up."

He fielded her glare with annoying equanimity. "And after I left?"

"As usual, I entered the shop through the stockroom." She gestured toward the door to her work area. "That way in is the shortest distance from the kitchen of my house."

"Who has access to this building when the shop is closed?"

"I do. And my aunt, Margaret Boyd. She lives in the upstairs apartment."

"And your parents?"

"They know where the keys are," Liss admitted, "but I'd like to point out that anyone could have come in here during business hours and taken that sword. I might have been in the stockroom, or the restroom."

He gave the bell over the door a pointed look. "Wouldn't you have heard them?"

Liss squirmed under his intense scrutiny. "Probably," she admitted.

"And *did* anyone come in when you weren't out front to see them? Anyone who had already left again by the time you poked your head out to see who was here?"

"Not that I know of." She was feeling testy again, and this time she didn't care if it showed.

"Any other theories you'd like to share?"

Liss fidgeted. She was pretty sure he was being sarcastic. She wondered if he'd asked Gordon Tandy about her. Her involvement in previous cases of murder was no secret. She offered a suggestion anyway.

"Maybe someone broke in here after hours. My locks aren't the greatest."

He didn't say anything to that. He'd probably already noticed.

"Look, I know you're investigating a murder. And it's obvious you think that sword was the murder weapon, but why on earth do you think my father had anything to do with it? And if he *did*, why would he put the sword in the trunk of his own car and then leave the car unlocked?"

"You'll have to ask him those questions, Ms. Mac-Crimmon."

Before she could come up with a suitably scathing reply to that suggestion, Franklin resumed his interrogation. He repeated all of his questions a second time. Cops did that, as Liss well knew, but that knowledge didn't make the experience any easier to endure. Finally, he seemed satisfied and closed his notebook.

"Where is Mrs. MacCrimmon?"

"Upstairs, in my aunt's apartment."

"If you'll show me the way?"

Given no choice, Liss led him to the door that hid the stairwell. She meant to accompany him to the second floor, but he wouldn't allow her to come with him. Politely but firmly, he told her he would talk to Vi alone.

Liss stayed put at the bottom of the stairwell, listening as he rapped on the door at the top and identified himself. When her mother opened the apartment door, Liss was ready. "Mom?" she called. "I can come up if you want me there."

"That's all right, Liss," Vi answered. "You have the shop to run." She had let Franklin in and closed the door again before Liss had time to remind her that the Emporium wasn't open and probably wouldn't be for the rest of the day.

"Great," she muttered.

With nothing better to do while she waited for the detective to finish interviewing her mother, Liss confirmed that it was okay to clean up after the other officers and got to work on the display window. The sooner she had all those weapons out of her sight, the better.

She paused in the act of reaching for a jewel-encrusted dagger. What she really wanted was to have them gone entirely. The minute she had them boxed up, she decided, she'd phone Caroline Halladay and tell her to come and get them.

* * *

All the while Liss had been working on the window, she'd kept an eye on the police car parked in front of her house. She'd half expected to see her father led out in handcuffs and put in the back of the vehicle. When the cruiser finally left, however, Mac MacCrimmon was not in it.

As soon as it was out of sight, Liss shut off the lights in the Emporium and made a dash for the stockroom. Vi must have been watching from an upstairs window. She scurried down the outside staircase just as Liss burst through the back door. She matched her daughter stride for stride across the driveway and the strip of lawn that separated the Emporium from Liss's kitchen door.

There was no sign of Liss's father downstairs.

"Bedroom," Vi said, and led the way.

The guest room door was closed. Vi reached for the knob, turned it, and frowned when it didn't open. Mac had locked himself in.

"Daddy?" Liss cringed at the helpless note in her voice. She cleared her throat and tried again. "Dad, we need to speak with you."

"Go away." His muffled voice was barely audible.

"No," Vi said.

"Not a chance," Liss seconded her. "You owe us an explanation."

Silence greeted this declaration. Liss and Vi exchanged a worried look.

"I don't suppose either one of us is strong enough to break down the door," Vi said. "Unless you think you can kick it in."

"I was a professional dancer, Mom. Not a martial arts expert."

But Liss had a better idea. Leaving her mother glaring at the guest room door, she entered her own bedroom. It occupied a front corner of the house, on the same side as the guest room. She opened the side window and stuck her head out. A narrow ledge ran below it, connecting to the balcony—a small porch, really—that was attached to the guest room.

Before she had time to overthink her plan, Liss went out the window. She could almost reach the porch railing while she still had one foot on her windowsill. She lunged over the short distance to the porch . . . and felt her feet slip out from under her.

For one terrifying moment, Liss thought she was going to fall. The ground wasn't *that* far away, she told herself as she started to panic. If she landed right and rolled, she probably wouldn't even break anything. She twisted her upper body in a last ditch effort to save herself. Her right hand connected with solid wood. She curled her fingers around the railing and clung.

She hung there, suspended over the strip of lawn next to the driveway, heart pounding and head spinning. Then she slung her left arm up and caught hold of the railing with that hand, too. She was just starting to pull herself up and over when her father gripped her shoulders to help her climb the rest of the way onto the small porch.

"Jesus, Liss!" His eyes were wide and all the color had leeched out of his face. "You could have killed yourself!"

A moment later she was engulfed in a bear hug. It squeezed the breath she'd just gotten back right out of her again, but she managed to hug him in return. Tears pricked at the backs of her eyes.

"I had to be sure you were okay," she mumbled into his shoulder.

She felt as well as heard his deep sigh. When he let her go, it was to walk straight through the guest room and turn the old-fashioned key in the lock. Vi all but fell through the door as it opened. When she'd righted herself, she smacked Mac, hard, on the upper arm.

"Don't ever worry me like that again!"

"We may as well go back downstairs and put on a fresh pot of coffee." He sounded resigned.

"You'd better not be planning to bolt," Vi said.

His laugh was humorless. "Can't. I've been ordered not to leave town."

Chapter Six

Liss's father wouldn't say another word until the three of them were seated around the kitchen table with steaming mugs of coffee on the table in front of them. Liss needed several reviving sips before she felt ready to start the inquisition.

"Why did the police take your fingerprints?" she asked.

"I answered that question this morning—for purposes of elimination."

"Well, they obviously didn't eliminate you!" Liss felt her temper spike and fought to keep it under control. "Why were your fingerprints at a murder scene?"

"Oh, Donald!" Vi wailed. "I *told* you talking to Lee was a mistake."

Mac scowled. "Talking to him wasn't the problem, Vi. It was going back to apologize. If I hadn't done what you asked, I doubt I'd be in so much trouble right now."

"This is *not* my fault!" She bounded to her feet, nearly overturning her chair.

"Whose is it then?" Mac rose, glowering.

"Yours, you stubborn, pigheaded—!"

"Stop!" Liss caught each parent by an arm and jerked, hard, until first Mac, then Vi, sat down again. She made the sign for a time-out. "Now, then, let's start at the beginning, shall we? Dad, are you telling me you went to Three Cities to talk to Professor Palsgrave? Why, for heaven's sake? And when?"

He shrugged. "It seemed like a good idea at the time. There are things you don't know, Liss. Things you don't need to know."

"I'm not a child, Dad." She shot her mother a challenging look. "Cards on the table. Did you . . . date Lee Palsgrave, Mom? Before you married Dad?"

Vi crossed her arms in front of her chest, leaned back in the chair, and sent fulminating looks toward both husband and daughter. "Yes." Defiance radiated from her. "*Before* we married. I hadn't seen him since. *Years* had gone by. Decades! We didn't meet again until Margaret and I went to talk to him about canceling the reenactment."

"You didn't know he was involved in the Medieval Scottish Conclave?"

For a moment Vi looked flustered. "Well, I . . . I recognized his name in the roster, of course, but that didn't have anything to do with . . . anything."

Deciding it was better not to pursue that point, Liss shifted her attention to her father. "So, then what? You didn't like the idea of Mom acting as liaison. I could see that for myself."

He shrugged again. "I didn't think it would hurt if I talked to the man. I reminded him that Vi wasn't a foolish young woman anymore. That she was my wife."

"In other words, you warned him off." Liss was having trouble taking all this in, but she persisted with her questions, determined to get the whole story. That was the only way she could hope to help her father. And it looked as if he was going to need her help. The police didn't tell people not to leave town if they didn't seriously consider them to be suspects.

"I confronted Palsgrave in his office last week," Mac continued. "I told him off, if you want to know the truth. And I expect people overheard us, as our voices were raised. There was a secretary nearby, and another woman. Maybe more people I didn't see."

"Honestly, Mac!" Vi snapped. "It is absurd for you to be jealous *now*. You've always known about my affair with him when I was a student. I told you about it before we got married."

"The nutty professor kept his good looks," Mac defended himself. "And you always said he was loaded with charisma."

Vi rolled her eyes heavenward. "Yes, Lee was always a charming man. And, well, sexy. But I *love* you, you dolt, although I'm beginning to wonder why! Besides," she added with a self-deprecating twist of the lips, as if she wanted to make a joke of it, "I'd hardly want to be seen naked by anyone else at this point in my life. Scars are so unattractive!"

"Scars?" Liss interrupted. "What scars?"

Vi gave a careless wave of one hand. "Nothing, darling."

"It's not nothing. What scars?"

"Oh, for goodness' sake! I had a radical mastectomy two years ago. Satisfied?"

The sucker-punch left Liss feeling queasy. "Why didn't you *tell* me?"

"Because it was none of your business. Besides, you had troubles of your own back then, what with your knee surgery and moving back here to Moosetookalook. And it's hardly important *now*. Not when we're trying to keep your father out of jail."

Liss stared at her mother as if she'd never seen her before. She'd had breast cancer and didn't think her daughter should be told? The mind boggled. With an effort of will, Liss dragged her racing thoughts back to the current dilemma.

"We're going to talk about this later," she warned her mother. Then she focused once again on her father's predicament. "Was that the reason the police questioned you? Because you went down to Three Cities last week and were overheard quarreling with Palsgrave?"

"Part of the reason. It would have been all of it if your mother hadn't insisted I apologize. To please her, I made an appointment to meet with him in his office."

"Without telling me a thing about it," Vi grumbled. "I'd have gone with him if I'd known."

"And I wouldn't have gone at all if I'd guessed that would end up being the day he'd get himself killed!"

Silently, Liss groaned.

"Anyway," Mac continued, "Palsgrave never showed. I waited in his office for a while. Touched things. That's why they needed to take my fingerprints."

"Please tell me you weren't also in his classroom."

Mac looked uncomfortable. "Wish I could, but I went there, too. His secretary seemed a little confused when I showed up and said I had an appointment. She told me that Palsgrave had a class that ran all morning. I figured maybe we got our wires crossed, so I stopped by there on my way out, but he wasn't there, either. No one was."

"Let me guess. You left more fingerprints."

Another shrug. "Looks like it. But I swear to you, I never saw Lee Palsgrave on the day he was murdered.

When I couldn't find him in his classroom, I drove straight back home."

"What about the sword in the trunk of your car?" Liss reached for her mug, found the coffee had gone cold, and set it aside.

"It wasn't in my trunk when I left Three Cities. The day had warmed up. I remember opening the trunk to toss my cardigan inside. I'd have noticed if there had been a great bloody sword lying there!"

"That means the murder hadn't yet taken place," Liss said, thinking aloud. "And that means that the quickest way to prove your innocence is to find someone who saw you *after* you left Three Cities—someone who can prove you were elsewhere by the time Palsgrave died."

"Surely the police will do that," Vi said.

"Maybe. And maybe they're only looking for evidence to prove that Dad *did* murder Lee Palsgrave."

"They won't find any," Mac insisted. "Unfortunately, I doubt you'll be able to locate anyone who can prove I didn't do it, either. I didn't stop anywhere on the way back here. I came straight home. Once here, I stayed in the house. I had a couple of beers and brooded. I didn't *want* to see anyone. And I didn't know Palsgrave was dead until Vi got back from the fitting, all upset, and told me. If you want to know the truth, when I first heard that, I was relieved. She may not have been interested in rekindling an old romance, but he sure as hell was!"

When Caroline Halladay exploded into the Emporium first thing the next morning, Liss assumed she had come to pick up the remaining swords. She was wrong.

"How dare you take down the display!" Caroline railed at her. "We had an agreement."

Liss gaped at her. Then it hit her. The police hadn't

yet made any public statement about how Professor Palsgrave had died. It seemed obvious to Liss that the reproduction of the hand-and-a-half broadsword had been used as the murder weapon, but Caroline would have no way of knowing that.

"Well?" The older woman stood on the other side of the sales counter, hands on hips, foot tapping with impatience while she waited for Liss to answer her.

Sometimes, Liss thought, the best defense was a good offense. "Don't tell me you're still planning to stage the reenactment! Talk about tasteless!"

Caroline's face blanched. "Well, no. Of course not. But the Medieval Scottish Conclave will still take place. Lee's battle wasn't the only attraction."

"It was, I hope, the only one featuring swords and knives."

"Well, yes, but—" Caroline broke off, eyes narrowing. "Say, what's going on here? Why *did* you take down the display?"

"How was Lee Palsgrave killed?" Liss countered.

"The police haven't said." But now she averted her eyes. She was a smart woman. She could connect the dots.

"I'm pretty sure the murder weapon was a sword," Liss said.

Caroline frowned. "Willa did say there was blood all over the place."

"Willa? *Willa Somener* was the one who found him?" No wonder Detective Franklin had known her name. Poor girl. What a terrible thing to stumble upon.

Caroline nodded. "For a while there she couldn't stop talking about the blood."

"And you wonder why I want those weapons out of my window!"

Still huffy, Caroline followed Liss into the stockroom. The large box that held the former contents of the display window sat on the worktable. Caroline opened it to make a quick inventory. "The hand-and-a-half broadsword is missing."

"Yes. The police have it."

"I beg your pardon?"

"I cleaned the fingerprint powder off the others as best I could, but you may still find some granules stuck to the decorative bits."

Caroline looked stunned. "Are you telling me that a weapon from your display window killed Lee Palsgrave?"

"The state police seem to think so."

"Good Lord!"

Liss hesitated. She should just let Caroline take the box and go, but since it was her own father who appeared to be suspect number one, she didn't think it would hurt to ask a couple of questions. "Who in your organization knew about the display?"

"Everyone." Caroline blinked, reconsidering. "No. That's not right. The subject didn't come up at any of our regular meetings. We had too much else to discuss."

"Then who did know, besides Palsgrave, you, and Willa?"

"Our arms master. He wasn't happy about our borrowing so many of his weapons, but I don't think he knew precisely where we were taking them."

"Does he have a name?"

"Kirby Redmond."

Liss wrote it down. "Who else?"

"Willa probably told her boyfriend. Gabe Treat," she added before Liss could ask.

Liss looked up sharply. The name Gabe rang a bell. "Big guy? Red hair? Lots of freckles?"

"That's right. How do you—?"

"He was in here. With his grandfather."

Caroline looked blank.

"The older man said his name was Alistair Gunn."

For a moment, Liss thought Caroline was having a seizure. Then she realized that what she was seeing was pure, unadulterated fury. Both plump, sturdy hands braced on the worktable, Caroline's knuckles went dead white with the force she was using to grip the edge. Head lowered, she took a series of deep breaths. Slowly, she got control of herself again, but she had a militant gleam in her eyes when she straightened.

"It appears," she said in a cold, precise voice, "that the conclave has a traitor in its midst. Thank you for your help, Ms. MacCrimmon. I'll be going now."

With that, she picked up the heavy box and barreled out of the stockroom, almost flattening Liss's neighbor, bookseller Angie Hogencamp, who had just entered the shop. The bell over the door was still jangling. With Caroline's departure, it rang again, this time sounding even more discordant.

"Whew," Angie commented, her gaze following the other woman's rush down the porch steps to her car. "What did you do to tick her off?"

"Not a thing." Liss hurried to the window, now minus the drape of black velvet as well as the weapons display. She watched in silence as Caroline tossed the box into her backseat, climbed in behind the wheel, and burned rubber in her rush to get away from their quiet little town square.

"I'm guessing she's upset about something," Angie drawled.

Liss shrugged. "She came to collect her swords. She's part of that Medieval Scottish Conclave. They just lost their head honcho." But that wasn't what had set Caroline Halladay off. Liss wished she knew what had.

"Oh, the murdered professor," Angie said. "Yeah, I saw that on TV."

"Please tell me the media coverage hasn't made a connection to Moosetookalook." The village didn't need that kind of publicity.

"Not yet," Angie said cheerfully, "but it's only a matter of time. I guess they won't be having their mock battle now, huh?"

"It's been cancelled. Definitely." Back behind the sales counter, Liss leaned her elbows on the smooth wooden surface. She felt twitchy, as if there was more she should be doing. Unfortunately, she didn't know what that might be.

"Was she close to the dead guy?"

"The woman who just left? No idea. But they did work together."

Angie wandered over to the window to study the uninspired display of Scottish imports Liss had hastily assembled the previous day. The result had a thrown-together appearance, with a scattering of Celtic jewelry on one side and a couple of colorful kilts on the other.

"I need to redo that display," Liss said, suddenly feeling embarrassed by the way it looked. Sure, she'd been distracted at the time, but a five-year-old could have come up with a better-looking arrangement.

"It's an improvement over what was there before," Angie reassured her. "I wasn't sorry to see the last of all those swords and knives. They gave me the willies. And it didn't help when you removed the big sword in the middle. That just made the others seem more ominous."

Liss froze. "You noticed a sword was missing? When?" She fumbled in the drawer beneath the sales counter, where she'd tossed the card Detective Franklin had given her. If Angie knew how long the sword had been gone, it might just clear Mac of suspicion of murder.

But Angie's answer was disappointing. "I have no idea when it was. Don't you know? I thought you must have sold it."

"It wasn't mine to sell. Think, Angie. When did you first notice it was gone?"

"I'm sorry, Liss. All I remember is glancing out my window and seeing the gap in the display."

"Okay, let's try this. Was it gone yesterday?"

"Well, yes, but—"

"How about the day before, when I was closed? Was it there that morning?"

This time a shrug answered her and she spotted growing irritation in Angie's eyes. They were big and brown, just like her daughter's, but they lacked Beth's innocence.

"Think, Angie. It's important."

"Read my lips: I don't know. And I smell a rat. What's the story with that sword?"

"I'll tell you in a minute. I promise. Right now I need to know if it was daytime when you last saw it. It must have been, right? It had to be light out or you wouldn't have been able to see the display at all." Liss didn't light her window at night.

"I suppose." Brow furrowed, Angie considered. "It wasn't yesterday. Maybe it was the day before when I first noticed it was gone. Maybe before that. What's going on, Liss?"

"Someone stole that sword and used it to kill Professor Palsgrave."

Angie folded her arms over her bosom but her glare was one of exasperation, not anger. She even made an attempt to keep things light, misquoting the famous sit-com line from *I Love Lucy*: "You got some 'splainin' to do, Lissy."

"Yeah, I do. And I think the explanation requires a hot chocolate and more than one of Patsy's muffins."

She flipped the BACK IN FIFTEEN MINUTES sign into place, locked up, and headed for the coffee shop with Angie in tow.

She left the detective's card behind.

Patsy's Coffee House was located next to the munici-pal building on the opposite side of the town square from Moosetookalook Scottish Emporium. Inside were three booths, two tables, and five stools at the counter. The smell of freshly baked breads and pastries filled the air. Patsy was renowned throughout Carrabassett County for her donuts and sticky buns. Liss easily picked out the enticing scent of cinnamon. Then she sniffed again.

"Are those blueberry muffins I smell?" she called out to Patsy, the tall, cadaverously thin woman in her mid-fifties who made everything she sold from scratch.

"Sure are, hon. Fresh off the farm."

"Isn't it kind of early in the season for Maine blue-berries?"

Patsy's gaunt cheeks momentarily flared red. "Now, did I say they were homegrown?"

"Patsy! I'm shocked," Liss teased her. "You're using blueberries from away?"

Hands on bony hips, Patsy gave her the evil eye. "You want a muffin or not?"

"Two, please. And hot chocolate."

Liss chose the corner booth for privacy, even though,

at the moment, they were the only customers in the place. When they had steaming mugs and a plate of muffins in front of them and Patsy had returned to the kitchen, Liss filled Angie in on what little she knew, ending with her admission that the police had found the sword in the trunk of her father's car.

"Obviously a setup," Angie said.

"Wicked, foolish way to do it," Patsy agreed as she slid into the booth beside Angie.

Liss jumped and nearly spilled her drink. "I thought you were still in the kitchen."

"You thought wrong. And that state police detective is just flat-out crazy if he suspects your father of wrong-doing. Mac MacCrimmon is as honest as the day is long. He's always been a real stickler for obeying the law. No way would he kill anyone. Ever."

The more upset Patsy was, the more she sounded like the old-time, native Mainer she was. Dropped Rs had her words coming out "sticklah" and "evah."

"She's right," Angie agreed. "If this Palsgrave was killed in a classroom and the weapon was a sword from your display window, then someone took it to Three Cities *planning* to use it to kill him. Anyone cold-blooded enough to do that would also be calculating enough to frame an innocent bystander for the crime."

Patsy's head bobbed up and down. "No way did Mac MacCrimmon do the dirty deed."

Liss felt her eyes well with tears. She blinked them away and managed a watery smile. The unstinting support of her neighbors buoyed her up in a way little else could have. "I only wish Detective Franklin could see things as clearly as you two do."

"He'll come around," Patsy predicted. "He's just somewhat slow."

Liss hoped she was right. "I don't suppose either of you saw my father on the day of the murder?"

"Sorry," Patsy said. "I don't have time to be looking out at the street."

But Angie nodded slowly. "I think I saw him drive away that day. Didn't he leave a little before you did? I remember seeing you go off with your mother and Sherri and Zara. To your dress fittings, right?"

"Yes. I closed the shop for the day." Liss sighed. "If only I'd glanced at the display on my way out of town."

"Well, I can tell you for certain that your father wasn't carrying any great honking sword when he left your house. I'll tell the police that, too." Angie gave a derisive snort at the very idea and took another swig of hot chocolate.

"The cops will just claim that he already had it stashed in his car." She considered for a moment. "It *must* have been gone by then."

"I'm sorry, Liss. I wish I could remember when I saw it last."

"Don't fret about it, Angie. There was no reason for anyone to pay attention to what was or wasn't in my window."

"Now that I think about it, I recall seeing your father come back home, too. It was about an hour before you returned. I can testify that he most definitely did not have blood all over him."

"That's great," Patsy said. "Isn't it?"

"Every little bit helps," Liss agreed. "Unfortunately, it doesn't prove his innocence. Unless someone saw Professor Palsgrave alive after my father was well on his way back to Moosetookalook, knowing when he arrived here doesn't help his case at all." She ran the chronology of events in her head and frowned. "Damn. Even if we find a witness, it may not help. News of the murder had already been announced before I left Three Cities. It takes an hour and a half for the drive home. The timing of Dad's return to Moosetookalook may even work against him."

Chapter Seven

The rest of Saturday and all day Sunday passed quietly. Almost too quietly.

"Why haven't the police canvassed the neighborhood?" Liss demanded of Sherri after the two of them, Dan, and Pete had demolished a half dozen large cartons of Chinese takeout. The smell of sesame chicken still hung in the air.

"Are you sure they didn't?" Pete asked. Dark haired and dark eyed, with the solid build of a linebacker, he personified the description "laid back," at least when he was off duty.

"No one has questioned Angie," Liss reminded him. She'd already told them about the bookseller's observations. In the end, Angie had not phoned Detective Franklin. She hadn't thought she had anything useful to tell him and Liss had been forced to agree.

Sherri and Pete exchanged a pointed look.

"What?" Liss demanded, intercepting it.

But it was Dan who answered. "You're too close to this, Liss. Hang back and let Franklin do his job."

"Even if he arrests my father for a crime he didn't commit? He must think Dad is guilty, that he took the sword and killed Palsgrave. That's the only reason I can think of for his failure to verify my father's movements on the day of the murder."

"*If* Mac is arrested—and that's a big if, because we all know your father isn't the type to go around killing people—we'll deal with it," Dan said. "There's no sense in borrowing trouble."

"For all you know, Franklin has already found a witness to give Mac an alibi," Pete put in.

"And if you stick your nose in where it doesn't belong," Sherri said bluntly, "you could mess up an ongoing investigation into some other suspect. Leave it alone."

They were right. Liss *knew* they were right. But it was hard to sit back and do nothing. She started to speak, then took a good hard look at the concern creasing Dan's face. He was working so hard to be able to take time off for their honeymoon. He didn't need to be worrying about what she got up to. She could give him that much.

"I haven't been snooping," she assured them in all honesty. It wasn't her fault that people like Caroline Halladay and Angie Hogencamp came into the Emporium of their own free will and talked to her. "And I promise I won't interfere."

"Thank you." The tension went out of Dan's shoulders and the muscles in his face visibly relaxed.

"Look at the bright side," Pete said. "There obviously isn't enough evidence to arrest your father or he'd already be in jail. Therefore, Franklin will keep following leads until he finds the real killer."

Liss dutifully put on a cheerful face and hid her continuing concern from her fiancé and her friends. It wasn't as if she didn't have other things to occupy her mind. July 25 was less than two weeks away and she still had a dozen items on her to-do list, everything from arranging the seating plan for the reception and writing out table and place cards to catching up on thank you notes for gifts that had already arrived. Dan had made all the arrangements for their honeymoon, but she still had to decide what to pack.

It was encouraging to look at that to-do list the next morning and see how many items had already been checked off, but there were enough that hadn't been to keep her busy well into Monday afternoon. She didn't stop thinking about her father's troubles entirely but, temporarily, she was able to push her worries about him onto the back burner.

Mondays the Emporium was closed, to make up for being open on Saturdays. While Dan was at work, Liss spent the entire day at his house, taking measurements and debating which pieces of furniture to keep. In the late afternoon, as she was standing in the kitchen, trying to decide between that room or the downstairs bath as a location for Lumpkin and Glenora's litter box, a loud banging sounded at the front door. Then the doorbell rang and kept ringing, as if someone was leaning on it.

"I know you're in there!" shouted a furious female voice Liss didn't recognize. "Open up!"

Curiosity drove her to a window that overlooked the porch. Two people stood just outside—Willa Somener and Gabe Treat. Willa looked ready to spit nails. If Gabe hadn't been radiating calm tolerance, Liss might not have risked letting them in.

"What seems to be the problem?" she asked when she'd opened the door to confront them.

"You're the problem!" Willa snapped. "I lost my job because of you." She pushed past Liss into the house, entered the living room, and plunked herself down on Dan's sofa.

Gabe, following, gave an apologetic shrug. "Sorry about this, Ms. MacCrimmon. She insisted on tracking you down. When Willa's determined on something, it's best not to get in her way."

"Yes, my father follows the same rule of thumb with my mother. Well, come on in. Can I offer you anything? Coffee? Soda?"

"We won't stay long," Gabe assured her, but he took a seat beside his girlfriend.

Liss remained standing, bracing her back against the side of the entertainment center Dan had built. Closed doors hid the television and the shelf underneath where the DVD player lived. Custom-made drawers held an assortment of movies and favorite TV series. Dan had an inexplicable fondness for Monty Python.

Willa appeared to be stewing. Liss wasn't sure what her problem was, but it obviously affected her deeply. "You said you lost your job?" she prompted. "What job?"

"Work-study." Willa spat out the words. "And I need that income to pay for my textbooks."

"Okay," Liss said slowly. "I'm still not following. What did I have to do with you being fired?"

"You told Professor Halladay about Gabe! And then she accused me of fraternizing with the enemy." Willa burst into tears and buried her face on Gabe's shoulder.

Liss handed her a box of tissues and waited out the storm.

It took a while to pass. The young woman was obviously very upset, but Liss didn't know what she could do to help her. The implication that she'd deliberately ratted Willa out was as unfounded as it was irrational.

"I'm sorry for your troubles," Liss said when she was reasonably certain Willa was calm enough to pay attention, "but I had no idea I was giving away state secrets. I met you and Gabe on separate occasions. I didn't know you two were an item. And I certainly couldn't have guessed that Dr. Halladay would react so strongly to finding out that your boyfriend's grandfather was one of the protestors."

Willa sniffed loudly. "I lost my job."

"Yes, you said that." Liss hesitated, then gave in to the impulse to be helpful. "I might be able to offer you an alternative. If you're going to be free during the highland games, I could use another pair of hands at the Scottish Emporium booth."

"Really?" The sun came out from behind the clouds as Willa smiled.

"Really. But aren't you still part of the medieval conclave?"

"Not anymore." The rain clouds regrouped and she sniffled in an attempt to hold back more weeping. "I'm not enrolled in any classes this summer. I was supposed to be Dr. Halladay's assistant for the whole semester, but I was going to get course credit for taking part in the reenactment. Now that's cancelled, too." On the last few words her voice rose perilously close to a wail.

"Shhhh, hon. It will be okay."

"Oh, Gabe! Everything is ruined! And she doesn't even care that Professor Palsgrave is dead. She'll probably dance at his funeral. She thought his theory was n-n-nonsense anyway. She only went along with it because he got that big grant and was willing to share it with the conclave. She said reflected glory was better than no glory at all."

"Now, now," he murmured, patting her on the back with one big paw of a hand when she once more dissolved into tears.

Liss cleared her throat. Darned if she didn't feel guilty about Willa's situation. And, guilt aside, she was in a position to help out. "Willa, pay attention. If the gig at the games works out, I can offer you employment during the last part of July and the first half of August—three weeks in all."

Liss's parents had volunteered to keep the Emporium open while she and Dan were away on their honeymoon, but Liss was sure they'd be delighted to have help while she was gone.

"Three weeks?" Willa sounded bemused but interested.

Liss nodded. "I'm getting married during the conclave. It's not an official event on the program or anything, but I'll be wearing a medieval gown and . . . well, anyway, we moved our venue to the hotel when the highland games did. While my new husband and I are in Scotland, my mother will be running Moosetookalook Scottish Emporium. You'd be her assistant."

"That's so romantic." The sparkle in Willa's eyes no longer came from tears. "Are you having a handfasting ceremony?"

"No," Liss said firmly, "but here's some good news: you and my mom are going to get along very well indeed."

She gave Willa and Gabe a brief overview of what working the Emporium's booth at the highland games entailed and then, never one to question good fortune, decided that she might as well take advantage of the fact that Willa had come to her. She crossed the room to take the chair at right angles to the sofa where Willa and Gabe sat and leaned in until she could see the young woman's face clearly. She'd back off if she had to, but for her father's sake she'd take a stab at asking questions first.

"I'd like to talk to you, Willa. About the day you found Professor Palsgrave's body." She made her voice gentle, well aware that Willa had been through a traumatic experience. Liss had been the first on a murder scene herself. Twice. She didn't wish that horror on anyone.

Willa slid closer to Gabe. "I don't even like to think about it."

"I'm not asking you to describe what you saw in that classroom," Liss assured her. "Only what you might have noticed before you went in."

"Is this really necessary?" Gabe asked.

"I'm afraid it is. You see, my father is one of the people the police are looking at as suspects in the professor's death. Dad went into Palsgrave's classroom that day, before the murder." Struck by a sudden notion, she spoke without thinking, completely forgetting the promise she'd just made. "At least, he didn't see anyone there. I don't suppose it's possible he overlooked—"

Willa's near-hysterical laugh cut the question short. "There's no way anyone could have stepped into that room and missed seeing there was something wrong. Blood was spattered on everything. And the body . . . it was covered in gore." She shuddered and covered her face with her hands.

Gabe wrapped an arm around her shoulders and murmured soft, comforting words, all the while glaring at Liss.

"I'm sorry. I understand that you don't want to think about that day, let alone answer more questions, but surely you don't want an innocent man to be arrested."

Willa sobbed harder.

It was Gabe who relented. "Babe? Come on. You need to help her out. She's helping you. Fair's fair, right?"

"What?" Understanding slapped Liss in the face and she reeled back. "Oh, no, Gabe. You've got it all wrong. Willa, the offer of a job stands. If you can't bear to talk about that day, then that's that. But I had to ask." She made a gesture of helplessness. "He's my father."

After a moment, Willa's whimpers subsided. With one last sniffle, she dried her eyes, looked straight at Liss, and nodded. "Family is important. I get that. What do you want to know?"

"Did you see anyone else around?" Liss asked, trying to tamp down her eagerness. "Anyone leaving the building just as you came in?"

Willa blew her nose, loudly, and tucked a scraggly lock of hair back behind one ear. "The police asked me that, too."

"What did you tell them?"

"That I didn't notice anyone in particular. There were people around. Other students. Professors. Even a couple of the demonstrators."

"The protestors? The same ones who were going to picket the highland games?"

Willa nodded. "They've been showing up pretty regularly just off campus. Sometimes they come on the grounds, but mostly they stay on the sidewalks."

"She saw me," Gabe interrupted. "We talked for a few minutes. I should have gone inside with her, but I had no idea—" He broke off, shaking his head.

Liss took Willa's icy hands in her own. "Which demonstrators did you see, Willa? Do you know their names?"

The young woman glanced at Gabe, waiting for his

nod before she answered. "Gabe's grandfather was one of them."

"Mr. Gunn must have been ecstatic when he heard that the battle had been called off," Liss remarked.

"Hey!" Gabe objected. "Don't go looking at Grand-dad for this. He's way too feeble to have done much damage to anyone."

"Do you know *how* the professor was killed?" Liss asked him.

"Well, no. But unless he was shot with a really light-weight gun, my grandfather couldn't have managed it. Besides, I was hanging around outside Lincoln Hall most of the morning to keep an eye on him and I'm sure he never went inside the building."

"Not even to use the restroom?"

Gabe's carrot-colored hair and fair skin made it impossible to hide it when he was embarrassed. A dull red stain crept up his neck and into his face. "He's got this bag thing," he mumbled.

Liss took pity on him. "Willa, you said demonstrators. Plural. Who else was there?"

Again Gabe answered for her, rushing into speech. "It was a mixed group, one from each of the organizations who had problems with Palsgrave's theory. There was John Jones. He claims to be one quarter Penobscot. Says he represents the extinct Massachusetts tribe that Palsgrave claimed Henry Sinclair wiped out. But I've got this friend who's a full-blooded Penobscot and he says Jones is as phony as a three-dollar bill. No Native American blood at all. Mike says Jones is just after free publicity for a book he self-published last year."

Liss wished she were in her own house, where there would be a lined yellow legal pad and a pencil in the end table drawer. Lacking either, she started a mental list. "Who else?"

"The Columbus First protestors sent Louis Amalfi. He's a good guy, but kind of flaky."

"I'm sensing a theme here," Liss muttered.

"Wasn't there someone new that day?" Willa asked. She seemed to recover from her bouts of weeping as easily as she succumbed to them. The resilience of youth, Liss supposed, suddenly feeling much older than she was.

"Oh, yeah. The religious nut." Gabe's brow furrowed. "Barry something. He doesn't represent any regular church, just a group that was upset because Palsgrave discounted the entire Templar treasure and Holy Grail business. You know about that?"

Liss nodded. "Some people believe that Henry Sinclair didn't cross the Atlantic simply because he was looking for rich fishing grounds and a new source of timber to build ships. They think he was secretly a Templar knight."

"A pretty good trick, given that the Templars were all wiped out more than a hundred years earlier," Willa said.

The young woman was a history major, Liss remembered. "I don't know about that, but I do recall hearing rumors of buried treasure in the New World."

"Holy relics," Gabe corrected her. His boyish grin put in a brief appearance. "The Holy Grail, in fact."

Liss's gaze drifted of its own volition to the drawer of the TV cabinet where the DVDs were stored. Inside, she was almost certain there was a copy of *Monty Python and the Holy Grail*. Not quite the same thing, she reminded herself, but equally outlandish. It seemed to her that the picketers held beliefs that made Lee Palsgrave look like the poster child for rational thinking.

"Did you give the demonstrators' names to the police?" she asked Willa.

"There wasn't any need to. They were all still hanging around."

"Everybody stayed to find out what was going on," Gabe agreed.

"Was there anyone else in the classroom building?" Liss asked.

Willa shook her head. "It's summer session. I'm pretty sure there weren't any classes scheduled after Dr. Palsgrave's morning seminar."

"What were you doing there?" In contrast to her earlier behavior, Willa now seemed perfectly composed and willing to answer questions. Liss had no problem taking advantage of that situation.

"Dr. Halladay sent me to find Professor Palsgrave. She said she wanted to talk to him about something and he hadn't come back to his office yet. Sometimes he'd stay late after the seminar to meet with individual students, so it made sense that he'd still be in his classroom."

Liss frowned. Her father had said that the room was empty when he stopped by. For the first time, she wondered what had happened to all the students. "What time did this seminar meet?"

"It was a three-hour session, eight till eleven."

But Gabe was shaking his head. "He dismissed class early. At least a dozen people left Lincoln Hall, more or less together, and then a couple more, separately, maybe a half hour before you went in. Maybe longer."

Liss's heart started to beat a little faster. "And you said you were outside all morning, right?" At Gabe's nod, she described her father. "Did you see anyone who looked like that go into Lincoln Hall?"

"I think so." Gabe's brow furrowed in thought. "I wasn't paying all that much attention. Not to who went in and out. I was there to make sure my grandfather stayed out of trouble, not to watch the building."

"So you don't have any idea how long it was before my father came out again?"

"Sorry. No."

"Do you think you'd have noticed him if he'd come out covered in blood?"

Gabe laughed at her sarcastic tone, then sobered instantly. "Sorry. Yeah. I'm pretty sure I would have twigged to that."

"Okay. Good. Remember that detail if the police ask you about it, okay?"

"Sure thing, Ms. MacCrimmon."

"What about the other protestors besides your grandfather. Did you notice any of them entering the classroom building?"

"I think both Jones and Amalfi took breaks. Probably to use the bathroom, like you said. But nobody came back out covered in blood. I'm sure of that. And no one carried in any weapons, either. Not that I saw." There was a question in his voice.

"Hand-and-a-half broadsword," she said succinctly.

Gabe gave a low whistle. Liss knew what he meant. Between the size of the weapon and the amount of spilled blood, how could *anyone* have gone into the building, killed Lee Palsgrave, and gotten away again without being seen?

There didn't seem to be anything else to say, and Liss had run out of questions. When Gabe said they had to get going, she escorted them to the door.

"If you come by the Emporium a couple of days before the highland games begin, that should give you time to familiarize yourself with the stock and fill out paperwork," she told Willa when they reached the porch.

"I really appreciate this, Ms. MacCrimmon."

"Make it Liss. Ms. MacCrimmon is my mother."

She watched the young couple cross the town square to a pickup truck parked in front of the Emporium. Her smile faded after they'd driven away. Had she just made a huge mistake by hiring Willa?

She was remembering, with sudden disconcerting clarity, the day that Willa and Caroline Halladay had set up the window display. Willa had picked up one of the swords—Liss couldn't remember which one—handling it easily as she mimed impaling an enemy.

What did she really know about the girl, Liss wondered, except that she had an ancestor who'd been an archaeologist? And Gabe? How could she trust anything he told her when his grandfather had been so fiercely opposed to Palsgrave's reenactment? All three of them—Willa, Gabe, and Alistair Gunn—had known exactly where to find a hand-and-a-half broadsword. And if Palsgrave had been stabbed instead of slashed or hacked, it wouldn't have taken all that much strength to kill him.

Willa could have done it.

Maybe even Alistair Gunn could have.

And a stab wound put her father back in the running, too.

"Aargh!" Liss closed the door and let her head fall against one of the wooden panels with an audible thump.

Almost anyone could have stabbed A. Leon Palsgrave to death. But the same problem remained, no matter who the killer turned out to be—how had he, or she, gotten to Lee Palsgrave, carrying a sword, without being seen, and then gotten out again, also without being seen? It wasn't quite a "locked room" mystery. The classroom had been open. But it did seem as if it fell into the "impossible crime" category. It was a subgenre Liss had never particularly cared for.

Think positive, she ordered herself. *At least in fiction, where there is a locked room, there is usually a secret passage.*

She just had to find it.

Chapter Eight

By the time Gabe Treat phoned Liss two days later with Barry's last name—Rowse—she had already spent many hours surfing the Internet, trying to find out more about the people on her list. To John Jones, Louis Amalfi, and Barry, she'd added Gabe himself, his grandfather, Willa, Caroline Halladay, and Kirby Redmond, the young man she'd been told was in charge of weapons for the mock battle.

Everyone seemed to have an online presence these days. Most of her suspects were on one social network or another. Some were on several. Those pages gave her entirely too much information about far too many aspects of their personal lives, but no single revealing tidbit to point a finger and shout, "Murderer!"

She also perused newspaper items, faculty bios, and articles in scholarly journals. As she'd read, she'd dutifully made notes, but now she just doodled on the pad in front of her, plagued by an uncharacteristic lack of direction.

She could almost hear the voices in her head—Dan,

Sherri, and State Police Detective and former boyfriend Gordon Tandy, the loudest—shouting at her to leave solving crimes to the professionals. But she'd seen what all the unanswered questions about Palsgrave's murder were doing to her parents. Vi and Mac barely spoke to each other. When they did, they were excruciatingly polite. Both of them seemed to be walking on eggshells. The constant tension did not create a comfortable living environment.

At the end of the day, no closer to finding a killer, Liss went home. She had to brace herself before she went through her own front door. As she'd expected, she found her father in the living room.

"How's it going, Dad?" she asked.

He shrugged, barely looking up from the jigsaw puzzle of a winter scene that he was putting together on the custom-made table—one of Dan's most popular woodworking creations—set up in Liss's bay window. He'd moved the Canadian rocker and footstool that usually occupied the space to a spot on the far side of the room and substituted a straight-back chair that didn't look at all comfortable.

Liss's mother bustled in from the kitchen. Her brittle smile and the dark shadows beneath her eyes were blatant evidence that she hadn't been sleeping well. "I made an apple pie," she announced.

"That's great, Mom." Liss managed a quick kiss to her mother's cheek before Vi, jumpy as a rabbit, scurried back the way she had come.

"She bakes when she's upset," Mac said. "Gives most of it away. The woman eats like a bird."

"I hope she lets you have some." Liss had to force the words out. Choked up over apple pie? Somehow, she doubted that was the real cause of what she was feeling.

Mac snorted. "Not often. She's forever fussing about my weight. If she's so damned concerned I might gain a pound, she shouldn't be baking in the first place."

He went back to sorting puzzle pieces in one of the four wooden drawers built into the sides of the puzzle table for that purpose. Liss wasn't surprised to see that the puzzle he'd selected from her supply was one of the more complex ones. She wouldn't be surprised, either, if he gave up on it before it was completed. She knew she had. In the end, all those hundreds of pieces the exact same shade of sky blue or snow white had defeated her. She preferred puzzles where the pieces contained clues, even if it was only a hint of some other color. At least that little bit gave her a starting place to figure out where the piece was supposed to fit into the whole.

Liss headed for the kitchen, intending to force herself to eat a slice of her mother's pie. That would cheer Vi up. Someone in this house should be happy. She stopped short in the doorway. Her mother sat at the table, her face buried in her folded arms. Her shoulders heaved with quiet sobbing.

As soon as she realized she wasn't alone, Vi sat up straight, dashing the betraying moisture from her eyes. "I wasn't crying. I never cry. I only put my head down because I felt a migraine coming on."

"You don't get migraines."

"How would you know? It's been a dozen years since you lived with your father and me."

Liss had to bite back bitter words. She hadn't known a lot of things, including the fact that Vi had undergone major surgery. She pressed her lips together so tightly that they formed a flat line. Anything she said now would be taken the wrong way.

Vi didn't seem to notice her daughter's silence. "He won't talk to me," she complained. "He won't explain about the hand-and-a-half broadsword." She left the table and started to clean the kitchen. Her baking spree had left traces of flour and sugar behind. The sink was filled with measuring cups, bowls, and the baking sheet she'd put under the pie pan to catch spillover.

"What is there to explain? Someone planted that sword in his car to make him look guilty."

Vi sent her an "oh, please!" look.

Liss stared at her, her heart sinking. "Mom," she said carefully, "you *do* believe Daddy's innocent, don't you?"

"I don't know *what* to believe." Vi slammed a measuring spoon into the sink to emphasize her frustration and turned the hot water on full force to start washing up.

Stunned, feeling as if she'd had her legs knocked out from under her, Liss sank into the nearest chair. No wonder Mac wouldn't defend himself to her. He must have sensed his wife's doubts about his innocence from the first. He didn't believe she'd listen to anything he had to say. And he was probably right. Once Vi Mac-Crimmon made up her mind, she rarely changed her opinion. How hurt he must feel. And how abandoned.

"Are you staying here for supper or going to Dan's?" Vi asked.

Liss cringed at the peevishness in her mother's voice. She'd originally planned to spend the evening with her parents. Now she knew she had to get out of the house before she did something drastic—like bang both their heads together in an attempt to knock some sense into them.

"Dan's," she blurted. "I need to talk to Dan about something." And before her mother could say another word, Liss fled.

She bolted out of the house through the back door. The balmy air of an early evening in summer was lost on her. She kept going at a fast clip until she was standing on the back stoop at Dan's place. He wasn't home yet, but she used her own key to let herself in.

Once inside the quiet kitchen, she felt calmer. It helped to indulge in a bout of cooking therapy herself. By the time her fiancé arrived, hot and grimy after a long day at the construction site, enticing smells filled the air. She'd added a healthy dose of garlic and herbs to the roasting chicken.

"I could get used to this," he murmured, leaning in for a kiss.

Liss started to move closer for a hug, but Dan laughed and evaded the clinch.

"Hold that thought until I've had a shower."

"Dan, I—"

But he was already gone, taking the stairs two at a time. Liss sighed and went back to putting together a green salad. The rice was the ninety-second microwave kind. When he came back downstairs she was ready to serve.

She asked him about his day, pretending interest but barely hearing a word he said. She ate without an appetite. She hoped Dan wouldn't notice. She should have known better.

"You're just picking at your food," he remarked half-way through the meal. "What's wrong?"

"What isn't?" She didn't really want to talk about it, not even to Dan, but everything spilled out in a rush. "Now I'm avoiding my own house," she added after she finished giving him a somewhat disjointed account of her day. "I'm spending long hours in the Emporium. I lied to my mother and said we had plans tonight so I could come over here instead of having supper with them."

"I'm sure your mother doesn't really think your father's a murderer," Dan said. "She's just upset by the uncertainty of the situation. That's only natural."

"I don't want to talk about it." When she realized she'd just piled all of her rice into a mound at the center of her plate, she hastily set down her fork.

"It will all sort itself out eventually, Liss."

She didn't want to hear platitudes, mostly because she couldn't believe in them.

Then an even more alarming realization came to her. If she couldn't talk to Dan about this, then what did that say about their potential for future happiness? They were supposed to be able to share everything. That had been what they promised each other when they decided to get married.

"What if it doesn't work out?" she whispered.

"We'll deal with whatever happens," he promised.

It took her a moment to realize he was still talking about the fact that the police suspected her father of murder. "I mean us," she said in a strangled voice. "What if *we* don't work out?"

He reached out a hand, but she shrank back. "Liss?"

"Maybe we should postpone the wedding. We may have to anyway, if the father of the bride is under arrest and—"

"Stop right there." He threw down his napkin and stood. "Amaryllis Rosalie MacCrimmon, you listen to me."

He flattened his palms on either side of her on the table and leaned in until they were nose-to-nose. He didn't look angry so much as determined, and Liss felt a little shiver of anticipation wash through her. "We are not postponing a damned thing. I've been working my butt off so that everything will be perfect for our wedding day and our honeymoon. I can't say I was sorry to move the ceremony to the hotel, but that's it. No other changes. Got it?"

"Got it," she echoed.

Then she seized his face in both hands and dragged him closer for a kiss to seal the deal. It was much, much later before she started worrying about her father again.

The next day, Thursday, Liss decided she had to be more proactive. She started by calling the cell phone number Willa had left with her and asked the young woman if she could come in for a training session. Willa's response was gratifyingly eager and she turned up at Moosetookalook Scottish Emporium early that afternoon.

"Is the commute going to be a problem for you?" Liss asked. "I know it takes about an hour and a half to drive from Three Cities to Moosetookalook."

"Oh, no." Willa's cheeks went pink. "We've already moved up here. Gabe and I."

Liss's eyebrows shot up. "You rented a place?" There wasn't all that much rental property available in the area. That's why Pete, Sherri, and Sherri's son, Adam, were in that cramped little apartment above the post office. There was the hotel, of course, but Liss was sure The Spruces was more expensive than Willa could afford.

"Not exactly." Pink turned redder and the young woman spoke in a rush. "We're at the campground. Gabe has an old pop-up. We were planning to stay there during the highland games anyway. After I lost my job, we decided to come early."

"Campground?" Liss repeated. "Do you mean Whispering Willows?" She tried to hide her dismay but doubted she was successful. "Are you sure you'll be okay there? It's not the most . . . salubrious place in the area."

Nor was it scenic. Curmudgeonly old Harold Cressy, his style of living crimped by a tight economy, had installed the minimum of required sanitary facilities on his back forty, paved a series of "streets" with gravel, run in a few outdoor electric outlets, and called it good. Most of those who stayed at Cressy's campground moved on after only one night.

Willa chuckled. "I know it's kind of a dump, but it's cheap, and I have a big, strong boyfriend to protect me from bears and moose and drunks."

Such assurances didn't stop Liss from feeling responsible. She resolved to introduce Willa to Sherri. At least then, if she and Gabe needed help, they'd know they had a friend at the local police station.

The paperwork didn't take long. Neither did training Willa on the cash register. She'd previously spent a summer working in a bookstore.

"Where was that?" Liss asked. She supposed she ought to check Willa's references. She'd get around to it . . . eventually.

"Boston."

"Is that where you're from?" When Willa nodded, Liss asked, "What brought you to Maine?"

"My grandparents have a place on the coast. Off the coast, actually. It's an island in Penobscot Bay." She didn't seem to notice Liss's astonishment. "And I wanted to attend a small college, not some big university." She grinned suddenly. "And I liked the picture of the chapel on the Anisetab College Web site. It's just the prettiest thing—like a little Gothic-style church in miniature. Gabe and I are thinking we might get married there after we graduate."

Most of the next hour was taken up with Willa's oohing and aahing over the many items Liss sold in her shop. The Emporium offered an eclectic selection of stock. Although all of it was related in some way to Scotland or Scottish American heritage, that still left a lot of room for variation. Liss's merchandise ran the gamut from delicate bisque figurines of highland dancers to bright chartreuse Loch Ness Monsters that straightened out to become draft blockers.

"You just put it at the bottom of a door or a window during the winter months," Liss explained, "to keep out the cold."

"I just love this place!" Willa's enthusiasm made Liss smile.

"You may have noticed we're not exactly swamped with customers," Liss said in a wry tone of voice after they'd adjourned to the stockroom for a quick course in packaging items for shipment. Not a single person had come in since Willa's arrival. "I do most of my selling online and spend a lot of time back here. If you're not out front when someone does come in, you'll hear the bell over the door so you'll know to go out."

At three, Liss declared a coffee break. Willa asked for tea instead. Once it was ready, they carried their mugs to the cozy corner.

"I encourage customers to browse and to sit here to look at the books I have for sale."

"Do you have a problem with vagrants?" Willa asked, taking her first sip of the tea. "At the bookstore we had two or three homeless people who'd come in and stay all day if you let them." She wrinkled her nose. "They smelled. The real customers didn't like going near them."

"That must have been a difficult situation for the store manager," Liss said. "Not only is it bad business to turn people out, especially if there's a chance that some hotshot newspaper reporter will get wind of it, but I know it would prey on my conscience if I had to be unkind to someone who was already down on his luck."

"You're kidding, right?"

Liss shook her head. "No. I think it would present a real dilemma. And I am very, very grateful that, being in a place as small as Moosetookalook, I'm not likely to have to face it myself."

"Don't you have any poor people here?" Willa sounded astonished.

"Of course we do. In fact, I'd say most of the population is 'poor' by city standards. But, for whatever reason, no one's sleeping on the park bench or coming into local shops to get warm."

"That's nice," Willa said, and helped herself to one of the cookies Liss had brought out to go with their beverages.

While Willa munched, Liss wrestled with her conscience. She had asked the young woman to come in so she could train her, but she'd had other reasons, too. She needed more information about the day of the murder. Willa could keep the shop open, allowing Liss to venture beyond downtown Moosetookalook in search of it. But she might also be a valuable resource herself. Still, Liss hesitated to upset her new employee. She probably shouldn't broach the subject of Palsgrave's murder with Willa at all. And yet, how could she not? Weighed against the possibility of proving her father's innocence, Willa's feelings had to come in a distant second.

Liss cleared her throat. "I don't know if you noticed, but I have copies of Professor Palsgrave's book for sale." She indicated the row of them on a nearby shelf.

To her dismay, Willa's cheerful, confident manner instantly crumbled. Tears welled up in her agate-colored eyes and her hands began to tremble so badly that she had to hastily set down her teacup.

"It was so terrible. So awful," she whispered. "Blood everywhere. I have nightmares. I don't want to talk about it."

"Of course not. I didn't mean to upset you. Drink some of your tea."

Willa obeyed. Either tea really was a sovereign remedy for everything, as the best British mystery novels seemed to imply, or the built-in resilience of youth kicked in again. After only a few sips, Willa calmed right down.

Once her new employee looked steady, Liss cautiously broached the subject of Willa's duties as a work-study student in the history department. She hoped this would be safer territory but still provide her with useful information. Willa might not have worked for the department head himself, but Liss felt certain she'd have seen and heard a good deal of what went on, perhaps more than she realized. With luck, Willa might even know something that would help clear Mac MacCrimmon of suspicion of murder.

Keeping the young woman on topic, however, proved harder than trying to teach Lumpkin to jump through hoops. Willa went off on tangents at the drop of a hat. Liss heard all about her archaeologist ancestor, one Serena Dunbar, who'd apparently made an important discovery on the family island and had then been discredited when her rivals—all men, of course—claimed she had seeded the dig site.

"I'm curious about something," Liss said, giving up on subtlety. It had never been her strong suit anyway. "If someone didn't go in through the front entrance of Lincoln Hall, how else could he, or she, enter and exit that building?"

"Which front entrance?" Willa asked, sipping her tea. "Oh."

Her eyes widened and her face started to scrunch up. The cup dipped and tea sloshed toward the rim. Liss caught it and set it down. She managed to refrain from catching Willa by the shoulders and shaking her, but it was a near thing.

"Don't you dare cry!" she ordered. "Don't think about the classroom. Focus on the other exits from that building."

Willa drew in one deep breath, then another, then nodded. "I'm okay."

"Look, Willa. Your job does not depend on assisting me with this, but I'd really appreciate it if you could help me visualize the inside of that building. Okay?"

Willa nodded again and managed a lopsided smile. "I may have to draw you a floor plan. *Try* to draw one," she amended. "Lincoln Hall is just the strangest building. Some places inside are a real rabbit warren."

"A what?" Liss thought she might have heard the term before, or maybe come across it in one of the historical mystery novels she'd read, but she had no idea what it meant.

"Oh, sorry. That's an expression I picked up from Professor Halladay. She's into all kinds of medieval arts and crafts and mysteries—that's mystery in the sense of a profession. Like Mystery Play?" At Liss's bemused look, she rushed on. "Anyway, what I meant by calling it a rabbit warren is that Lincoln Hall, the theater half anyway, has all these corridors with twists and turns and odd angles. It's because of the stage, you see—because of the way they had to build it for the acoustics? And because the auditorium is sort of V shaped, wider at the back and then it narrows down toward the stage."

Liss signaled for a time-out. "You've lost me, Willa." She went back to the sales counter and returned with a lined tablet and a pencil. "Show me how the theater end connects to the classroom section."

Willa was no artist. She drew two large rectangles connected by a third that was equally long but less than half as wide. "Classrooms," she said, pointing to one end of the drawing. "College theater, until they built that big, new arts center on the other side of the duck pond." She tapped the other end of the drawing.

"What's in the old theater section now?"

"It was converted into offices. Mostly. For the history department."

Oh-ho, Liss thought. *Now we're getting somewhere.*

"There's still a stage," Willa went on. "Some student-directed productions are put on there when the other facilities are booked for more important things. Gabe has performed on that stage a few times. But mostly the old auditorium is used as a lecture hall."

"Back up," Liss said when Willa drew breath. "Gabe's an actor?"

"He's a theater major." Pride radiated from every pore.

Liss filed that tidbit away to be considered later.

"What's this narrow section?" Liss indicated the long, thin rectangle that connected the other two in Willa's drawing.

"That's the art gallery. The entrance is in the same foyer as the box office."

"What about on the other side? The classroom side. Is there a door there?" Liss was beginning to see possibilities.

"Yes, but it's kept locked. Well, so is the one on the theater side, unless the gallery is open, and it hardly ever is."

"No exit that way, then."

"Well . . ."

"What?" Liss tried to tamp down on her impatience. There was no sense getting annoyed at Willa just because it was like pulling teeth to get information out of her. At least she was no longer teetering toward hysteria every time she thought about the grisly discovery she'd made.

"Dr. Palsgrave always used the art gallery as a shortcut from his office to the classroom and it didn't matter if it was open or not because he had his own key." She sighed. "Poor Dr. Palsgrave."

Liss scrutinized the young woman's face. "You're not going to cry again, are you?"

"No. I'm fine." There was a note of pleased surprise in her voice. "I really am."

"Are you up to talking to me about the professor?"

"I guess. What do you want to know?"

"Did he have any enemies?"

Willa looked blank.

"Did he quarrel with his coworkers?"

"Not when I was around. I didn't really have much to do with him, except for battle practice. Rehearsals, you know."

"With swords," Liss murmured.

Willa blanched and swallowed hard. "Yes."

Liss decided to veer away from that topic. Another matter seemed more pertinent now anyway. She picked up Willa's rough sketch of the building and studied it.

"Who else knows about this shortcut?"

Willa shrugged. "I have no idea. Everyone in the department, I suppose."

"Do they all use it?"

"Oh, no. Only Professor Palsgrave."

"Let me make sure I have this straight." She returned

the sketch to the coffee table so she could point to each area as she named it. "There's a door on each end of this art gallery. And the one leading into the classroom section is always kept locked?" She tapped that end of the long narrow rectangle.

Willa nodded.

"And this door from the theater foyer into the art gallery is locked whenever the gallery is closed, which is most of the time?"

"Right. I think it's only open weekend afternoons."

"So instead of having an open passageway between the two sections of this building, they're kept completely separate. Anyone who wants to get from one to the other has to go outside and back in again."

Willa nodded. "Crazy, huh?"

"Inefficient, to say the least. But Palsgrave, as chairman of the history department, with his office in one section and his classroom in the other, had a key that allowed him access to this shortcut."

"Right."

"Does anyone else have a key? Does Dr. Halladay, for example, use this shortcut to get to her classes?"

"I don't think so. I know I've seen her on cold winter days all bundled up like an Eskimo just to walk up the hill to teach a class."

Liss was still studying the sketch. She tapped the right side with the eraser end of the pencil. "So this is the street?"

Willa nodded and pointed to a spot on the lower left. "There's a parking lot here and this"—she traced the left side of Lincoln Hall—"is a paved path that runs between buildings. It ends in another parking lot. The classroom entrance faces that way, not out onto the street. Only the theater entrance faces the road."

"So someone could enter the building that way?"

But Willa shook her head. "The theater door and the one at the back of the building, facing the driveway that goes down to the lower parking lot, are kept locked. You can get out, but not in. The only entrances are here and here." Once again, she indicated the classroom building door off the upper parking lot. Then she pointed to a spot at the lower left-hand corner of her sketch, close to the lower parking lot. "That's the way in to the history department. Someone told me once that they put the offices in what used to be a scenery shop, which makes sense, I guess. That section of the building is directly under the stage."

And around and around we go, Liss thought in dismay. She was definitely going to have to make a trip to Three Cities.

"Where was the picket line?" she asked.

"Here. On the street. The demonstrators weren't supposed to set foot on college property, but no one could make them leave if they stayed on the sidewalk."

The spot she tapped was close enough to the front of Lincoln Hall that the protestors would have been able to see anyone entering or leaving the building. Liss sighed. She'd already assumed as much and that fact didn't help her one bit, not if the killer had followed Palsgrave through the art gallery.

That he must have done so was the only thing that made sense. And that he'd left the same way, unseen in spite of wearing bloodstained clothing and carrying a sword.

At least this wasn't a locked room mystery anymore, although Liss didn't feel that change brought her any closer to solving it. She had to learn more, not only about the building where the crime had occurred, but also about the people on her list of suspects.

"Can you come in to work tomorrow, Willa?" Liss asked. "I have some errands to run and it would be a big help to me if you were here to keep the shop open. My mother will be right next door if, by some fluke, there's too much business for one person to handle."

Willa leapt at the chance.

Chapter Nine

The next day, Liss faced her first challenge even before she left the house. She had to convince her mother to stay home. She finally persuaded Vi to do so by using the excuse that she needed her to keep an eye on their new employee.

"I'm just going to pick up my gown and the bridesmaids' dresses," Liss insisted. "No big deal." It wasn't a lie, but she had other business with Melly Baynard, as well.

For at least half the drive to Three Cities she expected her cell phone to ring—her mother calling to demand she come back and pick her up. When she realized she was obsessing about the possibility, she pulled over into the breakdown lane, fished the phone out of her purse, and turned it off.

She reached Three Cities at midmorning and drove straight to Melly's house. The seamstress was waiting for her, all three gowns ready for transport. After they'd been safely loaded into Liss's car, Melly offered coffee, the perfect entrée for Liss to ask questions.

"So what's the gossip around campus?" she asked

when they were settled at Melly's kitchen table, steaming cups in hand. She tried to sound casual, but her mother's old friend saw right through her.

"You mean you want to know who killed Lee Palsgrave if your father didn't?" She chuckled. "You should see the expression on your face! Don't worry. I'm not a mind reader. I've talked to Vi on the phone a couple of times since you were here last."

"If she's shared her thoughts with you, you're doing better than I am." Resentment stirred, but she tamped it down.

"Now, Liss, it's only natural that there are some things a woman doesn't want to talk to her daughter about. She needed a sympathetic ear and I could understand why she's upset."

"And I wouldn't?"

"You're Mac's daughter, too."

Liss's eyes narrowed. "We're all on the same side here."

Melly looked confused. "But Mac wasn't even in the picture when—Oh, I see. I do believe we're talking at cross-purposes." Her cheeks went pink with embarrassment.

"Are we? What did you and my mother talk about?"

Melly waved a dismissive hand. "Oh, you know. This and that. Reminiscing. We were students together at Anisetab College, you know."

If Melly's focus was on events way in the past, Vi hadn't confided nearly as much as Liss feared she had. She started to let it go, but her curiosity got the best of her. "Perhaps you could share?"

She soon regretted asking. Melly told her more than she wanted to know about her mother's college days and her relationship with A. Leon Palsgrave, the young and handsome professor. There had been secret meetings, since student-faculty fraternization had been frowned upon. There had also been lovers' quarrels and tears and tantrums.

"It was all a long time ago," Liss interrupted when she couldn't stand hearing any more. "What concerns me now is that the police are looking at my father as their prime suspect. He had an argument with Professor Palsgrave in Palsgrave's office a week or so before the murder and he was on campus the day the professor was killed. And then they found what they think is the murder weapon in the trunk of his car."

"Really?" Melly looked intrigued. "What was it? That detail hasn't made the news."

"A hand-and-a-half broadsword." She indicated with her hands just how long the weapon was.

Melly's surprise was obvious, but she made no verbal comment.

"My father didn't do it. He was framed."

"I have no problem believing that," Melly said.

"Does anyone in particular spring to mind as a likely murderer?" Liss whipped out a pocket notebook and a felt-tip pen, ready to jot down names.

"Well, just lately, there are all the people he pissed off with his theories about Henry Sinclair."

"You know about them?"

"Who doesn't? Lee was always up on his soapbox."

"You sound as if you didn't like him much."

"You're right. I didn't." Melly shrugged. "But I didn't dislike him enough to kill him."

"Did anyone?"

Melly considered this. "I don't know any of the demonstrators well enough to say. But I'd think the broadsword would rule out some people. You'd have to have the physical strength to heft one."

"It was a reproduction."

"A stage weapon? Still, they're pretty unwieldy. I sure couldn't manage one." Melly chuckled as she indicated her considerable girth. "Anything else you'd like to know?"

Aiming for nonchalance, Liss admitted there were one or two things she was wondering about.

"I'll just bet there are."

"What do you mean?"

Melly made a snorting sound. "I've read about you, Liss MacCrimmon. In the newspapers. This isn't the first time you've gotten involved in investigating a murder."

Liss winced at the reminder. "Never by choice. And I'm not involved in investigating this one."

Melly waved that off. "Of course you're involved. Your father is a suspect. How can you not be?"

Liss conceded the point. "That being the case, there *is* something you can help me with. You've worked in the theater department since you graduated from Anisetab, right?"

"More years than I want to count."

"So, you must be familiar with Lincoln Hall from the days before the arts center was built."

"Intimately familiar. I was a theater major as a student and worked in that building for the first dozen years I was on staff afterward."

"What I'd really like is a tour. I think that whoever killed Dr. Palsgrave got in and out through the art gallery. Is that feasible?"

"It's certainly a possibility." Melly abruptly stood and collected their empty coffee mugs. Liss couldn't even remember draining hers. "Come on. Time's a wasting. We'll take your car."

*   *   *

It was only a short drive to the college campus, with its tree-shaded green lawns and at least a dozen redbrick buildings. Liss recognized the stone chapel from Willa's description. She had no idea which one was Lincoln Hall, but parked where Melly told her to.

"This is not a classroom building," she said when Melly opened a door and the distinctive smell of French fries wafted out.

"It's eleven-thirty," Melly explained. "We're going to make our first stop the faculty/staff dining room."

"Why?"

The fried food aroma faded as they made their way deeper into the building. The next time Liss inhaled it was to catch the yummy scent of freshly baked lasagna. Her stomach growled loudly.

"That's why," Melly said. "I'm hungry, too. But more importantly," she added, lowering her voice, "this is where the history department's secretary always eats lunch, from precisely eleven-thirty until twelve-thirty every day. Ah, we've lucked out. She's at a table by herself. Go along with whatever I say."

Liss trailed after her mother's friend, feeling like an intruder. Everyone else in the room worked at the college.

"Hey, Norma," Melly said. "This is Lisa. She's going to be a visiting lecturer in the fall. Lisa, this is Norma Leeds. She's the secretary for the history department."

"Administrative assistant," Norma corrected, and accepted "Lisa" at face value. She seemed happy to have their company while she ate.

It didn't take long for Melly to bring the conversation around to the murder. "So, what's the latest scuttlebutt on Palsgrave's death?" she asked. "There sure hasn't been much on the news."

"Terrible, isn't it?" Norma asked in a hushed voice, but her dark brown eyes brightened with the avid gleam of a natural-born gossip. She was a horse-faced woman of indeterminate years—somewhere between thirty and fifty.

"How was he killed?" Melly asked.

"The police won't say, but I know for a fact that there was a lot of blood. Poor Willa Somener—that's Caroline's work-study student—she found the body. She was just hysterical. Well, I'm sure you can imagine."

Liss wondered if Norma knew that Willa was now Caroline's ex-work-study student.

Then she wondered how Norma had come to see Willa having hysterics. Had Willa returned to Caroline's office after the police questioned her? Somehow, Liss doubted it.

The more Norma talked, the more she reminded Liss of Dolores Mayfield, Moosetookalook's village librarian. Like Dolores, Norma didn't let the lack of verified facts keep her from embellishing a good story as she passed it on.

"I heard the police were questioning some guy Lee quarreled with," Melly said between bites of a club sandwich overflowing with sliced chicken and crisp strips of bacon.

"I'm not surprised. I told the officer about that, of course. And that the same man came back the morning of the murder. He *said* he had an appointment." She made it sound as if that was the most outrageous thing in the world.

Liss could no longer hold her tongue. "But he didn't see Dr. Palsgrave *that* day, did he? The day the professor died."

"Not in his office, he didn't. But he was headed for the classroom when he left, and that's where the murder took place, isn't it?" Norma's long, narrow face lit with a triumphant smile.

"Did you send him there?" Melly asked, dabbing her lips with a napkin.

"No, I did not."

"Who did?"

"It was Dr. Halladay who mentioned to that Mac-Crimmon fellow that Lee was probably still in class."

"So it wasn't yet eleven?" Liss interjected.

If Norma thought it odd that Liss would know when the class met, she didn't say so. "I suppose not, although the professor often stayed in his classroom after class, discussing projects with students and so forth. He was a very dedicated teacher."

"Didn't it worry you at the time?" Liss was finding it harder and harder to sound nonchalant. "That Dr. Halladay had told someone who'd quarreled with Dr. Palsgrave where to find him?"

"Why should it?"

She shrugged. "Well, if they fought the last time they met—"

"It isn't as if that was the first time I'd heard shouting from Dr. Palsgrave's office, although I must admit it was usually him doing the yelling." She frowned and even went so far as to stop eating. "Lee was prone to lose his temper, but he always smoothed things over afterward."

Hadn't Willa said she didn't know of *any* disagreements in the history department? Liss set that contradiction aside to think about later. "Could you hear what this argument was about?"

"Well," Norma said in a confiding tone, "I don't know for certain, but it sounded like Lee was up to his old tricks. That man was a tomcat, if you know what I mean."

"Cherchez la femme," Melly said with a laugh. When

Norma looked away, a tinge of pink in her cheeks, and began to shovel spoonfuls of her dessert into her mouth, Melly sent Liss an apologetic look.

"Did Mr. MacCrimmon *threaten* Professor Palsgrave?" Liss asked.

Norma nodded but didn't meet her eyes. "He shouted, 'You stay away from my wife, you son of a bitch, or I'll make you sorry you were ever born!' "

"You're upset," Melly said a few minutes later. They were back in Liss's car.

"Well, of course I'm upset." When Norma had repeated her father's threat, Liss had abruptly lost what little appetite she'd had. Although the department secretary had kept talking, Liss hadn't heard another word she'd said. She'd stayed put as long as she could stand to and then mumbled an excuse about not feeling well and bolted.

Melly reached across and turned the key in the ignition. "Norma always takes her full hour for lunch. That leaves us just enough time to take a look around Lincoln Hall."

Liss was silent during the short drive to the parking lot closest to the history department. She still felt shaky. She didn't believe her father capable of murder, but she was beginning to wonder if she knew him as well as she'd thought she did.

Melly unlocked a very plain door at the side of the building. Her attention caught, Liss zeroed in on the key her mother's old friend was holding. "Does everyone on faculty and staff have a master key to all the buildings on campus?"

"Oh, no," Melly said. "That wouldn't be prudent. But I have one for the arts center and another—this one—

that unlocks all the doors in this building. We still occasionally use the old stage for student productions and the like."

They entered a corridor with doors leading off on both sides.

"Way back when, there was only one office here, for the theater director." Melly indicated the first door to her right. "There was a classroom beyond. On the left there was only one door, leading into a huge open space situated directly under the stage. That's where we used to build sets."

The left side of the corridor now boasted two doors. Between them another hallway veered off in the same direction.

"Now there are all offices here," Melly continued. "Two floors worth." She chuckled. "If anyone tried to go through the trapdoor in the stage these days, they'd find themselves landing on somebody's desk instead of on the elevator platform that used to sit beneath it."

She sounded as if she missed the good old days, but Liss wasn't so much interested in the past as she was the present. "Where is Palsgrave's office?" she asked.

Obligingly, Melly led her into the side corridor and up a flight of stairs. On the second level, through another locked door, they entered an open space containing a desk and several file cabinets, along with the usual office equipment. "This is Norma's area," Melly said, "centrally located. Lee's office is through there."

Liss could easily understand how the secretary had been able to overhear the quarrel. Her work space was right in front of her boss's door. She was in a perfect position to act as guard dog, as well as to get a good look at any and all visitors.

Liss took a few minutes to look around and to read the names on the other doors. Dr. Halladay's office was opposite Dr. Palsgrave's, making it reasonable for her to have heard Liss's father asking for the professor and to have poked her head out to suggest he check the classroom. Liss wished Caroline hadn't been so helpful.

"Seen enough here?" Melly asked. "We need to hustle if we don't want to bump into Norma coming back from lunch."

"Where is the art gallery?" Liss asked.

"We'll get to that in a minute, but I thought you'd want to start from the same point Lee Palsgrave would have."

Their route took them along a zigzagging hallway, down a short flight of stairs, and past a number of closed doors. Melly pointed out one of them as having formerly led into the costume department. They came out into a small foyer containing public restrooms.

Liss felt thoroughly turned around. She thought they were at the back of the building and glanced through the glass in a nearby exit door to confirm her guess. Outside was the driveway heading down to the lot where her car was parked.

"You coming?" Melly was already halfway up the ornate flight of stairs opposite the exit.

At the top was the theater foyer. Double sets of double doors led to a porch on Liss's right and into the auditorium on her left. The box office and the entrance to the art gallery were straight ahead.

"Rabbit warren, indeed," Liss muttered. "I'm not sure I could find my way back to the history department without a trail of bread crumbs to follow."

Melly chuckled and once more whipped out her master key to open the gallery. She relocked the door behind them and hustled Liss past a handful of sculptures and dozens of paintings. Liss didn't get a good look at any of them. Melly hadn't bothered to turn on the lights.

At the far side of the art gallery was another locked door. In seconds, they were through and standing in a hallway flanked by classrooms. Most of their doors stood open and light streamed through from a multitude of windows. Only one door was closed. It also had yellow crime scene tape stretched across it.

Liss entered one of the other classrooms and crossed to the bank of windows. "We're on the first floor," she said in surprise.

"This section of Lincoln Hall is uphill from the theater wing. That's probably half the reason Lee liked to use this shortcut. He hated to exert himself."

"I'd think he'd get just as much exercise running through that maze." Liss studied the street outside. The sidewalk wasn't more than a few yards away from the building. "Whoever killed Dr. Palsgrave took a terrible risk of being seen. What if one of the demonstrators had looked in through a window at just the wrong moment?"

Melly studied the direction of the light, much as Liss had at her house on the day of her fitting. "Even if one of them came close enough, he'd have had a hard time seeing anything of the interior. And I don't imagine the killer took any longer about his business than he had to. Or stuck around afterward, either."

"No. I don't suppose he did. And if I'm right, he came in and went out the same way we just did. And he probably exited the building through that door near the restrooms in the theater wing."

"The one close to the pit," Melly mused. "That means he probably parked there. Too bad there aren't any surveillance cameras."

"The pit?"

Melly laughed. "That's the nickname for that lower parking lot. It overlooks the man-made duck pond that, once upon a time, separated the women's dormitories from the men's. Back in the dark ages when your mother and I were students here, before co-ed dorms became the norm, the powers that be tried to keep the sexes separated. That just made horny college students more creative. Those who had cars used them for parking, usually in that lot. Hence the name 'passion pit.' "

They left the building by the main entrance, after carefully relocking the door to the art gallery. As Liss had been told, the paved path that ran alongside Lincoln Hall sloped steeply downhill.

"About the master keys to this building," she began.

"I've already told you that I don't know who has copies, although I've no doubt that everyone in the history department was issued one. And Norma, of course."

"Anyone else? If Palsgrave locked up after himself, then his killer needed a key to use that route to get away."

"Unless he took Lee's."

Liss shuddered at the image of a murderer coldbloodedly going through the pockets of his victim. She had a good imagination, and no difficulty picturing the gory, gruesome scene. She only wished she could put a face to that vision of the killer.

"If only I had access to what the state police already know," she murmured. "They must have a list of everything that was in Palsgrave's pockets. They'd know whether or not he still had his key on him when they examined the body."

"The custodians also have access to all the buildings," Melly said, apparently still mulling over Liss's original question.

"What about work-study students? Are they given keys?"

"Some are. It depends on what jobs they're assigned. Back in the day, we used to hire a couple of boys just to do odd jobs in the theater department." She grinned suddenly. "Which makes me think there might be even more keys to this building floating around than I first supposed. Those boys weren't always good about turning in their copies back in at the end of a semester."

"You mean they'd forget and take them home with them?"

The grin got broader. "Nope. Those keys became legacies, passed on to a deserving underclassman."

Liss frowned. "I'm not following you."

"Ah, youth. You went to college long after the days when administrators believed they had to act in loco parentis for students. That means 'take the place of parents,' in case you didn't study Latin in school, which you probably didn't. Anyway, back in the day, we had curfews. Girls had to sign out when they left their dormitories after dark and sign in when they returned. If a girl wanted a little time in private with a boyfriend, they had to find someplace other than a dorm room—girls' dorms were off limits to boys and boys' dorms were off limits to girls."

"The pit?" Liss guessed.

"And, for those who didn't like freezing their butts off on a cold winter's night, or having a gearshift poke them in unfortunate places, there were always buildings that were supposed to be empty." She jerked her head toward the former theater as they got back into Liss's car. "In the wings, up a flight of metal stairs—handy for hearing if anyone was coming—there are a couple of rooms used for storing scenery. As far as I know, they're still used for that purpose." A reminiscent smile came over her face, erasing years from her appearance. "I have particularly fond memories of scenery storage loft number two—the one with the bed."

The car engine made a grinding noise as Liss turned

the key too hard in the ignition. It had been a fruitful day. She'd learned a great deal, even if she wasn't yet sure what it all meant. But she'd also heard *way* too much about what life was like on campus when her mother was a coed.

Chapter Ten

When Liss returned home from Three Cities, she found her parents on the little porch attached to the guest room—the same one she'd almost killed herself getting to on the day her father had locked himself in. The two of them looked quite cozy, sharing a late afternoon snack of iced tea and cookies. Apparently they'd talked while she'd been away. She hoped that meant her father had convinced her mother of his innocence.

Reluctant to shatter their rapport, she hesitated in the doorway. She might have retreated, had Vi not glanced up and seen her standing there before she could escape.

"Did you pick up the gowns?" she asked.

"Yes, I—"

"Did you hang them up as soon as you got home?"

"Yes, Mom. I—"

"We expected you back sooner. I hope there weren't any last minute problems."

"No problems with the dress, but I did take time to ask a few questions at the college."

"Really, Liss. There was no need for that."

Liss ignored her mother, keeping her focus on her father. "You were overheard threatening Dr. Palsgrave, Dad. His secretary says you yelled, 'You stay away from my wife, you son of a bitch, or I'll make you sorry you were ever born!' Is that what you said?"

Mac winced. "I'm afraid so, honey, but the worst I was threatening was to get a restraining order, not to kill him, and even that was a bluff because I wouldn't do anything to embarrass Vi."

Vi gave a disbelieving snort. "What do you think quarreling with Lee was, if not embarrassing me?"

"I didn't expect you'd ever hear about it."

Vi sputtered for a moment, then rolled her eyes.

"I'm sorry, Daddy," Liss said, moving closer, "but I need to know. Why were you so sure Dr. Palsgrave was out to cause trouble between you and Mother?"

"Because he tried once before, before we were married."

"I know they were . . . involved when Mom was in college."

Mac waved that away as unimportant. "It was a passing fancy. Sowing wild oats. Whatever you want to call it, it wasn't serious. What we had was. But Palsgrave didn't like losing. First he made a point of telling me about their affair. That was about a week before our wedding. He didn't realize that Vi had already confessed everything. Then he tried to convince me that he was better for her than I was. That I should break it off."

"He wanted to *marry* Mom?"

"He did *not*," Vi yelped.

Mac shook his head. "I doubt it. I seriously doubt it. He just didn't like letting anyone else have her. And recently, when he saw a chance to come back into her life, even after so many years, he was determined to seize it.

He wouldn't have been happy until he'd seduced your mother all over again."

"As if I'd have let him," Vi grumbled. She reached out to clasp Mac's hand. He squeezed hers in return.

Liss went back downstairs in a daze. It was disturbing enough to hear about her parents' sex life, but this new side to her father had her seriously freaked out. He loved her mother enough to want to protect her from a man he saw as a threat. Liss got that. What stunned her was that he'd reacted so irrationally. He'd never been one to lose his temper, but jealousy was a powerful emotion—powerful enough to drive men to kill.

Liss entered the library and closed the door. Once she was seated at the desk, she pulled out another of her ever-present lined yellow tablets and started the chronology of events that she'd been meaning to make for days.

July 2
*Dad quarrels with A. Leon Palsgrave;
    overheard by Norma Leeds and possibly
    others*

Before July 9
*At Mom's insistence, Dad phones history de-
    partment to make an appointment to apolo-
    gize*

Liss paused in her writing to study the last entry. She'd have to ask her father exactly when he'd made the appointment and who he'd talked to. Whoever had framed him for murder must have known he'd be going to Three Cities that day.

July 8 (?), probably in the middle of the night
*someone sneaks into Emporium and takes
    broadsword from the display window*
*Angie notices sword missing but she's not sure
    when*

July 9
Palsgrave's class starts at 8 AM
*Dad leaves Moosetookalook to go to Three
    Cities for appointment with Palsgrave*
*Protestors gather outside Lincoln Hall, know-
    ing Palsgrave's class meets there*
*Sherri, Zara, Mom, and I leave
    Moosetookalook to go to Three Cities for
    dress fitting*
Palsgrave dismisses class early
*Dad arrives for his appointment but Palsgrave
    is not in his office*
*Caroline Halladay suggests Dad go to
    Palsgrave's classroom*
*Dad finds the classroom empty, leaves and
    heads back to Moosetookalook*
*Palsgrave returns to his classroom—Why? And
    where was he?*

Again, Liss stopped writing. Palsgrave was supposed
to be in his classroom, teaching a three-hour summer
seminar that started at eight in the morning. Why had he
changed his routine? And had any of his students seen
anything before they left the building? She sighed. Her
time line was creating more questions than it answered.
Still, she went on with it. She didn't have any better
ideas.

Unknown party with broadsword probably uses
*   art gallery shortcut to reach classroom*
Palsgrave murdered
Killer probably returns the same way and exits
*   through door near "the pit"*
Caroline Halladay sends Willa Somener to see
*   if Palsgrave is still in his classroom*
Willa goes the long way around; stops to talk
*   to Gabe; finds body*

Liss tapped her pencil against the pad. According to
Gabe Treat, at least a half hour passed between Mac's
exit from Lincoln Hall and Willa's arrival. That was
plenty of time for someone else to find Palsgrave alone
and slaughter him, but a very tight time frame if the
murder was planned with the intent of framing Mac
MacCrimmon. The killer would have to steal the broadsword from Liss's display window in advance and know
exactly when Liss's father was due to arrive, and that he
would not find Palsgrave in the classroom when he
looked for him there. But how had he lured Palsgrave
away, then convinced him to go back?

To be honest, this scenario defied belief—except that
the only other possibility she could think of was that her
father really was the killer. That, Liss refused to believe.
She forced herself to finish listing events in the order
they'd happened.

local police arrive, then state police
reporters arrive
"breaking story" makes noon news
we head back to Moosetookalook
Dad arrives in Moosetookalook about an hour
*   before we do*

She quickly flipped the page and began a new list, copying all the names Melly had given her of faculty members who probably had a master key to Lincoln Hall. Melly had written them down for her after their visit to the scene of the crime. Liss added the name of the custodian assigned to Lincoln Hall. Melly had phoned her with that information during the hour and a half drive home.

Unfortunately, viable candidates turned out to be few and far between. At the end of an hour of checking online and making phone calls, she'd learned that most of the faculty members weren't even on campus for the summer session. Her history department list ended up pared down to the same few names—Caroline Halladay, Norma Leeds, and Willa Somener. Based on physical strength alone, none of them seemed likely killers.

That left the protestors. Liss wrote their names on a separate page: John Jones, Louis Amalfi, Barry Rowse, Alistair Gunn . . . and Gabe Treat. She circled Gabe's name. It was the one that kept cropping up. He was Gunn's grandson, Willa's boyfriend, and a theater major. Coincidence? Maybe. But the fact that he was in that last category meant he might well have his own key to open the doors in Lincoln Hall.

Perhaps, she thought, Caroline Halladay was the one she ought to talk to. Among other questions, she could ask the professor just why she'd been so upset with Willa that she'd fired her. On the surface, Willa's involvement with a young man whose grandfather was "the enemy" should not have been enough to cost the work-study student her job.

Saturday morning dawned clear and bright. Liss's wedding was only a week away. She went over her bridal checklist one more time. "Final guest count to catering department at hotel," she read aloud. "Check. Confirm details with florist . . . check. Write more thank-you notes." Liss made a face. She'd do that later.

Satisfied all was in order, she went to work. To her surprise, Willa showed up an hour later. "Do you mind if I just hang out here?" she asked. "The campground is pretty boring."

"Of course not, but where's Gabe?"

"Oh, he has to drive back to Three Cities every day to check on his grandfather." She trailed her fingers over a display of pewter figurines of bagpipers and Scottish dancers. "He's very devoted to Mr. Gunn."

Liss shooed Willa ahead of her into the stockroom so she could start processing orders. Willa pitched in to help, cutting off sections of bubble wrap as Liss put boxes together. "Have you known Gabe long?" Liss asked when they'd been working companionably for a while.

"Since we were freshmen."

Willa burbled on for some time about the early days of her romance with Gabe while she and Liss boxed, taped, and applied labels. Liss didn't really listen to the flow of words. She was biding her time, waiting to ask direct questions about the history department and about Gabe's grandfather. She started small, inquiring into Willa's duties as a work-study student.

"I ran a lot of errands. Dr. Halladay is doing most of the work of organizing the medieval conclave. It's going to be spectacular, especially now." Color flooded her face as she realized what she'd just said. "That didn't come out right. Of course no one's glad Dr. Palsgrave was murdered. All I mean is that without the reenactment of the battle, there will be more focus on the displays and craft demonstrations."

"What crafts?" Liss asked, more to keep the young

woman talking than because she had any deep interest in the subject.

Eagerness shone in Willa's eyes. "It's really going to be remarkable. There is a tanner and a glove maker, a brewer, a cobbler, a goldsmith, a weaver, and even a blacksmith. And Dr. Halladay learned to do almost every one of those things herself. She's very hands-on in her approach to studying history."

"Who will help her prepare for the conclave now that you're not there? Norma?"

Willa made a face. "Norma doesn't like to get her hands dirty. I'm sure she's hired someone else by now. Dr. Halladay is teaching two classes this semester. She wouldn't have had any trouble finding a student willing to do grunt work in the hope of a better grade."

"What is she teaching this summer?" Liss set another box on top of the pile ready to go to the post office.

"Medieval history." Willa laughed. "What else? One course is just Introduction to the Middle Ages, but the other is Women of Power in the Medieval World. Dr. Palsgrave used to tell her it should be called Medieval Roots of the Kick-Ass Heroine."

"I'm not much of a history buff," Liss admitted after she'd responded with the chuckle Willa clearly expected from her, "but I think I'd be more likely to enroll in a class that had *kick-ass* in the title than otherwise."

"Dr. Halladay says women have always been powerful. They just worked behind the scenes instead of center stage. And, of course, the history books always used to be written by men, so women's contributions were neglected."

"Not so much these days."

"No," Willa agreed. "Now a woman can do anything a man can."

"Unless it requires brute strength."

Willa didn't say anything for a moment. "Women can be strong. They just have to work at it." She sighed. "Not me, though. I've never been one for lifting weights. And those big workout machines are kind of scary looking, don't you think?"

A customer came into the Emporium before Liss could answer. She sent Willa out to wait on the patron and was gratified when, a short time later, she heard the cha-ching of the cash register.

"Tourist," Willa reported when she came back into the stockroom. "He bought a present for his wife. One of those thistle pins with the amethyst for the flower. Can I stay the rest of the day?"

"I'm not sure I have enough to keep you busy."

"You don't have to pay me," Willa said. "I just don't want to go back to the campground."

Liss agreed, but she was puzzled. Since when did poverty-stricken college students offer to work for free? Even more remarkably, after she dropped the packages off at the post office, Willa offered to treat Liss to lunch at Patsy's.

"You don't have to do that," Liss objected.

"But I want to. To thank you. And I already know that you sometimes close the shop from noon till twelve-thirty."

"Yes, but—"

"You *have* to eat."

Liss laughed and gave in.

At the coffee shop, Willa made a production out of selecting their booth. She didn't want Liss to have the sun in her eyes, she said, so Willa ended up facing the window, which left Liss staring at the passage that led to the kitchen and restrooms.

For the duration of the meal, Willa chattered incessantly, although she neatly avoided answering any questions Liss asked that had to do with Gabe or his grandfather. Just what was going on here? Liss wondered.

It was nearly one in the afternoon before they finally left Patsy's and headed back across the town square to Moosetookalook Scottish Emporium. Willa was so tense she was vibrating with it.

"More online orders to pack up, right?" she asked as soon as they entered the shop. She tried to herd Liss toward the stockroom, not even giving her time to flip the CLOSED sign on the front door to OPEN.

"I was thinking I should redo the window display." Liss dragged her feet. Her sense that something was off kilter grew stronger with every step.

At the entrance to the stockroom, Willa stopped and gestured for Liss to precede her. Liss frowned. The interior was black as pitch. Why wasn't any daylight coming in through the small window in the exit door?

She glanced warily at Willa. The young woman stared back at her with wide and worried eyes. She looked like someone on the verge of a panic attack.

Liss started to retreat, suddenly certain that she should not set foot in the stockroom. To prevent her escape, Willa grabbed her arm and, with surprising strength, shoved her over the threshold. The second they were both inside, Willa closed the door behind them, leaving them in total darkness.

At that moment, neither a blow to the back of the head nor a stab wound to the heart would have surprised Liss. She drew breath to scream, but before she could utter a sound, someone flicked the light switch.

She blinked in the sudden blinding brightness, unable to believe her eyes. Then her ears rang as a dozen high-pitched feminine voices shouted in unison: "Surprise!"

In her absence from the building, the stockroom had been transformed. Colorful streamers were draped over the shelves. A banner that said BRIDES RULE hung from the ceiling. Gifts were piled high on Liss's worktable, which had been shoved back against one wall. And all around her were her friends—Sherri, Zara, and Angie, among them—smiling and laughing and taking pictures. Her mother pushed through the crowd to give Liss a hug. Dan's sister was right behind her, beaming. Then the door from the shop opened again and Patsy joined the party.

"Did we truly manage to surprise you?" Vi asked.

"You truly did." Belatedly, she caught on. "You hired Willa to sandbag me!"

"I hear you had a bridal shower today," Dan greeted her that evening.

"My mother and your sister are sneakier than I gave them credit for." Liss slid into the passenger side of the pickup truck and buckled herself in.

She hadn't bothered to reopen the shop after the shower guests left. Instead, she'd sent Willa on her way and spent the rest of the afternoon attempting to get in touch with Dr. Caroline Halladay. She'd had no luck. Either the woman wasn't home or she was ignoring her messages.

Liss hoped Detective Franklin was doing better than she was at figuring out who had killed Professor Palsgrave. There had been nothing in the newspapers or on

TV about his progress in the case. It had now been eight days since he'd found the sword.

Two days later, or so Liss had heard through the grapevine, officers had finally shown up in Moosetook-alook to question the neighbors. No one in the village had caught so much as a glimpse of a state trooper since.

"I thought we'd drive out to the falls," Dan said. "It should be a pretty sunset."

"Sounds perfect," Liss told him, and meant it. She inhaled deeply, then turned to look behind the seat. A picnic basket nestled there atop a brightly colored blanket. "When did you have time to do all this?"

"You forget. I've got an in with the head chef at The Spruces. She thinks I'm too skinny."

"Fattening you up, is she?" She chuckled. Angeline Cloutier was also providing the food for their wedding reception. And the wedding cake. Liss and Dan had both been working hard to stay on her good side.

They ate cheese and crackers and opened a bottle of wine. Perfectly fried chicken with homemade coleslaw followed, along with biscuits still warm from the oven. By the time they topped off their meal with thick slices of chocolate cake, Liss felt relaxed and replete. All in all, she decided, it had been a lovely day.

They sat on the blanket, Dan's arm around Liss's shoulders, and watched the sun dip lower in the western sky over the waterfall. For the first time in weeks, Liss's world seemed peaceful and serene.

She was still in an excellent mood when they drove away from the picnic area. Perhaps her mother and Dan were right when they advised her to focus on the wedding—her big day, as Vi insisted on calling it. She wasn't making any progress in discovering who had killed Professor Palsgrave anyway. And Mac kept insisting that she had no cause to worry on his account.

She just wished he'd follow his own advice. Despite the fact that her father had said, repeatedly, that everything would sort itself out, new lines had appeared in his face, literally overnight.

Despite her best intentions, Liss found herself fretting again. If she and Dan went to Scotland for three weeks, it wouldn't be easy to get back home quickly in an emergency—like her father's arrest for murder.

She glanced over at Dan. He was in silhouette as darkness fell in earnest. She didn't have to broach the subject to know how he'd react to any suggestion that they postpone their honeymoon. He'd say the same thing he had about their wedding. Come hell or high water, they'd stick to the plan.

When they passed the road sign that told them Moosetookalook was five miles away, they also drove out of the "dead zone" they'd been in all evening. Liss burrowed in her purse for her cell phone and discovered she'd had two calls, both from her own land line. Each time, the call had gone to voice mail. The sound of a phone being slammed back into the cradle was the only audible message in the first. In the second, Vi's voice uttered a single expletive before she hung up.

Liss frowned, puzzled. It wasn't like her mother to swear. And her usual practice was to leave a long, detailed voice mail, especially when she was calling to nag her daughter to do something. Liss debated returning the call, but decided that whatever the trouble was, it could wait until they reached the house.

Then the phone attached to Dan's dashboard started to ring. The small screen lit up to display Liss's home phone number. Beginning to be alarmed, she hit the Speaker button.

"What is it, Mom?"

At first, she could barely understand what Vi was saying—or rather, screeching—into her ear. The words were liberally interspersed with sobs and curses. Then one sentence came through loud and clear, chilling her to the bone: "Your father's been arrested for Lee Palsgrave's murder."

Chapter Eleven

By the time Liss and Dan arrived back in town, Vi had conquered the worst of her hysterics and was sitting on the living room sofa, quietly sobbing. Liss took a firm grip on her own emotions. Her mother needed her to stay calm and levelheaded. She could always fall apart later. She put her arms around Vi's shoulders and was shocked by how violently the older woman was shaking.

"I don't deserve your sympathy," Vi whispered in a tremulous voice. "This is all my fault."

"Now, Mom, you know that's not true. But you need to tell us what happened. Where have they taken Daddy?"

"I don't know. I don't know anything. That policeman wouldn't tell me. He tried to shut me out." For a moment, she looked more indignant than devastated. "I have a right to know what's going on. Mac is my *husband*!"

"Did the police let him call a lawyer?" Dan asked.

"I don't know," she repeated. "One minute the detective was talking to Mac in the kitchen and the next he was taking him out of the house and driving off."

"Was it Detective Franklin?" Liss asked.

Vi nodded. "Terrible man."

At this particular moment, Liss was inclined to agree. Dan came back into the living room, having left to make a quick call on his cell phone. "Pete's coming right over."

"Good. Maybe he can help us sort this out. And Sherri must know something. Surely the local police would be informed in advance."

"Why should they be?" Dan asked. "The state police don't have to ask their permission to make an arrest."

"Courtesy? And it would have been nice to have given us some warning that this was about to happen."

"Would it have made any difference if you'd known ahead of time? Always assuming Mac didn't intend to skip town to avoid arrest."

Liss glared at him in exasperation. "That's not what I meant and you know it. I just can't help thinking that the arrest must have come as a terrible shock to my dad. He doesn't hear anything for over a week and then, boom! 'Hey you—you're under arrest for murder.' "

Dan started to say something, then turned away in relief as the front door opened to admit Pete Campbell. The fact that he was in uniform told Liss that he was on duty, or had only just reached the end of his shift. Either way, he was a welcome sight.

"Franklin arrested Mac?" he asked.

Fresh tears streaming down her cheeks, Vi nodded. "Just came in here and took him away."

"Any idea where they'd go?" Dan asked Pete.

"Back to Three Cities, I expect. To the county jail there, since that's where the crime took place."

"How do we get him out?" Liss demanded. "Will they set bail?"

Pete didn't want to meet her eyes. "Uh, probably not. Not if the charge is murder."

"You mean he'll have to stay in jail until his trial? That's preposterous. He's innocent!"

"They must have pretty solid evidence against him or the attorney general wouldn't have authorized an arrest." Pete's honesty earned him a basilisk glare from Vi and a tight-lipped frown from Liss. "Hey, don't kill the messenger! If the charge is murder, the accused stays put."

"I won't accept that." Liss strode to the phone on the end table. She only knew one lawyer, Edmund Carrier III. He didn't specialize in criminal law, but he'd know someone who did. And he'd answer her call even at this late hour.

Ten minutes later, Carrier had promised to check into the matter.

The next half hour passed with excruciating slowness. Pete made a series of phone calls but was unable to discover where Franklin had taken Mac.

"He hasn't been booked at any county jail within a radius of two hundred miles of Moosetookalook," Pete reported.

"Where else could he be?"

Pete was literally scratching his head. "No idea, Liss. Sorry."

By the time an hour had gone by, Liss was feeling desperate. "I'm going to phone Gordon Tandy."

"There's no need to bring the ex-boyfriend into this," Dan objected.

"Yes, there is, when he's also the state police officer for this area. I know he won't be pleased to hear from me, but I'm sure he'll help. And he ought to know how to contact Franklin, right? They probably have an in-house directory for phone numbers. Oh!" Liss felt her eyes go wide. "I'm an idiot! I already have Franklin's cell phone number. It's in the junk drawer at the Emporium."

Before she could leave the house to get it, her mother reached into the pocket of her slacks and pulled out a twin of the one Liss had treated so cavalierly. "I forgot I had this. Well, there's been a lot going on," she defended herself when Liss shot her an exasperated look. "You forgot, too! No one can be expected to remember everything."

Liss snatched the card out of Vi's hand and headed for the phone. Just as she was about to pick it up, it rang. She snatched it out of the cradle, relaxing only slightly when she realized it was Mr. Carrier on the other end of the line. He had no real news to report, but to the best of anyone's knowledge, Donald "Mac" MacCrimmon had not been arrested.

"That doesn't make sense," Liss objected. She turned at the sound of the front door opening and felt her jaw drop as her father walked in the house. He was alone, and he looked vaguely puzzled to find the living room full of people.

Everyone started to talk at once. Liss dropped the phone and flung herself into her startled father's arms. "We were so worried," she whispered. "I'm so glad they let you go."

"Let me go?" he echoed. "What are you talking about?"

"The state police. Mom said Detective Franklin arrested you."

Watching her father's face, Liss pegged his expression as incredulous, followed briefly by amused. Then the thunderclouds gathered and he put his hands on her shoulders to gently set her aside.

Vi was back on the sofa, sitting ramrod straight with her features arranged in a stoic mask. Mac went down on one knee, even though his arthritic joints popped loudly and the action made him wince. When they were eye to eye, he took her hands in his and finally spoke.

"Vi, you have to stop jumping to conclusions. Did you hear the detective tell me I was under arrest?" She shook her head. "Did you hear him read me the Miranda warning?"

"No, but—"

"What you heard was Detective Franklin asking you to leave us alone to speak in private. What I heard was you, in a snit, refusing. It was pretty obvious that even if he convinced you to leave the room, you'd be lurking just outside, listening to every word."

"I had a right to be there. I'm your wife."

He was more patient with her than Liss would have been. "Not in this case. And that's why we went elsewhere—to the police station down in Fallstown—to talk. Just to talk, Vi. He had more questions for me and he didn't want to share them with an audience."

That explained why no one had seen them, Liss realized. Pete had called around at the county level, since sheriffs ran the jails. He'd passed right over the local police department in the very same town as the nearest correctional facility.

"So, you weren't arrested." Liss's tone was flat.

"I was not arrested," Mac confirmed. "And we should all be relieved about that, right?" Patting Vi's hand, he hauled himself up again, only to sink down onto the sofa beside her. "That's not to say I may not be in the future, but for tonight the good detective just wanted to grill me without interference from my lovely wife."

"Do you think this is *funny*?" Vi demanded. "We were all worried sick about you."

Mac rolled his eyes. "There are definitely elements of humor involved, and I'd rather laugh over them than cry."

"We called a lawyer!" Now Vi sounded put out.

"Oh, Lord! Mr. Carrier!" Liss hastily retrieved the phone, which still dangled over the edge of the end table. She was both surprised and embarrassed to discover that the lawyer had not hung up on her. "How much of that did you hear?" she asked him.

"A fair amount." He, too, sounded amused, but when he spoke again, his voice was somber. "I think it would be a good idea if your father met with me first thing on Monday, Liss. Without your mother. I understand that he's innocent, but even the innocent need legal advice when the crime is as serious as this one."

She made the appointment without consulting either of her parents. And when she told her father of that fact, she also informed him that she'd be driving him to Carrier's office in Fallstown.

Sunday, thankfully, passed quietly and without incident.

On Monday morning, as Liss sat cooling her heels in the lawyer's waiting room while her father talked privately with Edmund Carrier III, she began to understand why her mother had become so agitated over being shut out. It was frustrating not to know what was going on, especially when it concerned someone so close to her.

The appointment had been for eight. The twentieth time Liss checked her watch, it was still moving unnaturally slowly. Mac had been in there less than an hour, but what little patience she had was already exhausted. She stood, ready to brave Carrier's dragon of a receptionist and storm the portal, but before she could put her plan into action, the street door opened and the most average-looking man Liss had ever seen walked in.

"Hey, babe," he greeted the receptionist.

"Good morning, Jacob." Her tone sounded frosty but

her eyes twinkled. Liss blinked. Was she *flirting* with him? The dragon, Danielle Phillipi by name, was sixty if she was a day.

"I keep telling you—it's Jake. Just plain old Jake."

Of course it was, Liss thought. Distracted, fascinated, she had no qualms about eavesdropping on the conversation. The waiting room was small. It wasn't as if they didn't know she was right there. They were just ignoring her presence.

Jake put both palms on the desk and leaned in until he was almost close enough to give Ms. Phillipi a peck on the cheek. "Come on, sweet knees. You know you want to."

"Want to what, Jacob?" she asked in saccharine tones.

"Call me Jake, of course." And they both smiled.

Another image superimposed itself over Ms. Phillipi and Jake Whatever-his-name-was. All of a sudden, Liss was seeing a scene from a James Bond movie—any one of them. The byplay she'd just witnessed had the same feel as the set-piece exchanges between Miss Moneypenny and 007.

She had to turn her back on the couple at the desk to banish the illusion. The thought that she might be losing her grip on reality spooked her. Although she was staring through the window at the tree-lined Fallstown street beyond, she didn't see the passing cars or the pedestrian traffic. Sounds faded from her consciousness, too, voices becoming as much a part of the ignorable background as the hum of the air conditioner.

She didn't hear the footfalls approaching directly behind her. When a hand touched her shoulder, she jumped.

Liss swung around, fists clenched, and found herself face-to-face with the man named Jake. He was almost exactly her own height, but short brown hair and brown eyes and an unlined face made it impossible to guess his age. Suddenly, the eyes went hard and calculating. *James Bond*, she thought again, before she realized that he was chewing gum. The big pink bubble he blew completely shattered the image of the suave superspy.

"You the guy's daughter?" Jake asked her.

"What?"

"The guy in with Carrier—you his kid?"

"Oh. Yes." And why was she talking to this man? She answered her own question—because she was more rattled by recent events than she'd thought. "Excuse me. I'm just going to sit down. To wait. He shouldn't be much longer now."

Jake trailed after her and took the chair next to the one Liss chose. "Jake Murch," he said, thrusting his hand toward her.

Automatically, she took it and shook. "Liss Mac-Crimmon."

"Well, Lisa—"

"Liss." The correction was also automatic. "L-I-S-S."

"Whatever. Carrier called me to come in. Thinks I can do a little legwork on your father's behalf." At her baffled expression, he added, "I'm Fallstown's answer to *Magnum, P.I.*" He chortled at his own humor. "Murch, PI, at your service."

Appalled, Liss could only stare at him. *This* was Mr. Carrier's investigator?

Murch grinned suddenly, as if he read her thoughts. "No joke," he assured her. "I'm the best you're going to get in these parts. And since Carrier hasn't called me in there yet, I may as well start working on the case with you. Want to tell me why I should believe your father didn't off that college professor?"

Feeling a little desperate, Liss looked to the dragon for help.

Miss Phillipi shrugged. "Mr. Carrier has already filled

Jacob in on the rough outline of the case. You should probably tell him what he wants to know."

It was a less-than-sterling endorsement, but at least it confirmed that Jake Murch was what he said he was. "My father was framed."

"They all say that."

"In this case, it's true. The murder weapon was stolen from the display window in my shop and planted in my father's car after it was used to kill Professor Palsgrave."

"And you know this because?"

"Because my father is not a murderer."

"Circular reasoning, sweetheart." Before she could explode, he pulled out a dog-eared notebook. "But let's suppose you're right. Who do you like for suspects?"

Her eyes narrowed as her hackles rose. Really, he was the most annoying man! "Why do you think I suspect anyone?"

"Because I did my homework. I know who you are and what you've been up to the last couple of years."

That was a sobering thought! Liss swallowed back her irritation, reminding herself that the important thing was to free her father from suspicion. If that meant sharing information with Jake Murch, so be it. She reached for her purse and the time line and list of suspects it contained.

She'd barely turned them over to Murch before the intercom on the dragon lady's desk buzzed and Ms. Phillipi announced that he should go on in to the lawyer's office.

"I'm coming with you," Liss announced, getting to her feet.

"Ms. MacCrimmon, Mr. Carrier only asked for Mr. Murch."

"Tough. He's getting me, too. I'm sure that Mr. Murch will vouch for my skills as an investigator."

Mr. Murch didn't appear willing to do any such thing, but short of tying her to a chair in the waiting room, he couldn't stop her. She steamed into the office ahead of him and before either her father or Mr. Carrier could object, held up a hand, palm out.

"If you don't think I have a right to be here as a daughter, then let me stay as someone who can help find the real murderer. I'm the one with a list of likely suspects. I can save Mr. Murch a good deal of time and effort."

"Liss, I don't want you involved in this," her father said.

"How can I not be?" She was prepared to enumerate the ways she was already involved, but she could see from his expression that he understood, perhaps more than she'd realized.

"This is such bad timing," Mac said with a sigh.

She rolled her eyes. "Is there ever a good time to be accused of murder?" She took the chair next to him, in front of Mr. Carrier's huge mahogany desk, leaving Murch to stand.

"I haven't been accused of any crime."

"Yet."

"I may never be. Have you considered the possibility that Detective Franklin is hesitating to arrest me because he sees the obvious frame-up as clearly as you do?"

"I'm not willing to bet your life on it."

His lips quirked into the ghost of a smile. "Relax, honey. There's no death penalty in Maine."

"No. Only life in prison. Are you willing to risk that on your faith in Franklin's common sense?" Liss shifted her attention to the lawyer. "What are the odds on my father being charged with murder?"

Edmund Carrier III was an overweight, balding gentleman in his midfifties. He was dressed formally in a three-piece suit but his ruddy complexion hinted at outdoor activities on the weekends. "The attorney general could probably make a case now," he said. "My best guess is that Detective Franklin is taking the time to dot his i's and cross his t's."

"Great. That's just great!"

Liss couldn't remain seated. She was too agitated. She bounded to her feet and paced to the window, then moved back past the wall of bookcases filled with lawyerly tomes and ended up leaning against the door with her arms folded in front of her chest. She glowered at the three men indiscriminately.

Murch, who had made himself comfortable in the chair Liss had just vacated, waved her list of names in the air. "You talk to any of these people since the murder?"

"With Willa, Gabe, Caroline, and Norma, yes." She gave him a brief recap of her conversations with each of them.

"Okey-dokey." He tucked the paper into his breast pocket and stood. "I'll reinterview those four after I have a little chat with each of the others." He tipped an imaginary hat to Carrier and Mac. "I'm on the clock."

"Okey-dokey?" Liss echoed, rolling her eyes. Feeling slightly frantic, she appealed to the lawyer. "Mr. Carrier, I—"

He cut her off. "I know. I know. Murch doesn't inspire a great deal of confidence, but I've worked with him before. He gets results. Think of Columbo."

"Columbo was a character on an old TV show. Real life is different."

"Less so than you might think."

"Let the investigator do his job, Liss," her father interrupted. "He's trained for it. You're not."

It was the same argument she'd been hearing right along for letting the police handle everything. She hadn't bought it then and she wasn't buying now. Her resolve hardened. Rather than stop talking to people, she would come up with logical excuses to question the others on her list. She'd track down each of the demonstrators and anyone else she could think of with a connection to the case. Who knew what she might find out under the guise of casual conversation?

But the first person she wanted to interview was her father. He'd entered Lincoln Hall through the front door. He must have noticed both the picket line and Gabe Treat. What else had he seen? Who else?

She started in on him the moment they returned to her car for the drive home. For once, he didn't object to being grilled, although he did insist she swing through the drive-up window of his favorite fast-food restaurant first. Fortified with a burger and fries, he took her step-by-step through his ill-fated attempt to meet with A. Leon Palsgrave.

"I was feeling pretty foolish by the time I left that classroom," he admitted, after he'd recounted the details she'd already heard elsewhere. "And I was more than a little irritated. I'd driven all the way to Three Cities to apologize—to please your mother—and then I couldn't find anyone to apologize to. I decided enough was enough and I headed home. I was completely wrapped up in my own thoughts. I didn't pay any attention to my surroundings before or after I left that empty classroom."

"You must have noticed the demonstrators." She took one hand off the wheel long enough to steal a few French fries.

When he didn't answer, she slanted a glance his way, taking note of the blank expression on his face. He had no idea what she was talking about.

"How did you get from the professor's office to the classroom?"

"There's a paved walkway between buildings. Goes uphill."

"And you went back the same way, to that lower parking lot?"

"Right." He took another bite of his burger.

Liss sighed. He hadn't gone near the street. Unless he'd looked that way as he'd entered Lincoln Hall, he wouldn't have noticed the picket line. There had only been four demonstrators. Even if they'd been chanting protest slogans, Mac might not have paid them any attention.

It was equally possible that none of them had noticed him.

"Were there any students around?" she asked.

Since he was fishing in the take-out bag for napkins, his voice was muffled. "Sorry, Liss. No idea. I really wish I'd known I was going to need an alibi. I'm sure I'd have managed to call attention to myself in some way. Maybe danced the tango in the middle of the quad."

She appreciated the dry humor, even while she lamented the fact that he had neither an alibi nor any details to add to what she already knew.

It was still early afternoon when they arrived back in Moosetookalook, but Liss felt utterly drained. If she hadn't had so much to do, she'd have considered taking a nap. Her father, too, appeared to be exhausted, but her mother, who came out onto the porch to greet them, was bubbling over with energy.

"Liss, dear," she announced in a cheerful voice, her smile blindingly bright, "Angeline Cloutier needs you to run out to the hotel and approve the final design on the wedding cake."

"Not now, Mom. It can wait."

Liss was in no mood to deal with wedding chores. And that begged the real question—how could she even think about getting married when her father might *really* be arrested at any moment? Mr. Carrier had confirmed what Pete had told them about bail. If the charge was murder, there would be no getting out of jail before the trial.

"No," Vi said in the firm mother voice Liss remembered from her childhood. "It can *not* wait. She's about to start baking!"

Chapter Twelve

Talking to Angeline Cloutier, head chef at The Spruces, was the last thing Liss felt like doing, but in the end she gave in to her mother's demands. A glance at her father reminded her that her parents needed time together without their daughter around. Once she'd approved the cake design, however—something she'd already done once—she planned to head straight home.

She started to feel more upbeat as soon as she stepped out of the car in the hotel parking lot and was greeted by the soothing scent of newly mown grass. The hotel kitchen smelled even better. Angeline had her sampling of the day's special as she trotted out the carefully drawn rendering of what she planned to bake and decorate. She'd added a few new flourishes, but Liss liked them. They shook hands on it and Liss left with the intention of making a quick getaway.

Caroline Halladay waltzed into the lobby at The Spruces just as Liss was passing through.

"I'm looking for Margaret Boyd," Professor Halladay told the desk clerk. "It's about the coming weekend's festivities."

"The highland games or the wedding?" Trisha Lynd asked. She'd been an intern at the hotel the previous year and had been taken on as a full-time employee at the beginning of the summer.

"What wedding?" Caroline sounded surprised.

"Mine." Liss came up behind her.

She hesitated a moment, wondering if Caroline would make the connection between the MacCrimmons she'd met—Liss and Vi—and the MacCrimmon who'd had an appointment with Leon Palsgrave on the day he was murdered. When no sign of distress showed on the older woman's plump features, Liss seized the opportunity to pump the history professor for information.

"I'll show you to Ms. Boyd's office if you like." Liss knew for a fact that her aunt was not there. Margaret had gone to Augusta for a hearing held by the state tourism board.

In contrast to Joe Ruskin's office, Margaret's was furnished with comfort in mind. The small room was painted a pretty pale green and three Carrabassett County landscapes, done in pen and ink by local artists, decorated the walls. Liss offered coffee or tea and then settled Caroline on a love seat upholstered in a bright floral pattern while she prepared the latter. As Caroline chattered about the arrangements for the Medieval Scottish Conclave and the half-dozen details that she wanted to confirm with Margaret, Liss used the small microwave behind Margaret's desk to heat water and pour it into the pretty Royal Doulton teapot her aunt liked to use.

"I suppose canceling the reenactment leaves a big hole in the program," Liss said in the most sympathetic tone of voice she could manage.

She put the tea tray on a glass-topped coffee table. Snagging a dainty wooden chair, she seated herself facing the love seat. She did not want the barrier of the desk between them.

"Personally, I think leaving it out is an improvement. The people who come to see our events and displays won't be distracted by those dreadful picket lines and can properly appreciate the richness of the medieval experience."

Caroline fluffed her short, curly, ash blond hair before reaching for the teapot. Liss found this evidence of vanity incongruous in a woman who so obviously took no care with the rest of her appearance. As had been the case every other time Liss had seen her, she wore bulky, shapeless clothing that only emphasized her lack of height and excess of pounds.

"If you don't mind my asking," Liss began, "I'm curious about something. You see, I've hired your former work-study student to help out at my booth at the highland games. I was wondering why you fired her. Her work record seems sound enough."

Not that she'd checked it before she offered Willa a job, although she had contacted the bookstore Willa had worked in since then. Initially, Liss had gone with her gut feeling about the young woman. She hoped she wasn't about to regret it.

Caroline set the teapot back down and took a moment to gather herself. "I suppose I may have overreacted," she admitted, "but I value loyalty above all else and when I learned, from you, that Willa had been fraternizing with the enemy . . . well, I was very upset, to say the least."

"Surely it isn't Willa's fault that Gabe Treat is the grandson of one of the demonstrators."

"Of course not." Caroline's bright blue eyes met Liss's, her gaze direct and her expression uncompromising. "It's that she wasn't *honest* with me about it."

"Perhaps she didn't think her personal life was relevant."

Liss took a sip of the tea Caroline had poured for her. She quickly put the cup down again. She wasn't much of a tea drinker and from the bitter taste she suspected that she hadn't brewed a very satisfactory pot of the stuff.

"You obviously knew Willa and Gabe were an item, even if you didn't know Alistair Gunn was his grandfather. What else do you know about Gabe Treat? He seems a nice enough young man to me."

"Spoiled," was Caroline's opinion. She sampled the tea and grimaced, but she continued to sip as she talked. "He's a rich boy. We get a lot of those at Anisetab College. He's majoring in theater, of all things. I ask you, what kind of job is he going to get after graduation with that training?"

"Learning to be at ease before a large group of people is always useful."

Caroline barked a laugh. "Well, yes. That's true enough. And I have to admit that I took a few speech and acting classes myself as an undergraduate. I was pretty good at it, if I do say so myself."

"If Gabe is all that rich, I don't suppose he has to worry about whether or not he finds a job."

"I wouldn't go that far. Most people, even the wealthy, are expected to do something with their lives."

"Does he do something at the college?"

"What do you mean?"

"Well, Willa had a work-study job. I just wondered—"

"No idea." Caroline cut her off before she could complete the question.

"I believe he spent time in Lincoln Hall on occasion. I understand theater students still use that stage."

"I wouldn't know. Why this sudden interest in Gabe Treat?"

"Idle curiosity."

Liss suspected that Caroline saw right through her lie, but she didn't let that stop her from steering the conversation back to the various groups picketing the campus. Unfortunately, the professor didn't seem to know anything about any of them, either. Except for Alistair Gunn, she didn't even know their names.

"I met Gunn because he came to my office once. He berated me in colorful terms for not doing more to rein in Professor Palsgrave. He was a fine one to talk! Gunn's an ancestor worshipper. You know the sort—my however-many-greats grandfather could do no wrong. Crackpots, the lot of them!"

She replaced her empty cup in its saucer with a clatter of china and glanced impatiently at her watch. "Where is Ms. Boyd? I can't wait around for her all day. Perhaps I'd better speak to your mother instead. She *is* still our liaison with the hotel, isn't she? There seems to be some confusion about that. When I phoned her yesterday, she said I was calling at a bad time and referred me to Ms. Boyd."

"Yesterday was Sunday," Liss pointed out, mentally giving her mother points for putting family first.

Caroline lifted her eyebrows, as if to say, "So what?"

How much, Liss wondered, should she tell this woman? Enough, she decided, to solicit answers to her questions.

"There was a man looking for Dr. Palsgrave on the day he was murdered. Tall, with salt-and-pepper hair. Did you see him?"

"Yes, of course. I told the police I had." She frowned. "Did they arrest him? I haven't been keeping up with the news. I've been too busy with the conclave."

"That man is my father, and I'm afraid the timing of his visit *has* made him a suspect."

Caroline's eyes narrowed. "That and the fact that Lee was killed with a sword from your display window?"

The woman was no fool. Liss warned herself that she'd be wise not to underestimate Caroline Halladay.

"That's right. Of course, he didn't kill anyone. All the evidence against him is purely circumstantial. But here's the troubling thing—later that same day, Dad also visited the very classroom where Dr. Palsgrave was murdered."

Caroline pursed her lips. "I am sorry to hear that. It makes his situation difficult, I'm sure. But you can't blame me. How was I to know?"

"Excuse me?" Liss blinked in confusion. "Why would I blame you?"

"Because I'm the one who suggested he try looking for Lee in his classroom," Caroline said. "Lee's seminar was meeting in that room and Lee had a habit of staying put to talk to individual students who wanted conferences with him, rather than make the trek back to his office." She rolled her eyes. "I won't say he was lazy, but he didn't like to walk farther than he had to. Of course, we found out later that he'd dismissed his students early. Heaven alone knows why."

So far, Caroline had contributed nothing new to Liss's knowledge of that day. "Why did you send my father to the classroom if you thought he'd be interrupting Professor Palsgrave's seminar?" she asked, probing blindly.

Caroline shrugged. "Why wouldn't I? As I recall, it was nearly eleven by then, so the class should have been almost over. And Norma—she's our department secretary—did say your father had an appointment." She toyed with her empty teacup. "I imagine I thought that he'd be willing to wait around outside the classroom for ten or fifteen minutes in order to speak with Lee after the students left. It never occurred to me that he had anything violent in mind."

"He didn't," Liss said through clenched teeth. "And when he got to the classroom, it was empty."

"So he's told you. And I understand that you'd believe your own father. But wasn't he the same man who quarreled with Dr. Palsgrave the week before he was killed? I'm sure Norma told me that he was." Caroline calmly poured herself more tea. Looking thoughtful, she added, "Even if I'd known that then, I suppose I'd have done the same. After all, why would I have thought he meant Lee any harm?"

Speaking clearly and distinctly, Liss said, "My father did not harm anyone."

"*Someone* did." She sipped.

Liss reined in her temper with an effort. Finger by finger, she uncurled the fist she hadn't been aware of clenching. Her defensive posture eased, but there was still tension in her voice.

"May I ask what you did after you sent my father to Professor Palsgrave's classroom?"

The corners of Caroline's mouth kicked up in a wry smile. "Are you asking for my alibi?"

"I suppose I am." Liss smiled back, but there was no warmth in it.

Caroline shrugged. "Very well. I spent the next half hour meditating. You can ask Norma to verify that I regularly do so and that I did so then. She was at her desk the whole time. She'd have seen me if I'd left my office."

"How do you know *she* was there? If you were meditating behind a closed door, Norma could have left and come back again and you'd never have missed her."

"True enough," Caroline conceded, "but I doubt that she did. In any case, she *was* there at the end of a half hour's time. And Willa had just arrived. At that point, I went to Lee's office. I needed to talk to him about the conclave. When I realized he hadn't yet returned from his seminar, I sent Willa to light a fire under him."

"So, it was what—eleven-thirty by then?" Liss angled herself forward so that she could see Caroline's face more clearly, but the older woman's expression was as bland and unrevealing as a bowl of oatmeal.

"My best guess is that it was no more than quarter past the hour."

"Then when you saw my father, it would have been around ten-thirty?"

"Closer to quarter to eleven. As I said, I meditate in half-hour increments."

"Dr. Palsgrave must have returned to his classroom within minutes of my father's departure," Liss mused aloud. "And the killer must have found him there almost immediately after that. But where was Palsgrave when my father was looking for him?"

"Perhaps he'd gone to the men's room?" Caroline looked mildly amused by the notion.

"What a pity he didn't just go straight back to his office after he dismissed his students. Professor Palsgrave might still be alive if—"

"Perhaps he was trying to avoid his appointment with your father," Caroline interrupted. She glanced pointedly at her watch and rose. "I can't wait any longer for Ms. Boyd. Please have her phone me as soon as she returns."

Liss also stood. She walked Caroline to the door, all too well aware that the other woman's patience with her probing had been exhausted. She was therefore surprised when Caroline paused on the brink of leaving the room to make a comment that was both unsolicited and unexpected.

"Lee Palsgrave was fortunate his killer attacked him in his classroom and not in the men's room." Her face crinkled with amusement. "Bad enough to be hacked to death, but think of how much more ignominious it would have been if he'd been found dead in what those living in the Middle Ages would have called the pissing place."

Momentarily speechless, Liss stared after her. She was still shaking her head as she closed the office door and started to clear away the tea things.

"You didn't like him much, did you, Dr. Halladay?" she murmured.

Liss looked with real longing at the pot of coffee her aunt had brewed that morning. It was far from fresh, either in smell or appearance, but it was hot. She picked up an empty mug, then put it down again. The last thing she needed was more caffeine. Her mind was working perfectly well without the added jolt.

Thought Number One was that although Caroline Halladay might not have liked her department head, she had an excellent alibi for the time of the murder. Lacking details, Liss had yet to finish her time line for the events of that morning, but she was fairly certain Professor Halladay needed to have been in two places at once to have killed Professor Palsgrave. Willa's involvement also argued against Caroline as a suspect. Surely, if Caroline had killed Palsgrave, she'd never have sent her work-study student looking for him, setting Willa up to make a gruesome discovery. Besides, Willa would surely have noticed it if Caroline had been spattered with blood.

Professor Halladay was definitely out of the running, Liss decided. Even if she hadn't had an alibi, there was still the matter of the strength one needed to swing a broadsword. Admittedly, Liss had never seen Caroline in anything but loose, shapeless clothing. She couldn't say for certain what kind of physical shape the professor was in, but it seemed far more likely that her bulky garments had been chosen to hide rolls of fat rather than well-toned muscles.

Thought Number Two was that the biggest question she had to answer was not where Lee Palsgrave had been when her father visited his classroom, but where the *murderer* had been. How, Liss wondered, had that murderer known that the man he, or she, planned to frame for the crime would conveniently show up at just the right time?

Someone had to have visited Liss's shop in order to figure out how to take the sword from the display window without being caught.

Someone had to have known that Mac had quarreled with Palsgrave and that he'd made an appointment to see him again.

Someone had to have known that Mac would also go into the classroom wing of Lincoln Hall.

No. Wait. Liss shook her head to clear it. Mac didn't *have* to go there. He only needed to be on campus at the right time. She frowned. That Palsgrave had been absent from the classroom at the precise moment Mac went looking for him there—that *couldn't* have been arranged. Besides, it would have served the killer's purpose just as well if Mac and Palsgrave *had* met, just so long as the murder took place right after Mac left.

Abandoning that conundrum for the moment, Liss added one more requirement to her mental list. The mysterious "someone" would have to have sufficient strength to wield a hand-and-a-half broadsword.

One candidate once again sprang immediately to mind—Gabe Treat. He'd been in the Emporium with his grandfather. His girlfriend had been a work-study student in the history department and could easily have told him about the quarrel and the appointment. By Gabe's own admission, he'd been hanging around the front entrance to Lincoln Hall on the day of the murder. And he was big and strong—perfectly capable of hefting and swinging the murder weapon.

But how had he hidden the sword, both before or after the crime? Liss's lips twisted into a wry smile. She doubted he'd used the same trick the fictional Duncan Macleod had in nearly every episode of that old cult classic, *Highlander.* The screenwriters never had revealed that particular secret. Or if they had, she'd missed it. And now she was clearly clutching at straws! She reset her focus on Gabe. How could he or anyone else have brought the weapon back to Moosetookalook and put it in the trunk of Mac's car without being noticed?

There was the matter of the blood, too. How had Gabe gotten rid of the inevitable stains on his clothing before Willa saw him? There was simply no way he could have butchered Palsgrave without looking as if he'd just finished a double shift at a slaughterhouse.

Liss's stomach twisted as the only possible answer occurred to her—Gabe and Willa had conspired to kill Palsgrave and frame Mac. The theory made sense. Willa could have lied about seeing Gabe before she went into the classroom and discovered the body. That would have given him time enough to clean up and change his clothes, then return to the scene of the crime in time to be found comforting Willa when the police arrived.

Willa Somener arrived for work at Moosetookalook Scottish Emporium on the morning of Tuesday, July 21, looking as if she didn't have a care in the world. When Liss had phoned her the previous evening to ask if she'd work at the shop again, she'd squealed with delight at the prospect of earning additional money.

"So, what wedding stuff do you have to do today?" she asked as she stashed her umbrella in a convenient corner of the stockroom. It was raining again, a soft mist that made the scene outside the window seem slightly unreal.

"Just odds and ends," Liss said evasively.

Now that Willa was standing right in front of her, she found it nearly impossible to believe the young woman could have willfully conspired in something as obscene as murder. And yet, that theory had made perfect sense to Liss the previous night. She'd worked it all out. Willa and Gabe not only had means and opportunity, they'd also had motive.

After much thought, Liss had come up with what she thought was a perfectly logical reason for Gabe and Willa to have killed Lee Palsgrave. She'd been chagrined to realize that she'd have thought of it much earlier if she hadn't been trying so hard not to dwell on her mother's past sexual relationship with the victim.

If Palsgrave had been involved with one student during his career at Anisetab College, Liss had reasoned, then surely there had been others. It seemed likely that he had seduced other young women over the years. If that were so, then he might well have made sexual advances toward Willa, giving Gabe a good reason to strike out at him.

Another reason, she amended as she watched Willa wield a dust rag. Gabe's primary motive might still have been to act on behalf of his grandfather. Who was to say that crackpot ancestor worship didn't run in the family?

Liss contrived to broach the subject with Willa by leaving a copy of Palsgrave's book on the coffee table in the cozy corner. At what seemed an opportune moment, she indicated the author photograph. "He was a handsome man," she remarked.

"You aren't the only one who thinks so." Willa barely glanced up from where she was rearranging Scottish-themed knickknacks.

"A bit of a ladies' man, was he?"

"That's the rumor."

Liss wandered closer to her temporary employee, trying to get a better look at Willa's facial expression. "Did he ever make a pass at you?"

"I wish," Willa said with a laugh.

"Really?"

Finally, the young woman looked up. Her cheeks had a hint of pink in them. "Oh, I know he was old and everything, but he still had . . . *something*." Her blush deepened to rose.

"Does Gabe know you had a crush on him?" Liss kept her tone light and teasing.

"Of course not! Besides, it wasn't as if I was ever going to *do* anything about it."

"Too late now."

Willa laughed again. "Well, yeah—unless I wanted to get real literal about the expression 'jump his bones'!"

The dark humor of Willa's remark caught Liss off guard, although she supposed it shouldn't have. The younger woman had already demonstrated a quixotic nature.

Shaking her head, Liss decided to quit while she was ahead and be grateful that her mention of the murder hadn't provoked Willa into another crying jag. Besides, the younger woman's comment had opened up an entirely new line of thought.

If Palsgrave had a reputation as a womanizer, was it possible that there were *more* angry boyfriends or husbands around? Men other than Gabe and Mac who might have objected to having their women hit on?

Liss knew just the person to ask. She left Willa in charge of the Emporium and went upstairs to her aunt's apartment. It was empty, since Margaret had already left for her office at the hotel. Liss had all the privacy she needed for an extremely enlightening phone conversation with Melly Baynard.

Chapter Thirteen

Liss returned to the shop after she talked to Melly, intending to stay only long enough to tell Willa she'd be gone the rest of the day. It was so quiet that at first she thought the young woman had left. Then she realized that Willa was curled up in one of the chairs in the cozy corner, so completely absorbed in Palsgrave's book that she didn't even look up at Liss's approach.

"Willa?"

"Mmmm."

"Willa, I could be a customer." More amused than annoyed, Liss waited for that possibility to sink in.

"No, you couldn't," Willa said. She used her finger to mark her place and finally met Liss's eyes. "The bell over the front door didn't ding."

Liss conceded the point with a chuckle. "What are you finding so fascinating about Dr. Palsgrave's book? I'd have thought you'd already know everything there was to know about his version of history."

"Not really. I was Dr. Halladay's student, not his. I just got roped into the reenactment because it was going to be part of the conclave and he needed bodies." A

bemused expression came over her face. "I hadn't realized . . . I think I should have told him about Serena
Dunbar, no matter what Professor Halladay advised."

"Your however-many-greats grandmother?"

Willa nodded. "She wasn't a fraud. I know no one believed her, but she really did find the effigy of a fif-
teenth-century European woman punched into the rock
wall of a cave on Keep Island—that's the family estate.
Punched—that's outlined with a series of holes made by
an armorer's tools, so that you connect the dots with
chalk to see the image. Just like the Westford Knight.
Only better, because the fact that there was a woman in
the party means they intended to colonize, not just explore. I don't know why I never put two and two together
till now. I suppose I was more interested in the curse."

"Curse?" Liss repeated, bewildered. The rest of what
Willa was saying confused her, too. There was a *second*
effigy on a rock? When did *that* happen?

"The curse was in the inscription under the woman's
effigy," Willa explained. "It said, 'Cursed be he who dis-
turbs my bones.' Silly, I know, but they used to believe in
that stuff back in the fourteen hundreds. And there was a
coin, too. Family legend says it was dated no later than
the year thirteen ninety-nine and it was found near the
cave. But someone stole it, so we don't have it for proof
anymore and the marks on the stone are really faint now,
just like with the Westford Knight. They could be natural. But they aren't."

Liss was having difficulty following Willa's rambling
explanation. She got the part about the Westford
Knight—the memorial allegedly left by Henry Sinclair
to one of his knights, who was supposedly Alistair
Gunn's ancestor.

"I was going to do a paper on Serena Dunbar," Willa

continued, "but I hadn't gotten started yet. There was too much else going on."

"And Professor Halladay's advice was . . . what?"

"Oh—that I shouldn't mention Serena to Dr. Palsgrave because—" She broke off, looking embarrassed. "Well, she seemed to think he'd steal the idea and write a paper about it himself. I thought she was trying to protect me."

Liss had heard of the pressure to "publish or perish" and supposed it could drive a particularly paranoid academic type to extremes to keep his or her original research secret until it was safely in print. Perhaps it was a good thing Palsgrave *hadn't* known about Serena Dunbar. Willa and Gabe didn't need yet another reason to kill him.

"If you ever do write that paper, you'll have to let me read it," she told Willa. Maybe then she'd be able to make sense of the story.

In the meantime, she still had her original plans for the day to complete.

Leaving Willa in charge of the Emporium, Liss once again made the hour and a half drive to Three Cities. The time passed quickly. She had a lot to mull over.

According to what Melly had told her on the phone, Professor Palsgrave had engaged in quite a number of inappropriate relationships with students over the years, although he'd always been careful to avoid attracting the attention of college administrators. In every case Melly knew of, however, the affairs had ended amicably, and all of his most recent conquests now lived too far away geographically to be likely suspects.

To Liss's mind, that didn't preclude the existence of a jealous boyfriend or husband. Melly had said she'd never heard any gossip to indicate that Palsgrave had been involved with a married woman, but did anyone ever know everything about another person? It wasn't as if Palsgrave and Melly had been close.

Or had they?

Since she was alone in the car, Liss groaned aloud. Did she really suspect *Melly* of being one of the professor's ex-girlfriends? She needed to get a better grip on reality.

All the same, she was glad Melly had an alibi for the time of the murder. Vi, Liss, Sherri, and Zara could vouch for her whereabouts and they had the bridal apparel to prove it.

After due consideration, Liss decided not to rule out the possibility that Palsgrave had a married lover, no matter what Melly had said. After all, her own father had told her that Palsgrave had threatened to go after Vi again. Liss contemplated that revelation. She wasn't sure she believed Palsgrave meant what he'd said. It seemed just as likely that he'd been lying—trying to get Mac's goat.

But what if he had been serious? That meant, Liss supposed, that she would have to question her mother. She ought to anyway, to find out more about the two times Vi had met with Palsgrave to discuss the Medieval Scottish Conclave. So far, she'd taken the coward's way out, repeatedly talked herself out of having that conversation on the grounds that Vi had not been alone with Palsgrave on either occasion. Aunt Margaret had gone with her the first time. The second encounter had been the day Palsgrave came to Moosetookalook with Caroline and Willa.

The harder Liss tried to form a clear picture of Dr. A. Leon Palsgrave, the fuzzier it became. He'd been a man full of contradictions, as she supposed most people were. There were only two facts about him that she could be sure of. He had possessed a certain charisma where women were concerned. And he'd been obsessed with the subject of his research, the six-hundred-year-old mystery of exactly what Henry Sinclair had done while in the New World.

She thought about what Willa had told her. If she'd understood that young woman correctly, Serena Dunbar's discoveries suggested a settlement on an island off the coast of Maine at an earlier date than anyone had previously suggested. Did that mean that Sinclair had returned home to Scotland and sent colonists back?

But if there *had* been a colony, what had happened to it? Had it vanished, like Roanoke? Liss supposed that was entirely possible. There was a wide ocean between the Old World and the New and a vast continent to get lost in if the settlers wandered far from the coast.

That sort of mystery, Liss realized, was the kind that might never be solved.

Once in Three Cities, Liss drove directly to Three Cities Free Public Library. Her earlier online search had revealed that Louis Amalfi, head of the Columbus First Society and the first name on her current list of suspects, was head librarian there. She found him in the stacks, reshelving books.

Amalfi was a hirsute individual with bushy eyebrows that cast shadows over eyes with deep bags beneath them. She watched him for a few minutes before she approached him. He moved slowly, shuffling along flat-footed from shelf to shelf. In spite of his ruddy complexion, he didn't strike Liss as being particularly healthy. She put his age upwards of fifty, since his hair was more steel gray than black. He did look strong enough to swing a sword, however, especially if he were in a rage at the time.

Rage did not seem likely, not when it must have taken such careful planning to kill Palsgrave and frame Mac for the crime. Liss doubted Amalfi was the killer, but he was still worth talking to. He might have noticed something useful while he was picketing Lincoln Hall.

Aware that she could hardly expect a stranger to answer her questions when she was neither a police officer nor a private investigator, Liss had worked out a cover story, one she hoped would prevent any of her suspects from growing suspicious of her. If one of them really was Palsgrave's murderer, the last thing she wanted was to appear to pose a threat.

"I'm here representing The Spruces," she told the librarian after she'd given him her name. "You've probably heard that the Medieval Scottish Conclave is now being held on the hotel grounds."

He pushed a big red book into place on the shelf in front of him and turned to give her a fulminating stare through beady black eyes. "I was aware of the change of venue." The words came out clipped and impatient, at odds with his slow, shambling movements.

"Yes, of course. Are you also aware that, due to the unfortunate demise of Professor A. Leon Palsgrave, the reenactment scheduled to be part of the conclave has been cancelled?"

"I assumed it would be. Good of you to confirm it."

"Yes, well, the hotel's concern is to make sure those who planned to demonstrate at the event are apprised of the change in plans. Without the interpretation of history the battle represented, I presume you will abandon your plans to protest." She did not make it a question.

Amalfi returned two more books to their places without answering, giving Liss time enough to begin to worry. "Probably not," he said.

"Probably *not*? What can you possibly have to object to if there is no reenactment?"

"Call it an informational picket." Shoving the book cart in front of him, he set off down another aisle.

Now in a quandary, Liss trailed after him. Given that preposterous statement, she ought to concentrate on trying to talk him out of demonstrating. She might have lied about being a representative of the hotel, but she would not be happy if her wedding guests had to cross a picket line. On the other hand, she was torn. Amalfi's stubborn determination to go forward in order to advance the cause of the Columbus First Society might be just the lever she needed to get him to talk about the day Palsgrave was murdered.

First things first, she decided. "Do you *like* walking a picket line?" she inquired. "I mean, I heard you were on campus the other day, right in the middle of all the excitement over the murder. I'd think that would put you off more demonstrations for a while."

"The one has nothing to do with the other. And we were not *on* campus. We were on a public sidewalk." He kept his back to her as he continued to shelve books. There were only a few left on the cart. Liss had a feeling she'd better talk fast.

"You mean you couldn't see the entrance to Lincoln Hall? You didn't see who went in and out?"

He glanced over his shoulder at her. "What are you getting at?"

She shrugged and tried to look innocent. "Well, it stands to reason that if you were right there, on the spot, you must have seen the murderer."

"If I did," he said stiffly, "I was certainly not aware of it. Palsgrave was a fool, but he didn't deserve death. To be discredited, yes. Ruined in academia. But killed? No, indeed. A long life spent in disgrace would have been a much more appropriate fate for the man."

"Did you hear a shot?" she asked. "Is that how he was killed? With a gun?"

"I have no idea. I neither heard nor saw anything untoward until that young woman came running out of the building screaming her head off."

"Willa Somener."

"Is that her name? Poor girl. I gather she found the body." Tut-tutting to himself, he resumed his work, shelving the last book on the cart with a decisive thump.

"I understand she stopped to talk to her boyfriend before she went into the building to look for the professor." Liss resumed following him as he pushed his cart toward a service elevator.

"Oh, yes?" He didn't sound even mildly interested, and in a moment he was going to escape.

"Gabe Treat? Alistair Gunn's grandson?"

Amalfi gave a short laugh at that. "That old coot? He's even more obsessed with the so-called Sinclair voyage than Palsgrave was."

"I suppose Gabe was there helping his grandfather."

"Not that I saw." He turned to her, frowning, after he shoved the cart onto the small elevator—more of a dumbwaiter than anything else, Liss realized, with no room for Amalfi to squeeze in.

"You didn't notice Gabe hanging around before Willa found the body?"

"I can't say that I did." He pushed the button to send the elevator back down to the main floor of the library and headed for the nearest stairwell with Liss still at his heels.

"Odd. I had the impression that Gabe kept a close eye on his grandfather."

"Someone should," Amalfi said, "but if the grandson was there that day, he stayed out of sight. Probably didn't want the senile old fool to see him and be insulted. Gunn's got a short fuse. He'd probably take the boy's head off if he thought he was looking out for him."

"Not literally, I hope," Liss mumbled.

She didn't think Amalfi heard her. He'd already gone through the stairwell door and started down the steps. She hurried to catch up and they entered the main lobby of the library together.

"What makes you so certain Palsgrave's theory was wrong?"

Responding to the challenge in Liss's voice, Amalfi turned on her, eyes flashing and nostrils flared. "The Zeno Narrative was a fraud. Everyone knows that."

It took Liss a moment to remember that the Zeno Narrative was the record left behind by Antonio Zeno, admiral of Henry Sinclair's fleet. It was an account of Sinclair's voyage to the New World. "Not everyone agrees with you, Mr. Amalfi. Some think the Narrative is a legitimate document."

"Oh, please. Aside from the errors on the so-called Zeno map—*obvious* errors—there's the fact that both narrative and map were supposedly 'discovered' by a descendant a couple of centuries after Zeno's death . . . in an attic, of all places! How much of a cliché is that? And, of course, the Zeno in question is accounted for, in Venice, during the same years pro-Sinclair people claim he was sailing to Nova Scotia."

Liss considered pointing out that recent scholarship, according to Palsgrave's book, suggested an alternate date for Sinclair's voyage, one that did allow for Antonio Zeno to go with him, and that the errors Amalfi spoke of could be attributed to a lack of knowledge on the part of the descendant who'd published the Zeno Narrative in the sixteenth century. Travel books were the best sellers of that age. It was not surprising that an enterprising Renaissance man had embellished the original.

Liss was not foolish enough to engage in a debate over such details, not when all she had to rely on was one quick reading of one book on the subject. "I'm afraid I don't understand," she said instead. "I'd think you'd be happy to advance the claims of this Zeno fellow, even at the expense of Christopher Columbus. After all, they both came from Italy, didn't they?"

Amalfi looked appalled by her suggestion. "My dear young woman! Bite your tongue. Zeno was *Venetian!*"

The second name on Liss's list was John Jones. He was home, but he refused to let her in. From the other side of his closed apartment door, he told her that he'd already talked to the police.

"I'm not with the police, Mr. Jones." She stared at the heavy wooden planks in front of her and raised her voice. "I'm from the hotel where the highland games are being held. We'd just like to confirm that you will *not* be demonstrating on Saturday or Sunday."

His response was loud and rude. "Get lost, girlie. I don't have to tell you diddly squat."

Prompted by a healthy sense of self-preservation—he did not sound like someone she'd want to be alone with in an apartment—Liss left. When she remembered what Gabe had told her about Jones's suspect credentials, she wasn't really surprised that he'd reacted badly to having people pry into his private business.

Next she contemplated hunting up Alistair Gunn. She talked herself out of it for three reasons. First, he was one scary old man. Second, on consideration, she decided that it would have been physically impossible for him to have killed Leon Palsgrave. Therefore, he wasn't really a suspect. And, third, if his "cause" was the motive for his grandson to commit murder, then it was hardly likely he'd roll over on that young man.

That left two names on her list. One was Barry Rowse, the one who believed Sinclair had secretly been a Templar knight and had buried the Holy Grail in New England. The other was Kirby Redmond, the "arms master" for the reenactment. She flipped a coin. Redmond won.

Liss made another phone call to Melly. She'd already discovered, online again, that Redmond, like Gabe Treat, was a theater major. His interest was in props, which fell into the same backstage arena as costumes. Melly was able to give Liss precise directions on how to find her quarry.

"He's a fine young man," Melly added. "And there isn't anything he doesn't know about stage weapons."

"I don't consider him a likely suspect," Liss assured her. "As far as I know, he was nowhere near Lincoln Hall on the day Professor Palsgrave was killed. But he does have a connection to the weapon. I'm hoping he can tell me something about the amount of strength it would take to use a hand-and-a-half broadsword to kill someone."

She found Kirby on the main stage in the arts center. All she had to do was follow the sound of steel ringing against steel.

Liss advanced down the aisle of the auditorium, mesmerized by the flash of blades. In spite of the fact that the two opponents wore protective face masks and clothing, they gave every appearance of trying to kill each other. The fencing foils in their hands looked lethal. Only the fact that one of the fencers kept up a steady stream of instructions reassured her that the fight was as carefully choreographed as any dance routine.

She applauded when the session came to an end. The "loser" got up off the floor and bowed to her. The "winner," a young man with a wiry build and fluid movements, looked nowhere near as pleased to discover that they'd had an audience for their bout. He whipped off his mask to reveal a face dominated by oversized ears, a broad forehead, and a wispy brown beard. "We're rehearsing here."

"Sorry to interrupt. Are you Kirby Redmond?"

"What's it to you?"

The other student laughed, revealing herself to be female. The padded jacket she was wearing had made it impossible to tell. "He's not always this surly," she called out. "I missed my mark. Twice. And I'm done for today, Kirby," she added, turning to her instructor. "I've got a class."

"Fine. Whatever." He turned his back on her and strode downstage toward Liss. "What do you want?"

"I have a couple of questions about medieval weapons, if you have the time."

"Maybe." He dropped down onto the edge of the stage, folding his legs beneath him, tailor fashion. His mild gray eyes stared intently into her face.

Liss moved closer, still wary. "My name is Liss MacCrimmon. I'd like to talk to you about the weapons that were, briefly, in my display window at the Moosetookalook Scottish Emporium."

He snorted. "Stupid idea."

"I don't imagine it was yours, but you are the local expert on arms and armor, isn't that right?"

He gave a grudging nod.

"Professor Halladay must have consulted you about which swords should go in the display."

"No need. Doc Halladay, she's got a pretty good working knowledge of weapons."

"Really?" Liss wondered if she'd been too quick to cross the older woman off her list of suspects. Then she remembered—Dr. Halladay had an alibi.

"Well, sure," Kirby said. "Blacksmithing is one of the crafts she's interested in promoting. Blacksmiths made swords," he added when she looked blank. "And when I told her she ought to include sword fighting as an art, because there were schools in just about every major city during the Renaissance, to teach the young noblemen how to fight, she arranged for me to do a demonstration at the Medieval Scottish Conclave."

"Congratulations."

"She's a real hands-on type. Got me to give her basic lessons in a couple of different types of swordplay. You wouldn't think it to look at her, but that old gal has the makings of a pretty good fencer. Too bad fencing wasn't popular in the Middle Ages. It didn't become fashionable until much later."

Liss tried to imagine Caroline Halladay wearing a practice outfit like the one Kirby had on and couldn't quite manage it.

"Are we done here?" Kirby's tone was so sharp and impatient that it knocked the half-formed image right out of Liss's head.

"Actually, no. What can you tell me about the hand-and-a-half broadsword?"

"Oh, not you, too?"

Liss's interest quickened. "Who else has been asking you about broadswords?"

"That old fart, Alistair Gunn."

"Gunn talked to you about the broadsword? When?"

"He buttonholes me every time he sees me. He's obsessed with the subject. Well, that's what is supposedly punched into that rock ledge in Westford, Massachusetts, isn't it?" His fingers drummed an impatient rhythm against the stage floor.

"You sound skeptical."

"I don't much care who did what that many years ago. My weapons, though—those I care about. Dr. Halladay says the cops confiscated my sword. I want it back."

"Have the police asked you about it?"

"No. Why should they?"

Liss sighed. Here was yet more proof that the state police weren't looking at other suspects. They thought they'd found their killer. "I need your expert opinion, Kirby. Could someone with severe arthritis in his hands heft that particular sword and kill someone with it?"

"Stab or slash?"

"I don't know." She hated working in the dark, but Detective Franklin was keeping details of the crime close to his chest. The general public still didn't know that the murder weapon had been a sword.

"It wouldn't take much strength to run someone through with a broadsword," Kirby said, "if you sharpened it and you had a good grip on it and you got a running start. Or if the other guy was moving toward you and you were trying to defend yourself. Slashing, though, that would mean lifting the blade over your head." He moved his arms to demonstrate. "That sword is a reproduction, so it's not as heavy as a real one would be, but you'd still tire out pretty fast if you were delivering blows from above."

"So, it *would* take someone with a good grip." That was a point in her arthritis-riddled father's favor. "The killer must have been a strong man in good shape to be able to—"

"Or somebody who was really pissed off at the professor." Kirby's grin showed off large, very white teeth.

"Do you have anyone in mind?"

"Not really." And he seemed to have lost interest in the topic. With an ease Liss envied, he stood, clearly ready to end the interview.

"Have you ever given lessons with a hand-and-a-half broadsword?" she blurted before he could bolt.

"Sure. I had all the students Palsgrave lined up for the reenactment practice with both broadswords and claymores. Some of the girls had a hard time with them."

"Willa Somener?"

"You know Willa? Yeah, she's game enough but she hasn't got much upper body strength. A couple of whacks and she was done for."

Liss nodded. "Yes, I can see that."

"Can't always."

"Can't always what?"

"Tell how strong someone is by looking at them, at least not when they've got clothes on." He grinned again. "Clothes hide muscles."

She smiled back. "Fight a lot of battles naked, do you?"

"Legend says the ancient Scots used to."

"Good point. Still, I don't think Willa is the one who used that broadsword on Professor Palsgrave."

"Naw." This time Kirby's smile lacked teeth, making it more smirk than grin. "If Willa wanted him dead, she'd get Gabe to do the wet work. That poor boob is so whipped he'd stab himself if she asked him to."

Chapter Fourteen

Given Kirby Redmond's comments about Gabe Treat, Liss reconsidered her decision not to talk to Alistair Gunn. It seemed foolish to drive all the way back to Moosetookalook without at least trying to interview Gabe's grandfather. She had his address. And, really—what was there to worry about? He was an elderly man. Unless he managed to whop her upside the head with his cane, she'd likely escape the encounter unharmed.

The deciding factor was that he might have noticed something. Old people and children often saw more than others gave them credit for.

Steeling herself for the encounter on the drive from the campus to the quiet, tree-lined street where Gunn lived, she debated the best way to approach him. She could use the "I represent the hotel" ploy. Or she could level with him and ask his help for her father's sake. After all, he already knew who she was. He'd been in her shop. She didn't have to let on that she suspected his grandson of murder in order to ask her question.

Gunn's house was set back from the street and surrounded by high hedges. Liss debated pulling into the driveway, which appeared to circle back on itself, curving around a large, colorful flower bed. Instead, she pulled in behind a dilapidated red pickup truck. It wasn't until she'd shut off the engine that she noticed the vanity plate. She let her forehead fall to the steering wheel and bumped it, hard, twice in succession. The plate read MURCHPI.

She'd managed to push the private investigator Mr. Carrier had hired to the back of her mind, but now she remembered that he'd planned to talk to everyone on the list she'd given him. Had he talked to Jones and Rowse and Amalfi, too? The latter hadn't mentioned answering questions for anyone else. Then again, perhaps Mr. Murch was more subtle than she gave him credit for. Maybe he'd disguised himself in some way. Maybe—

Murch emerged from Alistair Gunn's house and started down the driveway. Through the open window of her car, Liss could hear that he was whistling. She didn't recognize the tune, but she couldn't help but notice how cheerful he sounded. She wished she could feel more confident that he was in a good mood because he'd learned something significant from interviewing old Mr. Gunn, but she had her doubts. She opened the door and got out, then stood beside her car until Murch noticed her.

The whistling stopped abruptly. That and a slight hesitation in his step told Liss she'd taken him by surprise.

"Get in the truck," he said when he reached it.

"Why should I?"

"We need to talk." He swung up into the cab and turned the key in the ignition to start the air conditioner.

Liss debated only a moment. She didn't like the man, but Mr. Carrier trusted him. And he'd just talked to Alistair Gunn. He might have learned something useful.

The inside of Murch's truck was a surprise. It was a

total contrast to the clunker exterior. The seats were amazingly comfortable. A cooler, from which Murch pulled two cans of soda, filled most of the small space behind them. Liss didn't know the purpose of half the electronics she saw, both on and beneath the dashboard, and she wasn't sure she wanted to. She took the can and popped the top.

"What are you doing here, Ms. MacCrimmon?" Murch asked.

"Same thing you are, Mr. Murch."

"No. I'm working. You're butting in."

Liss sipped her drink and considered his tone of voice. Resentment, she decided. She supposed she could understand that. This was his livelihood. On the other hand, it was her father's *life*. "I have a right to talk to Mr. Gunn."

Now it was Murch's turn to sip, swallow, and ponder. "Maybe so, but I wouldn't advise it. He's on a tear."

"Did you say something to upset him?"

"Not so you'd notice. But I didn't get much sense out of him, either. Tell you what, sweetheart. If you want to help, give me the bullet points on this Sinclair the explorer thing. I couldn't make heads nor tails out of what the old man was going on about."

"Sure, *toots*," Liss shot back, "just as soon as you drop the macho PI act and talk like a normal human being."

He chuckled. "Busted. The little lady scores a bull's-eye."

"Murch," she warned.

He held up both hands in surrender. "I can't help it. Honest. It's what you call my signature style. I've worked real hard to develop a flexible persona over the years. It's second nature now. I channel whatever character will most put a suspect at ease."

"Columbo?" she asked, remembering what Mr. Carrier had said.

"Yeah. That's a good one. I lull them into thinking they've got nothing to worry about because I'm too befuddled to figure things out and then—boom! Gotcha!"

Liss sighed. "Okay. Fine. Just don't call me 'sweetheart,' okay?"

"You got a deal, swee—" He grinned. "Uh, make that Ms. MacCrimmon. Now, about this Sinclair business. What's with that?"

Liss settled herself more comfortably on the soft leather seat and took another swallow of her soft drink. "I don't get it, either," she confided, "but people can be passionate about the strangest things. In this case, what's at the heart of it is a debate over who really made landfall in North America first, a Scot sailing for Norway or an Italian sailing for Spain."

"This Sinclair guy is the Scot, right?"

"Right. And one of his men was named Gunn. Supposedly, Gunn died here. Or rather down in Massachusetts. Maybe killed by local Indians. Maybe not." Liss paused, trying to think how to simplify something about which entire books had been written. "Maybe I'd better go back to the beginning, but this may take a while."

"Knock yourself out." He gestured toward the cooler. "I've got provisions in there for a couple of days."

A smile fought its way onto her face. Good grief! She was actually starting to *like* Murch.

"Okay, but keep in mind that most of this is what they call speculative history. Some people think it happened this way and others insist the story has no basis whatsoever in fact."

"Gotcha."

Liss settled deeper into the seat. "The tale starts with a fisherman, around the middle of the fourteenth century." She slanted her gaze sideways and was gratified to see Murch's eyes widen slightly at the date. "Yup. Fourteenth. About a hundred and fifty years before 1492 and Columbus and all that. Anyway, this fisherman was shipwrecked somewhere in North America. He survived, wandered up and down the coast a bit, and eventually found his way back to his home, which was somewhere in the Orkney Islands, north of Scotland. The Orkneys belong to Scotland now, but back then they were claimed by Norway and the Scot who ruled them for Norway was the jarl of Orkney. His name was Henry Sinclair."

Murch fished a sandwich out of his cooler. "You want half?" The smell of onions filled the cab of the truck.

"No, thanks. I'm good. Bullet point number two: Sinclair heard the fisherman's story and decided to explore this new land, especially since it was supposed to be rich in timber and fish, both of which were profitable commodities in those days. He had a fleet of ships already, commanded by an admiral named Antonio Zeno."

"Italian?"

"So the story goes. Seafarers did get around in those days. Anyway, it's only because of Zeno that we know anything about Sinclair's voyage. He left letters behind. Now, flash forward. A descendant of Zeno's finds the letters and publishes them in the middle of the sixteenth century. By then, everybody had forgotten all about Henry Sinclair. In fact, the name of the northern lord Zeno worked for ended up as 'Zichmni' in the published book, probably because young Mr. Zeno couldn't read his ancestor's handwriting. That version also made Zichmni a prince. It was years before anybody figured out that Zichmni was really Henry Sinclair, jarl of Orkney."

"Just what is a jarl, anyway?" Murch interrupted.

"It's the equivalent of an earl."

"And how in blazes do you get Sinclair out of Zich—whatever it was you just said?"

"Beats me. The only language I read is English. But somebody better educated than I am apparently figured it out. The argument must make sense, because a whole heck of a lot of people nowadays are convinced that Henry Sinclair was the 'prince' Zeno sailed for. Oh, and there was a map in the sixteenth-century book. Unfortunately, Zeno's descendant decided to update it, which is why, later, some scholars decided it was a fake. And if the map was a fake, they figured that it stood to reason that the entire Zeno Narrative was a fraud, too—just something dreamed up to cash in on the sixteenth-century craze for travel books."

Murch paused in munching on his sandwich. "Wait a sec. You said nobody knew Sinclair made this trip? Why not? Didn't he come back?"

"That's a bit of a mystery, but the most logical explanation is that Sinclair himself kept his discoveries secret. He wouldn't have wanted other people encroaching on those rich fishing grounds. And he may have planned to send colonists over here. Some folks think he *did* send colonists. I'm not going to get into all the crazy scenarios people have come up with over the years. Suffice it to say that Palsgrave's theory wasn't popular with some of those who hold other views."

"What idea was the vic pushing?"

"Palsgrave thought Sinclair explored the coasts of Nova Scotia, Maine, and Massachusetts, lost one of his men to an Indian arrow, and massacred the natives who killed his friend, a member of the Gunn family. The reenactment Palsgrave had planned for the highland games was supposed to recreate that battle."

"And Alistair Gunn objected. Why?"

"Gunn claims he's descended from both Henry Sinclair and the Gunn who died and he doesn't accept that one of his ancestors could have killed innocent people, not even in revenge for a kinsman's death. What did he say when you talked to him?"

"Nothing that made any sense."

"Did you ask him about Gabe?"

"His grandson? No. Why?"

"Gabe claims he was hanging out near Lincoln Hall the day of the murder, keeping an eye on the demonstrators. I was hoping Gunn could confirm it." She started to tell Murch that she wasn't at all sure Gunn would answer truthfully. She was even ready to confide her theory that Gabe Treat had murdered Palsgrave at his grandfather's instigation, but the PI cut her off before she'd managed more than a tentative "I think—"

"Stick to the bullet points, okay, swee—ah, okay, Ms. MacCrimmon?"

"Fine." She drank the last of her soda first and tossed the can into the container labeled RECYCLE BIN that shared space with the cooler. "The debate over what really happened isn't new. The so-called Zeno Narrative has gone in and out of favor with scholars several times over the centuries. And everybody is passionate about it. Mr. Amalfi refuses to accept it as valid at all. Nor does he accept any of the other theories about early visitors to the Americas. His organization is called Columbus First, which pretty much sums up why he was on that picket line."

"Wait a sec. There were other early explorers?"

"Sure. Some of them well before Sinclair. The Vikings. An Irish monk. A Welsh prince. National pride is tied up in support for each and every one of them."

"Huh. The things you learn on this job." With precise movements he neatly folded the baggie his sandwich had been in and deposited it in the trash.

"Mr. Jones, who refused to talk to me, claims to be upset because the reenactment depicts Native Americans as savages." She gave him a quick summary of her conversation with him through the door of his apartment and followed that up with an account of her meetings with Amalfi and Kirby Redmond.

"Your turn. You must have gotten something out of Mr. Gunn."

"Not really, but at least part of what he was going on about makes a little more sense to me now. Unfortunately, I didn't learn anything that's going to be useful to your father. My guess? Gunn was so completely focused on walking that picket line that he didn't pay any attention to his surroundings until the cops arrived."

Maybe, Liss thought. Maybe not. "What's next on your agenda?" she asked aloud.

Murch fished a piece of bubble gum out of a pocket, unwrapped it, and popped it into his mouth before he answered her. "You say you haven't yet talked to this Barry Rowse?"

"He was next on my list, after Alistair Gunn."

"What nutty theory is he pushing?"

"He's the one who thinks Sinclair had a secret agenda in coming to the New World. It involves burying holy relics and a lot of other stuff that is way too far-fetched for me to make any sense of it."

Murch blew a big pink bubble. Liss wondered if that aided his thought process. When the bubble popped, he sucked the goo back into his mouth and nodded. "Okay. I'll talk to Rowse next."

"There's one more possibility," Liss said, and told him her theory about a jealous husband or boyfriend.

"Worth checking out," he agreed. Then he shifted in the seat so that he was facing her. "Here's the thing. From now on, you should stay out of this. You're an amateur. If you're not careful, you're going to muddy the waters."

"I hear that a lot," Liss said, "although not quite so colorfully put."

"So, let the professionals handle things from now on, okay?"

Liss smiled sweetly and promised that she would.

Liss left when Murch did.

Then she came back. This time she did park in the driveway, just where it looped back toward the street. *Pointing out, ready for a quick escape*, she told herself humorlessly as she marched up to the big front door with its ornate clan crest knocker.

She used the doorbell instead and heard a distant buzzing sound from inside the house. After a short interval, her summons was answered by a tall, middle-aged man Liss did not recognize.

"Yes?" He looked down his long, aristocratic nose at her.

The man wasn't dressed like the stereotypical English butler, but there was no doubt in Liss's mind that he saw himself in that role. Something about his snooty attitude made her wish she was armored in a dress and high heels instead of wearing comfortable slacks and a casual top, but it was too late to do anything about her clothing now.

"Ms. MacCrimmon to see Mr. Gunn," she announced.

He waited, as if he expected her to hand him a calling card. "And your business with Mr. Gunn?" he asked when she remained silent.

"Personal."

That earned her a disdainful sniff. "You may wait in the entry hall."

He strode away, nose in the air, to inform the master he had company. At least, that's how Liss thought of it as she watched him go. She wondered what Mr. High and Snooty had made of Jake Murch.

She was still cooling her heels in the entryway, waiting for the butler to return, possibly to throw her out, when a key turned in the front door lock and Gabe Treat entered the house. His eyes widened in surprise when he spotted her.

"Ms. MacCrimmon! What are you doing here?"

"Waiting to see your grandfather," she said, although that must have been pretty obvious.

"Why?"

And there, Liss thought, was the problem. She had no good excuse. Gabe wasn't likely to buy the reason she'd given Louis Amalfi, that she wanted assurance that the demonstrators no longer planned to picket the highland games.

"I . . . um . . . I . . . well, you know I'm trying to discover if anyone besides my father entered Lincoln Hall the day of the murder."

"Sure, but . . . oh, I see. You want to ask Granddad if he saw anyone."

"Right. I know it's a long shot, but sometimes older folks notice more than you think."

Gabe grinned, making his freckles stand out. He was like a grown-up Howdy Doody, Liss thought, which tended to cast doubt on the possibility that he'd murdered a man in cold blood.

"It's nothing to laugh about," she snapped. "My father could be arrested at any moment for a crime he did not commit."

"Sorry. But Granddad's half blind. I don't know what you think he might have seen. He didn't even notice me dogging his footsteps and with all this red hair, I'm pretty hard to miss."

"Humor me, okay. That is, if the guard dog will let me pass."

"You mean Henderson? He's a pussycat."

"Sure he is."

"Besides, you don't need to wait if you're with me. Come on. We'll beard the lion in his den."

He led her deeper into the mansion. They encountered Henderson en route. The butler frowned at Liss, but didn't seem inclined to get in Gabe's way.

"Hey, Henderson," Gabe greeted him. "How's it shaking? Where's the boss?"

"Mr. Gunn is in the conservatory." The stuffy formality was still present in the tone of voice, but Henderson's stiff-as-a-poker demeanor took a blow, literally, when Gabe clapped him on the shoulder on his way by.

"Good man," Gabe said, and took Liss's arm to lead her toward the back of the house.

"Conservatory?"

"Yeah. Granddad is filthy rich, in case you hadn't noticed."

"And yet you're living in a pop-up camper."

"It's a *nice* one."

"I'm sure."

Liss had never been in a conservatory before, although she'd certainly encountered plenty of them as settings in the mystery novels she loved to read. This one turned out to be a medium-sized, glass-walled room—a greenhouse furnished with comfortable furniture as well as an abundance of growing things. It was even hotter and more humid inside than it was outdoors, but Gunn seemed to flourish in that atmosphere. He was happily puttering with his plants, lopping off dead brown stalks, when they interrupted his labors.

"Hey, Granddad," Gabe greeted him. "You remember Ms. MacCrimmon, don't you?"

Gunn peered at her suspiciously. "Come closer, girl. Let me get a look at you."

She obliged, and found her hand grasped by bony fingers that were surprisingly strong. The backs of his hands were liver spotted and blue veins bulged, but he had the grip of a much younger man. *Never make assumptions*, she warned herself. Maybe Gunn had wielded that sword, after all.

Then she noticed the cane propped against the worktable. The hands might be strong, but the legs were weak. If Gunn had been behind Palsgrave's death, he'd had help, and Gabe was the most likely accomplice.

Alistair Gunn, having acquired a captive audience, gave Liss the grand tour of his indoor garden. Since Liss could barely tell a tulip from a rose, most of it went right over her head. Gamely, she pretended to be interested and bided her time waiting for a chance to change the subject. Gabe trailed after them, paying as little attention to his grandfather's rambling spiel as Liss did.

She wondered what Gabe was doing in Three Cities. Then she remembered what Willa had told her, that Gabe made the hour and a half drive from Moosetookalook every day to check in on his grandfather. That seemed to Liss to be taking the role of devoted grandson a bit far, especially when Mr. Gunn had a majordomo and probably other staff, too, to look after him.

At last the old man wound down. Liss seized the moment. "I wonder if you could help me out with something, Mr. Gunn."

"Depends on what it is." He sounded suspicious.

"The other day, when you were picketing at the college, were you or the other demonstrators paying any attention to who went into and came out of the building where Professor Palsgrave was teaching his class?"

"Some reason we should have been?"

They were back at his worktable. Rather than meet Liss's eyes, Gunn picked up the gardening sheers he'd been using earlier. He turned them over and over in his hands—hands, she reminded herself, that were stronger than they appeared.

Liss shook off a shiver, telling herself it was totally irrational to be afraid of Alistair Gunn. She was letting her imagination run away with her. She was perfectly safe.

"Mr. Gunn," she blurted out, "a man was murdered in that building while you were only yards away."

"Yep. A. Leon Palsgrave." He said the name with distaste. "Good riddance, I say."

"Granddad!"

Gunn wagged a finger at his grandson. "You didn't know him like I did, boy."

"I'll level with you, Mr. Gunn. The police think my father had something to do with Professor Palsgrave's death. I'm trying to discover who else went into that building at about the same time. Can you help me?"

He pointed to his eyes. "You see these, girlie? Cataracts. I'm half blind."

"And the other half?"

Surprised into a laugh, he nodded. "Got me there. I can see some things." He jerked his head toward Gabe. "I can see well enough to know that there young fool has been wasting his time watching me every time I walk a picket line. You think I didn't know, boy? I may be old but I'm not senile!"

"I never thought you were, Granddad. And if I'm keeping an eye on you, it's only because I worry about you overextending yourself."

Ignoring Gabe, Gunn addressed himself to Liss. "Thinks I'm going to wander out into the road and get myself hit by a truck. There's nothing wrong with my hearing!"

"Well, then, did you *hear* anything that day?" Liss asked. "You were right outside the classroom windows and it was warm, so they were probably open."

"Oh, you're a sharp one, you are." He chuckled and reached out to pat Liss's hand. "We could hear Palsgrave lecturing, and the racket his students made when they left. We figured he was still in there, though. None of the others saw him leave." He shrugged. "It wouldn't have mattered if he had. We planned to picket all morning, so we were committed to staying till noon."

"So, you heard the students leave. Anything after that?"

"Not much, but now that you mention it, there was something." He frowned. "About an hour before the police came, I heard someone call out, 'Hello? Is anyone here?' Might have been inside the classroom. Hard to tell."

Liss's heart rate quickened. "That must have been my father. He was looking for the professor. Did anyone answer?"

"Nope. Nary a peep."

"And you didn't hear anyone else speak after that? No grunts? No sound of someone falling?"

"You ever walked a picket line?"

She shook her head.

"Thought not. The whole point is to keep moving. We were going back and forth, back and forth on the sidewalk. We walked down to the driveway that leads to the parking lot below the old theater and then back to the entrance of the parking lot in front of Lincoln Hall. At least half of the time, I was out of earshot of anything that went on in that classroom."

Liss sighed. Another dead end.

A short time later, Gabe walked her to her car. His pickup truck was parked behind her in the curving driveway. "It's too bad Granddad couldn't help you. Have you talked to the others?"

"Most of them."

"No one saw anything?"

"I'm afraid not." She sighed again as she slid in behind the wheel. "It was a long shot anyway. Whoever killed Palsgrave probably used the same shortcut he did, through the art gallery. Certainly, he must have escaped that way."

She sent Gabe a wary look. The more time she spent with him, the more she wanted to believe he was the nice young man he appeared to be. At the same time, she didn't dare let down her guard. She'd been fooled before by a killer who presented a pleasant facade to the world.

"Did you ask the demonstrators if any of them saw someone leaving the building by the back door?" Gabe asked.

"I didn't think to, but I don't suppose they did. I'm sure they would have mentioned it to the police if they'd seen someone go out that way, especially since he'd have been wearing bloodstained clothing and carrying a sword."

Gabe looked thoughtful. "What if he wasn't carrying it? What if the killer hid the weapon somewhere in the building before he left? There are plenty of places to stash things in that old theater."

"I'm sure the police have already done a thorough search."

"Why would they, once they found the sword?"

Liss pondered his question. She began to wonder if the state police had searched the theater wing at all.

What if they'd assumed no one could get into that section of the building, since the door to the art gallery had been locked?

Had the sword been hidden and retrieved later? Gabe's suggestion made a certain amount of sense. The killer could have concealed it somewhere after he committed the crime and retrieved it when he was ready to plant it in the trunk of her father's car.

"I should talk to the detective in charge," Liss murmured, but she hesitated to reach for her cell phone. Would Franklin listen to anything she had to say? He wouldn't be happy to hear she'd been investigating on her own. That much she could guarantee.

"You could take a look around the theater for yourself first," Gabe said. "I can help. I know the place inside and out. And I've got a key to the building." He produced a metal key ring with at least a dozen keys attached to it and fingered the one that had a bit of red tape stuck to it.

"The weapon is long gone," Liss reminded him. "Assuming it was ever there."

"There might be some traces left." Gabe's enthusiasm put Liss in mind of an eager puppy.

Bloodstains, she thought. Blood was hard to get rid of. Gabe was right. There might still be something to find. She was sorely tempted to take him up on his offer. Common sense held her back. Exploring the backstage area of a deserted theater in company with a muscular young man who might have an ulterior motive for luring her there was *not* a smart idea.

"This is a matter for the police," she told him in the firmest voice she could manage. Then she started the engine and put the car in drive.

His face fell. "Okay. If you're sure. But if you change your mind, just ask." Jingling the keys in one hand, he gave her a little wave with the other before heading toward his own vehicle. An easygoing smile had already replaced the look of disappointment on his face.

Gabe's truck stayed in Liss's rearview mirror as she drove back to Moosetookalook. As the miles passed, the sight made her increasingly uneasy. At one point, she considered pulling over to the side of the winding rural road and using her cell phone to call Detective Franklin. She talked herself out of it only because, if she stopped, she'd be even more vulnerable to attack.

She told herself she was overreacting. Gabe meant her no harm. But there was very little traffic anywhere along their route on this weekday afternoon and in a little while she'd be coming up on the spot where she'd once had a near-fatal not-so-accidental accident.

Liss gradually increased her speed and didn't let up on the gas until she reached the 35 mph sign on the outskirts of Moosetookalook. Gabe was still right behind her.

"Well, of course he is," Liss scolded herself. "How else could he pick Willa up when she gets off work at the Emporium?"

Chapter Fifteen

On the nerve-racking drive back to Moosetookalook, in between bouts of paranoia during which she imagined that Gabe was about to run her off the road to prevent her from discovering proof that he was Palsgrave's killer, Liss had tried to think logically about the suggestion he'd made. She had no idea if Detective Franklin had searched all of Lincoln Hall or not. If he hadn't, someone should point out to him that the sword could have been stashed, temporarily, somewhere in the little-used theater.

The problem, as she saw it, was that Franklin was convinced that the murder weapon had gone straight from the classroom to the trunk of Mac MacCrimmon's car. He was not going to be interested in hearing an alternate theory, especially if it came from Mac's daughter. Better, Liss decided, to call Mr. Carrier, inform him of Gabe's suggestion, and add to it that she thought the art gallery had been used as the killer's escape route. Surely the lawyer could find a way to pass both tips on to the police, hopefully in a way that would compel them to follow up on those leads. This plan had the added advantage of forestalling accusations that she was interfering in the investigation.

Liss phoned Edmund Carrier's office as soon as Gabe and Willa drove away and she had Moosetookalook Scottish Emporium to herself. She flipped the CLOSED sign over to prevent interruptions. And she locked the door.

"I'll relay your thoughts to Detective Franklin," Carrier agreed when he'd heard her out, but he sounded distracted.

Liss gripped the phone more tightly, feeling her anxiety return. "Will Franklin listen? Or is he too fixated on my father as the killer to look at anyone else?"

Carrier made soothing noises. "Have a little faith, Liss. If the police were going to arrest Mac, don't you think they'd have done so by now?"

After she hung up, she brooded. Would Mr. Carrier follow through? She was no longer certain of it. And even if he did pass the information on, there was still the possibility that the state police would ignore it.

Liss went to bed early that night, in part because she wanted to avoid talking to her parents. She didn't have to hide her agitation from Dan. She hadn't seen him. He was spending the evening and half the night filling in for a sick receptionist at the check-in desk at the hotel.

She slept poorly at first, but eventually dropped into a deeper slumber. She dreamed of an army of freckled redheads brandishing swords. They all had Gabe Treat's face and they were all wearing kilts.

Wednesday morning dawned clear and bright. Liss stretched and smiled . . . until she remembered that her wedding was only three days away and she wasn't any closer to proving her father's innocence than she had been when she started investigating.

How could she focus on getting married, and then relax and enjoy a three-week honeymoon, with her father's imminent arrest hanging over her head? As she dressed for the day, she once again considered postponing the trip to Scotland. Once again, she could almost hear what Dan's reaction would be to such a suggestion. "Come hell or high water," he'd said about taking their vows on Saturday. He'd undoubtedly give the same response if she broached the idea of rescheduling their honeymoon.

Or would he? He couldn't have been all that jazzed about going to Scotland in the first place, given that he couldn't stand the sound of bagpipes. He'd picked their destination to please her.

Liss sat on the side of the bed, dashing moisture from her cheeks, embarrassed to find herself in tears. This was *so* not like her. She didn't get weepy, especially over things that were within her power to fix. She wouldn't change their plans. Not yet, anyway. Not while there was hope of resolving the situation with her father. Squaring her shoulders, she marched downstairs and into the kitchen. She'd simply work harder and faster, especially faster, to find the real killer before the wedding.

Her mind busy with plans, she fed the cats and fixed her own breakfast by rote. The smell of coffee helped her think more clearly even before she tasted the first glorious sip. Step one, she decided, was to check out the old theater in Lincoln Hall for hiding places. She'd do that on her own . . . unless she arrived and found the police were there ahead of her.

When the phone rang, Liss ignored it. Let the answering machine deal with any new crisis. But she'd reckoned without her mother. Vi, already up for the day, picked up the extension in the living room.

A moment later, Liss heard a wail of dismay. She'd barely scrambled to her feet before her mother burst into the kitchen.

"There you are!" she cried upon spotting her daughter. "Oh, Liss—this is a disaster!"

Liss braced herself, fearing the worst. "What is it? Are the police on their way?"

"The police? What have the police got to do with it?"

"I thought—"

"It's the flowers for your bouquet. The orchids I special-ordered aren't going to arrive in Moosetookalook by Saturday."

The relief that washed over Liss was so intense that she had to sit down again. For a moment she'd thought that her father's arrest was imminent. A change in floral arrangements? *That* she could handle.

"Substitute something else," she suggested. "In the great scheme of things, what does it matter if I carry pansies or petunias?"

"Pansies or—? Amaryllis Rosalie MacCrimmon, I swear, sometimes I despair of you." Violet braced her hands on her hips and rolled her eyes heavenward.

Liss couldn't help but smile at the picture her mother made. "It's your own fault, you know. You should never have named me after a flower. I'm sure that's what's given me a lifelong disinterest in the subject. And I know for certain that I'm cursed with a black thumb. Every time someone gives me a houseplant, it up and dies on me."

"That's because your wretched cats always eat the poor things."

"Oh, unfair! Plants died on me long before I inherited Lumpkin."

She'd never been any good at identifying flowers, either. If it hadn't been for the little markers stuck in next to each plant in the flower beds in the town square, she'd never have known what was in bloom.

"We need to find another florist," Vi said. "Fast. There must be someone who carries orchids in the right colors."

"Must they be orchids?" Liss frowned, struck by a thought. "Did they even have orchids in medieval Europe?"

"Oh, I'm certain they did," Vi said, but she avoided meeting Liss's eyes.

"They didn't!" Liss exclaimed, amused and exasperated at the same time. "How about roses instead? I know they had roses in the Renaissance."

"But I like orchids." Violet pouted.

"You like roses, too. And violets. Whatever flower you decide to substitute is fine with me. I'm sure the result will be lovely."

"Oh, Liss—where did I go wrong?"

It was either laugh or cry. Liss went with laughter. "Nowhere, Mom. You're the best."

"It's just that I've always envisioned you carrying a bouquet of orchids as you walk down the aisle on your wedding day."

"You'll figure something out. I have faith in you." Liss gave Vi a hug and a peck on the cheek for reassurance and then beat a hasty retreat.

A glance at her watch when she was safely inside Moosetookalook Scottish Emporium told Liss that Willa was due in at any minute. As soon as she arrived, Liss intended to head back to Three Cities. She'd had enough of a tour of Lincoln Hall with Melly to be fairly certain she could reach the theater without being seen by Norma or anyone else in the history department. The only problem she could foresee came from the fact that so many doors were kept locked. Still, a master key would solve that problem, and she was certain she could persuade Melly to let her borrow hers.

While she waited for Willa to arrive, she punched in Melly's number on the shop's phone. It rang a dozen times before Liss gave up. No Melly, no key. That was a setback she hadn't anticipated.

The bell over the door jangled loudly. Liss glanced up as Willa breezed into the Emporium, closely followed by Gabe.

"I brought muscle along," Willa announced. "I thought he could lift that heavy box on the floor in the stockroom up onto a shelf, so I don't keep tripping over it."

Liss had no idea what box she was talking about and didn't care. Her attention was riveted to the key ring Gabe was jiggling in one hand as he crossed the shop. Since he needed both hands free to lift the box, he set the keys down on top of Liss's worktable.

The one marked with a bit of red tape beckoned to her. The clasp on the key ring was the kind that was easy to open with the thumb tab. Without giving herself time to think better of what she was doing, Liss slid the taped key off the ring and into her pocket. By the time Gabe and Willa turned around, Liss was three feet away from the worktable and wearing an innocent smile.

"Thanks, Gabe," she said, meaning it. "I have to be away again today. Wedding stuff. If you want to hang around with Willa, I have no problem with that."

"That's great, Ms. MacCrimmon."

"Liss," she insisted.

She couldn't fault him for being polite. Her mother would say he was showing respect for his elders. But Liss wasn't quite ready to be considered an elder by someone less than a decade younger than she was.

"Liss, then. I appreciate it." Once again, he reminded her of a big puppy dog, only this time she was one who'd just been offered a treat.

"I'll put him to work," Willa promised. She ran one hand possessively up Gabe's well-muscled arm.

"I do have to run down to Three Cities late this afternoon and check on Granddad," Gabe said as Liss started to leave.

"Oh, I'll be back long before that," she called over her shoulder.

I'd better be, she thought. *And I'd better hope I can find a way to get that key back onto Gabe's key ring before he discovers it's missing.*

For the present, however, she had a more immediate goal in mind. She was going to search the theater wing of Lincoln Hall for places where a killer might have hidden a bloodstained sword.

There was no sign of the state police when Liss drove past Lincoln Hall and turned down the driveway to park in "the pit." There didn't seem to be anyone else around, either. Only a half dozen cars occupied the parking lot. One was Norma's, she imagined, but Norma would be at her desk.

Liss tried the door closest to the history department first and found it locked. Satisfied that this meant students would be unlikely to troop through the building while she was conducting her search, Liss circled around to the door that led into the small auxiliary lobby containing the restrooms.

Gabe's key turned easily in the lock and the door opened without a sound. Glancing once over her shoulder to be certain she hadn't been observed, Liss slipped inside and scurried up the flight of stairs that led to the main lobby in front of the auditorium.

She half expected the doors to the theater itself to be locked. They were not. It took only a moment to step inside. When the door closed soundlessly behind her, the auditorium was plunged into nearly total blackness. The only illumination came from exit signs. It was eerily quiet, too.

Liss fished for the small but powerful flashlight she'd stashed in her shoulder bag. She wore it slung across her chest so that both hands were free.

The beam of the flashlight showed her an aisle leading to the stage. The auditorium was wider at the back than at the front, narrowing down to the width of the stage. The back of the theater was also higher than the front. Liss felt as if she were descending a ramp as she walked slowly forward. Her soft footfalls on the carpeted aisle made little padding sounds. Nothing else stirred.

Halfway to the stage, Liss paused to shine her flashlight into the rows of seats on either side of the aisle. If the sword had been hidden beneath one of the seats, she'd never find a trace of it. She didn't have sufficient light to see around and under them all, let alone the time to make such a careful examination of each one. It would be difficult to do a thorough search for bloodstains even if she turned on every light in the place.

"Luminol," Liss murmured. Was that the right name? She thought so. Whatever it was called, the police used it all the time on cop shows to make blood glow in the dark. Or maybe it only glowed under black light. She wished now that she'd paid more attention, but dramas that featured forensics weren't really her cup of tea. She much preferred to lose herself in the adventures of an amateur sleuth. Still, that glowy stuff was what she needed and she didn't have any.

But *would* the killer have hidden the sword in the auditorium? Probably not, she decided. Surely a murderer who'd planned so carefully to frame someone else for his crime would not take the risk that some stray theater student checking sight lines or acoustics in the auditorium might stumble over the weapon. Bloodstains might be hard to spot, but a sword that big would have stuck out, at least a little. That meant that, if the sword had been left in the theater at all, it must have been hidden somewhere else.

Liss continued on down the aisle and climbed the short flight of steps to one side of the stage. She stood on the apron and shone her flashlight into the wings. The backstage area looked exactly like hundreds she'd seen during the years she toured as a professional dancer.

No production appeared to be in progress at the moment. Liss observed that someone kept the place clean, either a custodian or a work-study student. She sighed. What a shame he'd been so diligent. The stage had been swept recently, which meant that there was no chance of discovering a handy set of footprints in the dust and following them straight to the place where the killer had concealed the sword.

She poked around the backstage area, looking behind the flats stacked against one wall and into an empty trash barrel. On stage left, a flight of stairs led down to a locked door. The area beneath the stage, she recalled, had once been a shop for making sets. These days, it housed the offices of the history department. She saw no point in unlocking that particular door. It would be just her luck to run straight into Norma Leeds on the other side.

Instead, she ascended again and shone her light on the bare boards of the stage. Since she knew what she was looking for, she quickly found the outlines of a series of trapdoors. They, too, had once given access to the shop below, opening downward over a platform, or perhaps over moveable scaffolding. Unlike the exit she'd just examined, however, they no longer led anywhere. Once the offices had been built below, the trapdoors had ceased to function. Nowadays, if a production called for a ghost to appear, the actor would have to enter from the wings, rather than rising up from below.

It was also a pity that the trapdoors didn't open upward. There must be an open space a few inches in height between the floor of the stage and the new ceiling below. What a great place that would have been to conceal the murder weapon!

Losing interest in the trapdoors, Liss turned in a slow circle. There were surprisingly few really good hiding places for something the size and shape of a hand-and-a-half broadsword. If she was right and the killer had left it somewhere in the theater for several hours, long enough for the police to finish with Palsgrave's body and go away, then he had to have hidden it someplace where no one was likely to find it by accident.

She stared out through the proscenium arch at the rows of seats, once again rejecting them as a hiding place, and then shifted her gaze upward to the control booth at the back of the auditorium. Could the sword have been secreted there? She didn't see an entrance at the back of the auditorium, so the door to the stairs that led up to the booth was probably located just off the lobby. Still, stashing the sword up there would be just as problematic as slipping it under a row of seats—there was a good chance that some theater student would stumble over it. Liss had gathered that this theater was used, even during summer sessions, for student projects. Even for a rehearsal, someone would probably have gone up to man the light board in the control booth.

Liss's background had made her familiar with all sorts of theaters. She knew there had to be a way to get to the lights that hung between the booth and the stage—probably a walkway above the ceiling. When she looked directly overhead she found, as she'd expected, flies and a catwalk. She doubted that the sword had been flown like a piece of scenery or a curtain. Once again, that scenario presented too much risk that someone would glance up and spot it hanging there. Worse, the sword might have slipped loose and ended up impaling the stage floor. Aside from spoiling the killer's plan to frame Liss's father, that would have left a nasty gouge!

The catwalks had the same argument against using them as a hiding place—they were too open to view. But as Liss's gaze roved the space above her head, she belatedly remembered something Melly had said. There were storage rooms up there, just off the catwalk on stage right. She considered for a moment. Would the killer have taken the time to climb way up there? Maybe, she decided. A disused storage loft would make a good hiding place, and it could also have provided the killer with a place to change from his blood-spattered garments into clean clothes.

Liss scrambled up a metal ladder and made her way carefully along the narrow walkway at the top. It passed in front of two closed doors labeled, appropriately, #1 and #2. She found scenery storage loft #1 unlocked and nearly empty. The floor was covered with a thick layer of dust, clearly undisturbed. No one had ventured inside the room for a very long time.

Liss expected scenery storage loft #2 to be the twin of #1, but this door was locked. She fished Gabe's key out of her pocket and let herself in. A quick survey by flashlight showed her a room filled with odd pieces of furniture and assorted props. It was also windowless. When she located a switch, she flipped it, blinking when bright overhead bulbs flickered to life.

Intrigued by the contents of the room, Liss began to explore. She doubted that the storage loft had ever been arranged in any sort of order. Smaller items were piled in a haphazard fashion atop larger pieces. Behind a tall screen, liberally draped with discarded curtains and mismatched lengths of silk cord, she found a narrow cot topped with a thin mattress.

Melly's comments came back to her: *I have particularly fond memories of scenery storage loft number two—the one with the bed.*

Apparently, some things never changed, not even in the modern world where students could visit each other's dorm rooms without fear of expulsion.

Liss started to turn away. Scenery storage loft #2 was not a place the killer could reach in a hurry, and surely he'd have been in a rush to get out of the building before the body was discovered. Besides, anyone who knew the theater well enough to be aware that this storage room existed would also know that some hot-blooded young couple looking for privacy might blunder in and discover the sword before he could come back for it.

But even as she dismissed the possibility that the sword had been hidden in the storage room, Liss's gaze returned to the cot. The mattress was a disreputable-looking thing, stained and ratty. What had once been blue ticking had long since faded to gray. But not all of the *stains* were old. She bent to take a closer look. Could that really be dried blood?

Liss frowned. A small bloodstain on a mattress in

scenery storage loft #2 shouldn't surprise her. It was probably the result of another fine old college tradition—losing your virginity. But this particular bloodstain, if it *was* blood, seemed to her to have the distinctive shape of a sword blade.

Liss's heart began to beat a little faster. Had she really found the evidence she'd been looking for? At first she was certain her imagination was playing tricks on her, but the more she studied the suggestive stain, the more certain she became that she was right. She reached into her shoulder bag, hunting for her cell phone.

If the sword had lain there, temporarily hidden until the killer could plant it in her father's car, then this discovery would clear Mac of suspicion once and for all. The police could match the blood to the murder victim's. Maybe they'd even find the killer's fingerprints on the door handle or the light switch. She winced. That is, they might if she hadn't obliterated them with her own. Even if she had, she knew for a certainty that no one would find her father's fingerprints in this room. She doubted that he knew this place existed, but even if he *had* heard of it—in what context she didn't care to speculate—he wouldn't have been able to get in. Besides that, Angie could testify to the time he arrived home on the day of the murder. If the sword had been left here, it couldn't possibly have gone straight into the trunk of his car.

Calm down, Liss warned herself. She had to present the facts in a logical manner when she talked to Detective Franklin.

Her hand closed around her phone. Another minute passed as she searched for Franklin's card. She'd found it and entered the first three digits of his phone number when she heard the first ominous thumping noise from below. She froze. Someone was onstage. Heavy footsteps moved ponderously across the bare boards.

Until that moment, being alone in a dark, deserted theater had not made Liss uneasy. She'd been far too accustomed to performing in strange houses to be spooked by shadowy shapes in the wings or imaginary watchers at the light ports in the auditorium ceiling. The possibility of encountering another person hadn't worried her much either. At worst, her right to be in the building would have been challenged and she'd have been hauled into the campus security office to explain herself. That might have been embarrassing, but she'd have been in no physical danger.

Liss glanced nervously toward the door she'd left open. No one had turned on the stage lights. That probably ruled out campus security as the source of the footsteps.

She listened harder, all the while trying to tell herself that she was imagining things. At first she heard nothing more. Then came a sound that dashed her last hope of remaining undiscovered. The clang of leather against metal meant someone was climbing the stairs to the catwalk. They were coming up fast, and still without turning on any lights.

Anyone with legitimate business in the theater would already have called out. That certainty sent shivers down Liss's spine. Her gaze darted frantically around the storage room, seeking a place to hide. There were plenty of things she could duck behind, but there was no way out except through that one door. She was well and truly trapped.

Fighting full-blown panic, she ducked behind the screen. It would not conceal her presence for long. That the overhead lights were on was a dead giveaway that someone was in this room.

Belatedly, she remembered the cell phone she still held in one hand, but before she could do more than tap in the next two digits of Detective Franklin's number, she heard the approaching footsteps cross the catwalk and stop in the doorway.

Through a narrow gap between the two sections of the screen, Liss had a limited view of the room beyond. With bated breath she waited for the intruder to walk into her line of sight. She still hoped to see a stranger, preferably one wearing the uniform of a campus cop. Instead, she recognized Gabe Treat, and he was very obviously searching for her.

Even though she knew that he'd hear her the moment she spoke into the phone, Liss punched in the remaining numbers on Franklin's card. Gabe rounded the screen just as the number started to ring.

"Did you really think I'd let you get away with it?" His nostrils flared with anger and his eyes were hot.

Liss winced and shrank back when he took another threatening step closer. She couldn't move far. The bed was in the way.

Very faintly, she heard Franklin's voice as he answered her call. She drew breath to scream for help, but before she could make a single sound, Gabe grabbed her wrist and wrenched the cell phone out of her hand.

"Sorry," he said into the mouthpiece. "Wrong number."

He ended the call and tossed the phone onto the bed. Liss inched sideways, truly terrified now. His angry glare had been bad enough, but now it was reinforced by hands clenched into tight fists at his sides. Gabe Treat was big and powerful. Although Liss had acquired a few self-defense skills over the years, she knew she was no match for someone with his sheer brute strength.

"Never surrender. Never give up," she muttered, and

had to tamp down hard on a bubble of hysterical laughter when she realized she was quoting dialog from *Galaxy Quest*. It didn't matter where the words came from, though. When push came to shove, she was fully prepared to fight for her life.

Chapter Sixteen

For a moment, they faced off in total silence. Neither moved. Then the fury vanished from Gabe's eyes as if it had never been and he cocked his head, studying her as if she were an interesting specimen in a zoo.

"Are you planning to karate chop me or something?"

Liss blinked and looked more closely at his face. The anger was gone, replaced by nothing more frightening than annoyance with a touch of exasperation . . . and a disconcerting hint of amusement.

Embarrassment flooded through her. She straightened up, nervously wiping her palms on the sides of her jeans. Now that the moment of sheer panic had passed, she realized that he'd never intended to kill her. And that he was now just as uncertain what to say next as she was.

"What are you doing here?" she asked.

"I was about to ask you the same question. Except that I pretty much figured out the answer when I realized that you'd stolen my key."

She fished it out of her pocket and tossed it to him. He caught it on the fly and took a moment to return it to his key ring. Liss could have escaped then, if she'd still been worried about his intentions.

She wasn't.

"You gave me a scare," she admitted.

"I meant to. You had no business being in here on your own. You could have gotten hurt. There are all kinds of traps for the unwary lying around backstage."

He didn't know she'd been a professional dancer, Liss realized. "Is that why you were so angry? I appreciate your concern, but I would have been fine. I'm very familiar with scenery, props, fly lines, ballast and the like. I wasn't in any danger of catching my ankle on a rope and ending up suspended over the stage. Besides, I was just about to leave when you turned up."

He raked his fingers through his bright red hair and his face colored up to match. "I've got a temper. I apologize. But you *stole* from me. Why didn't you just *ask*?" Hurt and bewilderment came through his words, as well as lingering irritation.

"I apologize for that. But look at it from my point of view. I wasn't sure I could trust you."

Gabe's gaze shifted to the phone on the bed as it started to ring. "Who did you call?"

"Detective Franklin." She scooped it up, glanced at the screen, and repeated, "Detective Franklin." Apparently she'd been connected long enough for him to capture her number and call back.

While Gabe listened, she told the state police officer where she was and what she thought she'd found. She had to hold the phone away from her ear when he exploded. Predictably, he was not happy to hear that she'd been meddling. In the end, however, he told her to stay put and wait for him to arrive.

"Are any of the outside doors unlocked?" Liss asked Gabe after she hung up.

He was staring at the stain on the mattress.

"Gabe?"

"It's like the memorial to the Westford Knight." His awed whisper sounded loud in the quiet storage room. "Look at it—the outline of a hand-and-a-half broadsword, just like on that ledge of rock in Westford, Massachusetts."

"Yeah, okay. I'm sure that's what the killer had in mind. Pay attention, Gabe. You need to go down and unlock one of the exit doors so the state police can get in."

"Yeah, okay," he echoed, and went.

It was some time later, after the state police forensics team had arrived to do their thing in scenery storage loft #2, that Liss found herself sitting next to Gabe at the back of the auditorium. Franklin had told them both to wait there until he gave them permission to leave. He'd already chewed Liss out for acting on her own and potentially destroying evidence. At the same time, he'd been skeptical that there was any evidence to destroy. Unlike Gabe, he did not immediately see the shape of a sword.

"If you'd asked to borrow the key, I'd have loaned it to you," Gabe grumbled, still belaboring that issue. "You didn't need to sneak it off my key chain."

"Give it a rest, Gabe."

She wondered when he would twig to the fact that she'd considered him a suspect. That he hadn't, she supposed, argued for his innocence, not that she needed any further proof. She was now convinced that Gabe Treat was exactly what he'd first appeared to be—a nice young man who was kind to his elderly grandfather and treated his girlfriend with respect.

"What if I'd been the killer?" Gabe asked.

"What?" She swiveled to stare at him.

"You'd have been trapped up there if whoever killed

Professor Palsgrave had seen you come into the theater and guessed what you were looking for."

She opened her mouth, then closed it again, deciding that, for once, she'd better think before she spoke. After a moment, she reached out to close her hand over his forearm. "You're right. And I'm glad you showed up to protect me. Thank you for that. But I have to confess that, for just a minute there, I thought *you* might be planning to do me in."

As she'd hoped, he laughed at the very idea. Then he blushed again. "I'm sorry about grabbing your phone that way. I didn't know you were calling the cops. I thought . . . well, I don't know what I thought. I was just upset, because you'd taken my key, and I wanted to get things sorted out between us, you know?"

"I think I do, yes. Don't worry about it. And the upside is that the police have to listen to us now. They'll test that blood and find out it's Palsgrave's and then they'll know that my father couldn't possibly have killed him."

That was all that mattered, Liss told herself. From now on the ball was in Detective Franklin's court. It was up to him to find out who'd really murdered the nutty professor.

A little more than an hour later, Detective Franklin allowed them to leave, but not before he'd given Liss a lengthy lecture about interfering in police business. He flat out refused to speculate as to whether her discovery would free her father of suspicion. When she ran through the time frame she'd worked out, he just shook his head.

"Your reasoning depends largely on a suspect's wife and daughter as witnesses."

"And I suppose that means you assume that the said wife and daughter are lying to protect their husband/father?"

He shrugged. "Wouldn't you, if you were in my shoes?"

Liss was still steaming when she stepped outside. The first thing she saw was Jake Murch's truck parked next to her car. Murch himself got out when he spotted her approaching. He waited for her, hip resting against the side of the truck bed, arms folded across his chest. He did not look happy.

"Don't start," Liss warned him. "I've already had an earful from the state police."

She watched Gabe, who had parked on the other side of the lot, get into his pickup and drive off to check on his grandfather. She envied him. For all intents and purposes, he didn't have a care in the world.

"You want to fill me in?" Murch asked.

Leaning against the trunk of her own car, Liss grudgingly did so. "How about you?" she asked when she'd brought him up to date. "Any useful discoveries?"

"Only negatives, but we can rule out both Rowse and Jones as suspects. I located a couple of students who were sitting under a tree—studying, they said, but I suspect the guy was mostly studying the girl. Anyway, they had a good view of both the picket line and the front door of Lincoln Hall. They remembered Gabe Treat hanging around, and they say the only demonstrator who went inside the building was Amalfi, and that was well before your father showed up. Probably had to use the can."

"Whoever killed Palsgrave entered and exited by way of the art gallery. He left the sword in the storage room and went out the back way. Your witnesses were in the wrong place to catch a glimpse of him."

"Are you thinking the killer is someone in the history department? Because I talked to the secretary—"

"Administrative assistant."

"Whatever. Norma Leeds, right?"

Liss nodded.

"She backed up what you told me about Professor Halladay being in her office during the relevant time period. No one else who works in that department came in that day."

"I don't suppose Norma herself had a motive?" Liss asked without much hope.

"Strangely enough, she did, but I don't think she's our killer."

"What motive?" Liss took in Murch's smirk and groaned aloud. "Oh, no. Don't tell me *Norma* was one of Palsgrave's conquests."

"Okay. I won't tell you. But I've got a source who says they went at it hot and heavy for about six months."

"When?"

"Two years ago. There must have been a dry spell in the cute student department."

"Or else Palsgrave was getting too old to attract coeds."

"There is that." Murch fished in a pocket for a fresh hit of bubble gum.

Liss's nose wrinkled when he unwrapped it. Even from a few feet away, the sweet, fruity scent was cloying.

"Anyway," he continued as he started to chew, "the scuttlebutt is that Norma and her boss remained friendly after they broke off the affair. From what I can learn, Palsgrave always managed to stay on good terms with his ex-ladies when he moved on." Murch shook his head over the oddity of that. "I sure would expect there to be some jealousy, but if there was, I haven't found it yet."

"What about ex-girlfriends' current love interests?"

Murch shrugged. "You sure you want me to go on with this investigation? It's not that I'm trying to talk you out of keeping me on the payroll or anything, but it sounds to me like your father's off the hook."

"Franklin hasn't said so yet."

"He will," Murch predicted.

"You didn't answer my question. Did you find any suspicious husbands or boyfriends?"

"There is one possibility, but it's a long shot." Murch opened the door of the truck and reached inside for a file folder.

The light breeze that had been blowing Liss's hair into her eyes while they talked now caught the contents as Murch opened the folder. One page, printed with a photograph, flew upward and straight into her hand. She clutched it, on the verge of laughter until she recognized the face looking up at her.

"I know this man."

"Yeah? Where from?"

"That's what I'm trying to remember. Who is he?"

"His name is Martin Edgerley. He's a professor here at the college. He teaches philosophy, if you can believe that. I'd have thought that subject would have gone the way of Latin and Greek."

Liss continued to stare at the printout. The face seemed familiar, but she couldn't place where she'd seen him before. In the photograph he was staring directly at the camera. His arm was slung around the shoulders of a much younger woman. Liss assumed she was his daughter. Edgerley appeared to be in his fifties, with a receding hairline and salt-and-pepper hair. His eyes were a pale blue. His most distinctive feature was a hawklike nose. His build, she noted, was muscular enough to allow him to swing a broadsword.

"He's the husband of Palsgrave's most recent conquest," Murch said. "See the girl? Her name is Gaylene. She was Edgerley's student before she married him. Apparently, she likes older men. She took up with Palsgrave about three months ago."

So, Liss thought—not Edgerley's daughter, after all.

"I'm impressed, Mr. Murch," she said aloud. "This is the first time I've heard anything about an affair with a married woman, and I thought I was fairly well plugged in to the gossip on campus." She wondered how Melly had missed this tidbit. Or had she? Maybe she'd had reasons of her own not to share the information with Liss.

"I have a gift," Murch said with a hint of sarcasm in his voice. "And good instincts. They're telling me that Edgerley isn't a likely suspect. He has no history of violence. Besides that, he seems to have known about his wife's affair from the beginning. But if you saw him somewhere near Palsgrave, or near the sword—"

"That's it!" Liss felt a surge of relief as the elusive memory surfaced. She tapped the photo. "This man was in Moosetookalook. He didn't come into the shop, but he stood outside for a long time, his nose all but pressed to the window, staring at the display of weapons. I don't remember exactly when it was, but I don't suppose that matters. The important thing is that he knew the sword was there."

"That's pretty slight evidence to tie a man to murder."

"It makes him a viable suspect, Murch. He needs to be investigated."

"I'm already on it." He tipped an imaginary hat to Liss and climbed back in to the cab of his truck.

Belatedly, another thought occurred to her. She banged on the passenger side window until he pushed the button to lower it. "Did you actually talk to Jones and Rowse, or just take that student's word for it that they weren't in the building?"

Murch blew an enormous pink bubble and let it pop before he answered her. "No and yes. You agreed with me that they were out of it, Ms. MacCrimmon."

The window rolled back up before she could remind him that either or both of the demonstrators might have seen someone leave Lincoln Hall by the back door. Now that she knew the killer had not been carrying a sword, it seemed even more likely he'd exited the building that way. From a distance, any bloodstains on his clothing would not have been noticeable, but perhaps Rowse or Jones had seen him leave, or noticed his car as he drove away from the scene of the crime.

It was worth taking the time to ask.

Stopping only long enough to order something to eat at the drive-up window of a fast-food restaurant, Liss headed for Melly's house. Her mother's friend was just unloading groceries from the trunk of her car when Liss pulled in behind her in the driveway. Hastily polishing off the last French fry and wiping her fingers on a napkin, Liss killed the engine and got out.

Melly sent her a considering look. "Shouldn't you be at home getting ready for your wedding?"

"Mom has everything well in hand."

Melly headed for the side door. Liss grabbed the last two grocery bags, slammed the trunk closed, and followed her.

"Leave it up to Vi and you're likely to end up with that handfasting, whether you want it or not."

Liss gave a theatrical shudder. "I'm counting on Reverend Browne to fight that battle for me."

"Vi can be very persuasive." Melly waved Liss into the kitchen and started putting foodstuffs away.

Liss settled onto one of the tall kitchen stools and gave her mother's friend an edited account of the day's disclosures while she worked. She waited until Melly was folding the empty bags before she dropped Martin Edgerley's name into the conversation.

"So, you heard about that," Melly said.

"You already knew Palsgrave was having an affair with his wife?" Unspoken was an accusation: *and you didn't tell me?*

Melly shrugged. "I know Martin pretty well. He's just not a likely suspect, especially for such a violent murder. I didn't want to cause him any trouble. Besides, the way I hear it, the affair with Palsgrave has been over for a while now. He got tired of Gaylene always clinging to him."

"You don't sound like you're a fan of the wayward wife. What about this Gaylene as a suspect? Was she angry over being dumped?"

"I have no idea," Melly said. "I'm friendly with Martin, not his wife."

Liss thought about the photo Murch had shown her. Edgerley's wife was skinny, with thin, weak-looking arms, although she was generously endowed in the bosom department. "Does Gaylene work out?" Liss asked Melly. If Gaylene went regularly to a gym, it was possible she had strength that wasn't readily apparent.

Melly's lips twisted into a wry smile. "Maybe you should ask her your questions directly. I can give you her address."

Ten minutes later, Liss pulled up in front of a Cape with dormers. Gaylene Edgerley herself was in the front yard, watering a flower bed. She was wearing very short shorts and a crop top that left little to the imagination.

And if she had any great strength in her arms, it was indeed well hidden. Still, Liss figured that, since she was there, she might as well talk to the woman. As one of Palsgrave's former lovers, Gaylene might have some idea who had hated him enough to kill him.

"Mrs. Edgerley?" Liss called out as she crossed the perfectly manicured lawn.

Only when she got closer did she realize that the woman couldn't hear her. Any sound but the music Gaylene was playing was blocked by her earphones. Gingerly, Liss tapped the woman on the shoulder.

Startled, Gaylene jumped. She turned, wild eyed and fist swinging. Liss barely ducked in time to prevent the other woman from planting a facer.

Hastily backing up, both hands held in front of her to ward off further blows, Liss tripped over the garden hose and nearly landed flat on her backside. She saved herself from the fall just in time, but it was at the expense of her weak knee. She heard it pop as she twisted her body to stay upright.

"Who the hell are you?" Gaylene demanded, ripping off her headset.

"Sorry. I didn't mean to startle you. My name is Liss MacCrimmon. I was wondering if I could ask you about—"

"Oh, no. No more questions."

"*More* questions?" Liss echoed. Drat! Did that mean Murch had been here?

"Yes, more questions. First it was the police, and then that annoying man with the bubble gum, and now you. And I don't know anything. So just leave me alone."

"Did the police also question your husband?" Liss asked.

Gaylene's face flushed, the change in color apparent even beneath her heavy application of makeup. Her eyes narrowed to slits. Liss backed up again, prepared to make a run for it. If ever she'd seen a woman who looked like she was about to explode, it was Gaylene Edgerley.

Liss would not have been surprised if Gaylene shoved her, or even clawed at her eyes. Instead, the potential for violence proved an impotent fury. Gaylene stamped her feet like a toddler getting ready to have a temper tantrum. Then she threw down the hose, still spewing water, and burst into tears. Before Liss could do or say anything, her quarry had fled into the house.

Mulling over Gaylene's reaction, Liss found the outside spigot and turned off the water. Then she got back into her car and drove away.

Convinced that Murch did not intend to interview either John Jones or Barry Rowse, Liss glanced at her watch. She still had time before she needed to head back to Moosetookalook. She tried Rowse's address first.

It was a storefront in the seedier section of Three Cities, on one of the streets near the old textile mill. Making blankets had once been a major industry but the factory had closed down decades ago and most of the buildings had stood empty ever since. Only one had been given new life as a minimall. Rowse's store was several blocks away from that attempt at urban renewal. The siding on the building needed painting and the display window could have done with a good washing. Liss could barely read the letters that spelled out ROWSE AND SON USED FURNITURE AND HOUSEHOLD ITEMS.

The inside of the shop was a jumble of chairs, tables, and lamps. They were stacked on every side with reckless abandon. Liss followed what looked like a narrow aisle between towering piles of furniture. Mazelike, it wound back on itself several times before finally taking her to a display case with an antique cash register sitting on top of it.

"Hello?" she called, tentatively at first and then in a louder voice.

Like an apparition, a scarecrow of a man rose from behind the counter. He blinked at her with bloodshot eyes, frowning as he swiped at his long, unkempt hair, pushing it behind his ears. "Can I help you?" he asked.

"Mr. Rowse? Barry Rowse?" For some reason, Liss had expected him to be older, but the man behind the makeshift counter was somewhere in his midtwenties. She supposed he must be the "and son" advertised on the window.

Warily, he nodded.

"I'd like to ask you a couple of questions."

"What do you want to know?" His frown had morphed into a scowl.

Liss thought about turning around and leaving, answers be damned. Standing this close to him, she could tell that there was something not quite right about his pupils. Her best guess was that Rowse was taking drugs, and that made her nervous. On the other hand, she'd come this far. She might as well push ahead. She was pretty sure that if he turned violent, she could outrun him.

"I heard there was a Barry Rowse who's interested in the Templar treasure," she said. "Is that you?"

"Well, yeah," he said, as if she should know that just by looking at him. "Would you believe there's a guy at the college who thinks the dude only came here for the fish?"

"The dude? You mean Henry Sinclair?"

"Who else. Sinclair's the man." He leaned forward

and gave her a conspiratorial wink. "Brought the trea-sure to the New World. Left a clue in the Newport Tower."

At her blank look, he expanded on this. The Newport Tower, it seemed, was a structure in Newport, Rhode Is-land, that appeared to predate colonization by the Eng-lish. Rowse thought Sinclair had built it. Liss didn't care.

"You know the guy at the college got killed, right?"

"Oh, yeah. Forgot." He scratched his ear.

"You were there that day," Liss reminded him. "Pick-eting."

He shrugged. "Guess so. Days run together some-times."

I'll bet they do, Liss thought. "So you didn't see any-thing? Maybe someone running away from the build-ing?"

He started to giggle. "Wouldn't turn him in even if I did. The dude deserved it for trashing my man Sinclair."

Liss gave up. "Okay. Thanks. I'll be going now."

Rowse seemed unhinged enough to have killed Pro-fessor Palsgrave over the Sinclair debate, but aside from the fact that he clearly lacked the planning skills neces-sary to have framed her father, his arms were as skinny as the rest of him. He'd have trouble lifting one of the lamps he had for sale, never mind a broadsword.

Although she doubted she'd find out anything more this time than she had on her last visit, Liss returned to John Jones's address before she headed home. She got lucky. A man with a dog on a leash was just coming out of the apartment. He didn't look like a Native American. Then again, according to Gabe's friend, he wasn't one.

"Mr. Jones?" she hailed him.

Once again she was met with suspicion, but the out

and out rudeness was absent. The dog, a cocker spaniel, seemed delighted to make a new friend. He pranced right up to Liss and rose onto his hind legs to put his front paws on her thigh. The next thing she knew, he had his nose in her crotch.

"Down, Tonto," Jones said.

Liss knelt to pat the spaniel on the head. She looked up at Jones through her eyelashes, trying to assess him and decide the best way to proceed. He was of medium height and chubby, with dark eyes and hair, one of those people for whom *nondescript* was an accurate description.

"I understand you've written a book," she said, remembering another of Gabe's comments.

It was as if the sun had come out after a long rainy spell. Jones's eyes sparkled. His mouth curved into a bright smile. Even his teeth gleamed. "Why, yes, I have," he said.

Ten minutes later, Liss was the proud owner of ten copies of *Norumbega Defiled*, a collection of original poems that Jones claimed to have written after making contact with a distant ancestor during a séance. Liss had her doubts. And she thought it likely that all ten copies were destined for the Dumpster.

"You're familiar with the place-name Norumbega, of course," Jones said.

"That's the old name for New England," Liss replied, grateful for the course in Maine history every student in her middle school had been required to take.

Jones seemed more interested in the distant past than in the present. It took a little doing to turn the conversation to the day of the murder. When Liss finally managed it, she was pleasantly surprised to discover that Jones was far and away the most observant of the four demonstrators.

He had seen her father go in and come out again. He was certain Mac's clothing had been free of bloodstains and that he had not been carrying a sword.

He had noticed Gabe and guessed that he was there to keep an eye on his grandfather.

He reluctantly admitted that he thought Barry Rowse was high on drugs.

He recalled that Louis Amalfi had gone into Lincoln Hall to use the men's room and come out again within minutes, and that this had occurred before Mac arrived.

He had seen Palsgrave's students leave the building, but not Palsgrave.

He'd seen Willa arrive, talk to Gabe, and go into Lincoln Hall. He'd heard her come out again.

"She was screaming like a banshee," he said as he and Liss walked Tonto down the street to a small park.

Jones had left the little dog in her care, waiting on the sidewalk in front of his building, while he'd gone back inside for the books. Now he held the leash and she carried the thin, overpriced volumes. They were clothbound with garish covers. Never in a million years would they sell to her usual clientele.

"So Gabe Treat never left his post and never went inside Lincoln Hall?" Liss prompted when Jones failed to add anything else.

"Not that I saw."

She nodded. She'd hoped she could exclude Gabe as a suspect. This went a long way toward allowing her to do so.

"Did you notice anyone else around, anyone you recognized?"

He shrugged. "Students. Professors. I don't know everyone's names."

"But you know some?"

"I've taken a few classes on campus—they offer what

they call adult enrichment programs from time to time. Oddball stuff. Theater of the Absurd. Classics of Science Fiction. A seminar on the life of William Faulkner. Now there was a weird guy. Did you know that he never answered a question the same way twice? My guess is that he just lied about everything personal because he figured his private life was nobody's business but his own. That was an interesting class. So was the one I took in ancient religions from Dr. Edgerley."

Liss's thoughts had started to drift, but now her interest quickened. "Martin Edgerley? Is there any chance you saw *him* hanging around Lincoln Hall that day?"

Jones frowned. "Come to think of it, I did see him the day Palsgrave was offed, but it wasn't there."

"Okay. Where *was* he when you saw him?" Tonto had found a bush he liked and they stopped while he tended to his business.

"He was parked in the lot they call the pit. I saw him getting into his car when we were down that way. You know . . . picketing."

"Was that before or after you saw my father leave?"

Jones's frown deepened. "I'm not sure. I think it was after, but I wasn't paying much attention. It was definitely before the body was discovered, though. I'd remember if it had been after that."

Good enough, Liss thought, and moved Martin Edgerley to the top of her revised suspect list.

Chapter Seventeen

When Liss arrived home an hour and a half later, it was to hear that she'd just missed a phone call from Edmund Carrier.

"He wanted you to call him back as soon as you came in." Vi had a vaguely disapproving look on her face and lingered in the background as Liss punched in the number.

While she waited for the lawyer to answer, Lumpkin and Glenora appeared as if by magic to let her know they'd noticed that she'd been away for the entire day. The small black cat wound herself so enthusiastically around Liss's legs that Liss decided it was the better part of valor to take a seat on the sofa. Otherwise, should she take a step in any direction, she was likely to trip over the cat and wind up in a heap on the living room floor. The moment her new position made a lap available, both felines leapt into it. Lumpkin, more savvy and twice as large, made short work of shoving his "sister" aside. His rumbling purr announced his satisfaction with the result.

Liss was absentmindedly stroking a furry back by the time Mr. Carrier came on the line. In her peripheral vision, she saw that her mother now held Glenora cradled in her arms. Vi showed no inclination to leave the room.

She forgot all about her mother's eavesdropping when Carrier explained the reason for his call. She was so surprised by what he told her that she had to ask him to repeat it.

"It's simple enough, Liss," Mr. Carrier said. "Mrs. Gaylene Edgerley has made a formal complaint about you to the state police."

"All I did was talk to her," Liss protested. "She'd already answered questions for the detectives *and* Mr. Murch."

"That is precisely why she considers your appearance on her doorstep as badgering. She took her objections straight to Detective Franklin and Detective Franklin contacted me. I'm under orders to rein you in. You're interfering in an official investigation."

In her agitation, Liss tightened her fingers on the fur beneath her hand. Lumpkin made a loud sound somewhere between a hiss and a yelp, kicked her in the stomach, and abandoned her lap. She winced as she touched a hand to her midriff and made a mental note to clip the big cat's back claws at her first opportunity.

"On the positive side," Carrier's voice continued in her ear, "you can take heart from the fact that the state police did question Mrs. Edgerley and her husband before you even knew of their existence. I take that to mean that they've been looking at other suspects all along."

"I don't understand why Mr. Murch can talk to people and I can't," she complained.

She heard a deep sigh on the other end of the line. "Liss, you've been a great help. You provided Murch with a number of useful suggestions. And I don't discount that you found a thing or two on your own that he missed. Detective Franklin as good as admitted that he might not have searched the theater as thoroughly as you did. But for all intents and purposes, your father is in the clear now."

"Did Franklin say that?"

"Not yet. He has to wait for the results of lab tests before he can make any official pronouncement. I'm sure you can understand that."

"I understand, but I don't like it," Liss muttered.

Even if her father was in the clear with the police, the mud would stick to him until the real killer was arrested. Liss knew small towns. Early on, everyone had been supportive, but the longer the investigation went on without an arrest, the more people would look at her parents askance, even those who'd known them for decades. There were already sudden silences when any MacCrimmon entered a room where the locals were gathered. In time, the situation could well become so intolerable that it would drive Mac and Vi away for good.

"Show a little faith in the system," Carrier advised. "In the meantime, don't you have other things to occupy your mind? I believe your mother mentioned something about an orchid shortage."

The flower situation was still cause for crisis mode the next morning. At ten, Vi invaded Moosetookalook Scottish Emporium with yet another report of dismal failure.

"It's hopeless," she wailed. "I found a florist who has miniature canary panda butterfly orchids but not a single one I've contacted can supply orange marmalade phalaenopsis in time. I don't understand it."

"Orchids need special growing conditions," Gabe said absently from his seat in the cozy corner, "and they don't bloom all that often." He was reading one of the copies of John Jones's book.

Vi had him in her crosshairs before he had time to draw another breath. "How do you know so much about orchids?" she demanded.

"My grandfather grows them."

"Mom," Liss protested. "I don't think—"

"Hush, darling. Mother's busy. . . . Your grandfather, you say?"

Liss wasn't surprised to find herself en route to Three Cities again by eleven that morning. This time, however, she wasn't going with the intent to snoop. Her mother was in the passenger seat. Gabe was in the back.

The stuffy butler let them in without argument and led them straight to the conservatory. Vi was in seventh heaven at the sight of all those flowers. Liss still couldn't tell a daffodil from a carnation, but she took her mother's word for it that Alistair Gunn had propagated exactly the right color in orchids. Vi flitted from plant to plant, uttering rapturous little squeals.

"Intelligent woman, your mother," Gunn remarked.

"If you say so." Liss knew she sounded disgruntled and made an effort to show more enthusiasm for the details of her own wedding. It wasn't easy, not when Vi was clearly the one making all the decisions.

"Women weren't so interesting when I was young," Gunn added.

"Maybe you just didn't notice, Granddad," Gabe kidded him.

"Nope. All the ones I knew were dull sticks. Only interested in fashion and society. Nowadays, though, every woman I meet is full of surprises. You got this one here, hell-bent on proving her daddy innocent of murder. And then there's that one there, who clearly knows her orchids."

Liss hid a smile. Her mother had learned everything she knew about the subject by surfing the Web. Unwilling to disillusion Mr. Gunn, however, she let him keep his rose-colored glasses.

"Willa's pretty unique, too," Gabe offered.

Gunn gave a disbelieving snort. "Pale copy of her mentor, if you ask me."

"Mentor?" Liss asked. "Are you talking about Caroline Halladay?"

Gunn nodded. "Now there's a really interesting woman, one who knows a lot about the old ways of doing things. And you could have knocked me over with a feather when I walked into her office and saw what she had there."

"An illuminated manuscript?" Liss guessed. "A medieval tapestry?"

"You see, that's the thing," Gunn said with a laugh. "You'd expect something like that. Or maybe a shield and crossed swords on the wall behind her desk. Nothing of the kind. She's got this great, honking exercise machine taking up half the space in the room."

Liss smiled, imagining a tiny office dominated by an exercise bike or a treadmill. She had no doubt that someone of Caroline's proportions would try to keep the pounds under control by a few minutes here and a half hour there on one or the other.

"She has one of those padded floor mats, too," Gunn said. "She told me it was for meditating."

"Yes," Liss said. "I understand that she often meditates in her office." From the look of the woman, she did more meditating than exercising.

Vi reappeared at the end of the worktable. Clutching two abundantly flowering potted plants, she wore a huge smile on her face. "These," she said. "These are perfect."

Gunn beamed with pleasure at the compliment, but his expression quickly turned stormy when he heard what Vi wanted to do with his precious babies. "Cut off the bloom stalks for a bouquet?" he yelped. "Are you mad, woman?"

Vi set the plants down, took his arm, and went to work on him in a quiet, persuasive voice. Liss caught only a word or two, but what she did hear alarmed her. She would have interrupted had Gabe not caught her arm and hauled her out of the conservatory.

"Hey!" she protested. "I had something to say to her."

"Quarrel with your mother later. I haven't seen my grandfather enjoy himself this much in a dog's age."

"She's talking to him about holding a handfasting ceremony. I've already vetoed that idea."

"Well, then, there's no problem, is there? You're the bride. You don't have to do anything on your wedding day that you don't want to do. Right?"

"Damn straight," Liss muttered, but in her heart of hearts she wasn't so certain. Violet MacCrimmon was a force of nature, capable of overwhelming the most vehement protests and sweeping them away. Any flotsam left behind was too waterlogged to voice further objections.

Twenty minutes later, they were on their way back to Moosetookalook with two of Alistair Gunn's potted orchids carefully stored in the trunk of the car. When they had duly delivered them to the florist in Fallstown who was handling the wedding flowers, they returned home.

As far as Liss was concerned, the entire day had been a waste of time, but her mother was happy. Liss supposed that counted for something. Carrier and Franklin would be happy, too. Liss hadn't done a single thing to interfere in the official investigation of A. Leon Palsgrave's murder.

On Friday morning, Liss awoke with a hangover. The previous evening, after she and Willa had closed up shop, she'd gone toe to toe with her mother over the handfasting ceremony. She'd laid down the law. No silken cords. No anvil. No broom. And definitely no sword.

Vi had burst into tears.

An hour after that, at the wedding rehearsal, they'd both pretended that everything was just fine. That was the only way either of them could have survived both the rehearsal and the supper afterward.

Now Liss stared forlornly at her bloodshot eyes in the mirror. She'd imbibed a bit too freely of the champagne Joe Ruskin had provided. She had a feeling she'd be paying for that overindulgence for the rest of the day.

The sight of the rumpled bed behind her, now in possession of Lumpkin and Glenora, tempted her to return to oblivion. What would it matter if she caught a few more hours of sleep? But the strong work ethic that had been instilled in her from childhood, by both her mother and her father, propelled her to her closet and got her dressed. She had a great deal to do on this, the day before her wedding.

With Willa's help, she packed up the items slated to go to the hotel for the Moosetookalook Scottish Emporium booth at the Western Maine Highland Games. By four in the afternoon, when they put out the CLOSED sign, everything had been loaded into two trucks—Dan's and Gabe's. Ten minutes later, they were parked on the hotel grounds next to the space Liss had been assigned. Their first task was to erect the sturdy canvas tent with its roll-up sides, a purchase Aunt Margaret had made years ago for just such occasions as this one.

Similar tents and a smattering of awnings had already sprung up on every side. Cheerful shouts, the steady thwack of hammers pounding in nails on the stage being erected for the dance competition, and the sounds of bagpipers tuning up filled the air. Just a glimpse of Janice Eccles, a.k.a. the Scone Lady, setting up her portable oven, made Liss's mouth water. Except for the dignified old hotel rising in the background, the grounds would soon have the look, feel, sound, and smell of every other Scottish festival Liss had ever attended.

"Are you nervous?" Willa asked as they set up a display of kilt pins and other clan jewelry.

"About what?" Liss asked, stepping back to study the effect.

Willa giggled. "Your wedding. That *is* why the gazebo is decorated with flowers, isn't it?"

Liss felt herself flush. For a moment, she'd actually forgotten she was marrying Dan the next day. She glanced toward the gazebo and started to smile. It did look gorgeous. "Yes, indeed," she murmured. "Tomorrow is the big day."

Her headache had disappeared without her noticing. So had any trepidation about getting married with an unsolved murder hanging over her head. Franklin had the investigation under control. Liss had the Emporium booth in order. All was right with the world.

Willa, shading her eyes to see better as she surveyed their surroundings, suddenly frowned.

Liss followed the direction of her gaze. The Medieval Scottish Conclave contingent had arrived. They were just starting to set up their tents, far more ornate structures than those used by most of the exhibitors and vendors. In the course of the next hour, that section of the grounds came to more closely resemble a Renaissance Faire than a Scottish festival.

The program had called the displays living history and contained a list of all the crafts that would be represented. Caroline Halladay's students would be out in full force. Did Willa regret not being part of that? Liss wondered. For the first time, she also considered the possibility that Willa's rift with Dr. Halladay might have seriously damaged the young woman's future in the field of history.

She started to ask about Willa's plans for the next semester, then thought better of raising uncomfortable topics. Willa was placidly unpacking boxes. Remembering how quickly her moods could shift, Liss decided to leave well enough alone. Later, after she returned from Scotland, she'd see what she could do for her. Perhaps student and mentor could be reconciled. After all, Professor Halladay had already admitted, when she'd talked to Liss in Margaret's office, that she'd overreacted to learning that Willa's boyfriend and Alistair Gunn's grandson were one and the same.

On Saturday morning, Liss's wedding day, the bride-to-be was up at the crack of dawn. It didn't take her long to get ready to go out to the hotel. She planned to wear her hair loose under a circlet of flowers, so all she had to do was make sure it was clean. She'd never been one for heavy makeup, so that took only a few minutes to attend to. Once she'd fed the cats and dawdled over toast and coffee, she still had *hours* to fill.

"I'm going out to the hotel," she announced when her

parents appeared in the kitchen. Apparently neither of them were experiencing any bridal jitters. She was happy for them, but too impatient to sit still while they billed and cooed at each other.

Vi glanced at the kitchen clock. "It's too early," she protested.

"I'll take my dress out and leave it in the room Joe booked for us to change in. Then I'm going to take a walk around the grounds. I want to check the Emporium booth and make sure there aren't any last minute problems."

"Leave the girl be," Mac said. "She needs to keep busy."

"Really, Liss, just this one day, couldn't you let someone else worry about the business?"

"I'm not worried, Mom. Willa and Gabe will be fine without my supervision. But I'll be climbing the walls by the time I'm scheduled to say my vows if I don't have something to occupy my time."

Reluctantly, Vi let her go. She had plenty to do herself, Liss knew, starting with an appointment at the most expensive hair stylist's salon in Fallstown. For her only daughter's wedding, Betsy Twining at the Clip and Curl, a shop that shared space with the Moosetookalook post office, just wasn't good enough for Vi MacCrimmon.

By the time Liss arrived at The Spruces, the main parking lot was already full and the overflow was being directed onto an open section of lawn. Fortunately, wedding parking would have its own space—the staff parking lot.

Liss made short work of stashing her gown and shoes. Thanks to Vi's organizational skills, there was nothing more she had to do before she actually got dressed. The flowers were ready. So was the cake. And the hotel's kitchen staff was even now preparing the food they'd serve after Liss and Dan exchanged their vows.

She had more than two hours to kill.

Her route from the hotel to the Moosetookalook Scottish Emporium booth took her through the medieval conclave tents. She heard them before she saw them. In the best tradition of London street vendors, someone was calling out, "Hot cross buns! Get your hot cross buns!"

The clang of metal against metal and the smell of smoke gave her the location of the smithy, a shedlike structure made of wood. A young man she didn't know was manning the bellows, attempting to get a fire going in a stone-lined pit. So far, only wisps of smoke drifted up toward the opening in the roof.

The interior of the smithy had the look of a stage set. Hooks hammered into the back wall held a variety of implements, everything from mallets to long-handled tongs. On a small table were an assortment of horseshoes, some rather strangely shaped, as if the blacksmith who'd made them hadn't yet mastered his craft.

The other medieval craftsmen operated out of tents. Liss had never seen anything quite like the displays spread out before her. The closest she'd come had been on a long-ago visit to Maine's Common Ground Fair. There had been a blacksmith and a leatherworker there, too, and scores of crafters. She remembered that she'd bought a handmade trainman's cap from a vendor that day . . . and watched the llama drill team perform.

At the Medieval Scottish Conclave, signs in the "ye olde" tradition pointed tourists to various WORSHIPFUL COMPANIES. The occupants of each tent were hard at work, demonstrating how various goods had been made in the distant past. If any passerby showed the slightest interest, the reenactors launched into detailed explanations of what they were doing and why.

Hard by the blacksmith's shop, Liss encountered a display of swords and knives. Flyers printed by very modern methods listed the hours when Kirby Redmond would be giving demonstrations of fighting techniques using various medieval weapons. She passed by without stopping or picking one up.

In the next tent, a shoemaker hammered hobnails into the sole of a boot. Across the way, an apothecary had set up shop, displaying phials and vials in all sizes, shapes, and colors. A scrivener was hard at work nearby. His spiel explained that he wrote letters for people who could not do so for themselves.

A pie man joined the woman selling hot cross buns. To the background accompaniment of bagpipes being tuned and the more melodious sound of someone playing a lute and singing "Greensleeves," he was loudly hawking his wares.

Everyone was in costume.

Liss silently applauded the results of Caroline Halladay's efforts. Intrigued, she stopped to watch a tanner at work. The young man, another she'd never seen before, dropped a deer hide over what looked like an ordinary log that had been tilted to a forty-five-degree angle. Then he took up a large curved blade with handles at each end and began to run it over the hide's surface.

"This is an unhairing knife," he explained, seeing that he had an audience of one. "This hide has already been soaked in a solution of wood ash to loosen the hair. Now it has to be scraped before it can be tanned. Tanning is a long process—nine to eighteen months from start to finish. And smelly, too. The tanning pits contain a solution

of tannin made from the bark of oak, beech, and birch
trees and oak galls, acorns, acacia pods, or sumac."

"Uh-huh," Liss said, moving on when he started to
explain the difference between a tanner, who worked on
cattle hide, and a whittawer, who "tawed" the skins of
sheep, goats, deer, horses, dogs, and even cats.

There was such a thing as too much information! She
passed by the next tent, where the sign read WORSHIPFUL
COMPANY OF GLOVERS AND WHITTAWERS, without stopping.

She was about to leave the medieval encampment and
head over to the Emporium booth when she heard someone call her name. A couple hurried toward her, holding
hands. As she waited for them to reach her, she studied
them with undisguised curiosity.

It was the first time she'd seen Gordon Tandy and
Penny Lassiter together, although she'd known for some
time that they were dating. More than dating, from the
look of it.

Gordon, who topped six feet by an inch or two, kept
his thick reddish-brown hair cut very short. That and an
ingrained military bearing made his occupation—state
police detective—all too easy to guess. Liss had dated
him for several months. She knew that he had a gentler
side. It showed in eyes of a brown so dark that they
looked black and in boyish good looks that made Gordon appear younger than his early forties.

Penny Lassiter, a medium-sized woman around 5'5"
tall, was about the same age. Her build was wiry, except
for very feminine curves, and her almond-shaped eyes,
high cheekbones, small up-tilted nose, and pointy little
chin sometimes prompted those who didn't know what
she did for a living to refer to her looks as "elfin." They
never made that mistake twice. Penny Lassiter was the

duly elected sheriff of Carrabassett County, as her father had been before her. She had years of law enforcement experience under her belt.

"Liss," Gordon said, "I'm glad we ran into you."

"You'd have seen me later," she reminded him. "I know you both RSVP'd to the wedding invitation."

"True. We came out early to enjoy the games. But I was also hoping I'd have a chance to talk to you in private."

Penny drifted off to inspect the wares of the glover and listen to his spiel—something about a seven-year apprenticeship and how he only tawed the white skins of deer, sheep, and goats, but not those of cattle or swine, which went to the tanner. Liss stepped aside with Gordon, seeking the shade of the cooper's tent. On the other side of the canvas, that gentleman sang the praises of the barrels, baskets, and casks he'd made himself. He explained to a potential customer that he was making another wooden cask even as he chatted with passing tourists.

"I want you to understand that I'm not speaking officially," Gordon said in a low voice. "In fact, I shouldn't be saying anything to you at all, but I wanted to set your mind at rest. I know you're going to be away for the next few weeks." His lips quirked. "Consider this an extra wedding gift."

"Okay. What is it I'm not supposed to know?" Behind her back, she crossed her fingers. She thought she knew what was coming and hoped she was right.

"Your father is no longer a suspect."

"Yes!" She pumped both fists in the air.

Gordon fought a smile. "He was pretty well in the clear even before you went exploring in the college theater."

"Well, I knew that," Liss said, grinning at him, "but I wasn't so sure that Detective Franklin did."

"The blood on the sword had dried well before it was placed in the trunk of Mac's car. Forensics took the trunk lining at the same time they confiscated the murder weapon. That information didn't jibe with the idea that Mac had killed Palsgrave and driven off with the broadsword in his car. Not to mention that, if he *had* been the murderer, it would have been pretty stupid of him not to get rid of the weapon before he got back to Moosetookalook. He'd have had miles of heavily forested land to hide it in."

"So what I found was just confirmation of what Franklin already knew?"

"Pretty much. All the results aren't in yet." His lip twitch turned into a rueful smile. "It takes a lot longer to process these things than it does on TV. But the blood type was right for Palsgrave and the shape of the stain on that mattress was dead on."

Liss hesitated, then blurted out the question she'd wanted an answer to from the first. "*How* was he killed?" At Gordon's bemused expression, she clarified. "Was he stabbed? Or . . . you know?"

"Ah." He grimaced, but answered her. "Palsgrave was hacked to death. Your original argument about Mac's arthritis also had weight with Franklin—your father might have managed to do that much damage in an adrenaline-fueled fury but he'd have been obviously crippled up afterward. All in all, Liss, you can stop worrying that Mac will ever be arrested for murder."

"I don't suppose you can tell me if Franklin has another suspect in mind?"

"Not a chance. Now, go get married." He refrained from adding a warning to stay out of the investigation, but she could tell that the words were on the tip of his tongue.

She went up on her toes and kissed his cheek. "I will. Thank you, Gordon. Excellent wedding present."

While he went off to find his new lady love, Liss resumed her trek toward the Moosetookalook Scottish Emporium booth. She glanced back only once, smiling when she saw that Caroline Halladay had arrived and was pitching in to get the fire going in the blacksmith's forge.

Everyone had said she was a hands-on teacher, and here was the proof of it. When she was satisfied that the flames were hot enough, she used long tongs to hold a horseshoe in the fire until it glowed red. Extracting it, she then hefted one of the mallets and brought it down on the metal shoe with a resounding clang.

Liss continued on her way and was pleased to discover that Willa and Gabe were already doing a steady business. She pitched in to deal with another customer, and for the next little while all her focus was on selling and building goodwill. It was not until there was a lull that she remembered Caroline and mentioned the professor's skill to her crew.

"It was a very impressive demonstration," she said, opening a bottle of water and taking a hearty swig. She hoped Caroline was well supplied with liquids. She'd work up quite a sweat if she kept at the blacksmithing very long. "The entire medieval conclave is more interesting than I expected it to be."

"It ought to be," Willa said, grabbing a water bottle of her own. "Professor Halladay got big bucks to buy materials the minute the battle reenactment was cancelled."

Slowly, Liss put the water down. In her mind's eye, she once again saw Caroline swinging that mallet.

"She's got considerable upper body strength," she murmured.

"No surprise there, either." Willa was watching a browser turn over tartan scarves. When she started to head his way, Liss caught her arm.

"Let Gabe wait on him. Why is it no surprise that Dr. Halladay is strong?"

Willa shrugged. "Because she's got that humongous exercise machine in her office, of course."

The one Willa had earlier referred to as scary looking, Liss remembered. The one Alistair Gunn had mentioned as taking up half the space in the room. "It's what?" she asked. "A bike? A treadmill?"

But Willa shook her head. "Dr. Halladay says she has to deal with a lot of tension. That's why she meditates so often. And that's why she works out. It's one of those great big exercise machines that are supposed to build strength." She put her fists together and then mimed forcing her arms apart against a heavy-weight setting.

Liss's eyes widened. It appeared that she'd been wrong. Caroline's loose clothing concealed muscle rather than flab. And, according to Kirby Redmond, she'd taken lessons from him, learning how to use a variety of medieval weapons.

Liss tried to tell herself that she was being ridiculous. Caroline Halladay was the one person who had an alibi for the time of Palsgrave's murder. Murch had verified it with the history department's administrative assistant, Norma Leeds. Caroline had not left her office during the crucial half hour. She couldn't have done so without being seen.

Unless . . .

Suddenly Liss realized that Caroline *could* have managed it . . . if one of the trapdoors in the stage was directly above her office. At first, the idea seemed too far-fetched, but the more Liss thought about it, the less able she was to dismiss it out of hand.

"I've got to go," she told Gabe and Willa.

"Have a wonderful wedding!" they chorused.

Liss promised she would, but she had something else to do first.

She had to find Gordon Tandy.

Chapter Eighteen

The grounds at The Spruces had never seemed so vast nor the crowds so dense. Liss hunted in vain for the first ten minutes. She couldn't find Gordon anywhere.

She did spot Jake Murch. He was wearing a Royal Stewart kilt complete with a sporran to keep his wallet in. He was one of those men, Liss decided, who should not show off bare knees. She was almost desperate enough to recruit him when she finally caught sight of her real quarry.

Gordon was feeding a warm buttered scone to Penny and laughing as she took what was clearly her first taste of the delicacy. She had her eyes closed in sheer bliss. Crumbs landed on her shirtfront as Liss grabbed Gordon's arm, jostling his hand.

"Hey!" he protested.

Liss didn't let go. "I've got to talk to you. Now. I know who did it."

Gordon and Penny exchanged a speaking glance. Then they both came with her. The three of them found an empty picnic table at the edge of the lawn near the tree line. Looking back, Liss saw that she had a clear line of sight to the forge where Caroline Halladay still labored, demonstrating the blacksmith's art.

"Talk," Gordon said.

"Caroline Halladay."

His eyes narrowed.

Encouraged by the fact that he didn't immediately dismiss her accusation, Liss kept going. "I know she has an alibi, but I think I've figured out what happened."

"Go on."

Across the table from them, Penny fished in her fanny pack and came up with a pen and paper. At Gordon's nod, she took notes as Liss talked.

"Okay. Here's what I think happened. I don't have any proof, and I won't even be in the country twenty-four hours from now, so I'm trusting you to convince Detective Franklin that the idea isn't as crazy as it sounds."

Gordon's expression was skeptical, but he gave another curt nod.

Liss held up one finger. "Caroline Halladay was in her office the day my father visited Dr. Palsgrave. She overheard them quarreling." A second finger went up. "She knew he had an appointment with Palsgrave on the day of the murder. I'm not sure how."

"She answered the phone while the secretary was on a break." Gordon shrugged when he saw Liss's eyebrows shoot up. "Franklin talked to me about the case. We sometimes bounce ideas off each other."

"Good. That's good. I think." She didn't have time to picture Gordon and Stanley Franklin as brainstorming buddies just now. "So, Caroline could have made the appointment for a time when she knew Palsgrave would be teaching his seminar, if she was already planning the frame-up. And she's an administrative assistant," Liss added. "Norma, I mean."

"Stick to the point, Liss."

"Okay. Okay." She was surprised to find her hands were trembling. Everything was falling into place, but it was happening so fast that she was afraid she'd leave out some crucial step and fail to convince her listeners. "Give me a sec."

"Take your time," Penny said, reaching across the table to pat Liss's forearm. "You're doing great."

"I don't know why I'm so nervous."

"You're fingering a killer," Gordon pointed out. "It's a heavy responsibility. And for once, you're not doing it on the run."

A choked laugh escaped her. "Will wonders never cease! Okay. Here's how I think it went down. Somehow, Caroline knew Palsgrave planned to dismiss his class early that day. I don't think he'd told anyone else that. Maybe Caroline's the one who asked him to stay in the classroom, so they could talk out of Norma's hearing. I don't know. But what you just told me means she deliberately lied to me when she said Norma told her about the quarrel and the appointment. Anyway, she knew where the sword was. It was her idea to set up the display in my shop window in the first place. She stole the sword, intending to use it to frame my father."

"How did she get into the Emporium?" Penny asked.

Gordon answered before Liss could. "A ten-year-old kid with a piece of plastic could break into Liss's store."

Liss made a face at him, but she didn't dispute the assessment. "Caroline planned to be in her office when my father arrived for his appointment, so she could suggest to him that he check the classroom." She frowned. "Or not. That part's a little fuzzy, because how could she know that Palsgrave wouldn't be there?"

"Maybe it didn't matter one way or the other if your father met up with Palsgrave," Penny ventured.

Liss had already considered that possibility. If they'd

met, would anything have changed? Either Mac's apology would have been accepted or they'd have quarreled again. Either way, Palsgrave would still have been a sitting duck once Mac left.

"There's one big problem with Caroline Halladay as the killer, Liss," Gordon said quietly, "even if she did make the appointment for your father and then lie about it. She has an alibi. She was in her office at the time of the murder."

"But that's just it. That's what I realized." She explained about the trapdoors in the stage above the old scenery shop, now converted into two levels of offices for the history department. "She could have gotten out through that trapdoor unseen. If she removed a ceiling panel, she could release the bolt holding the trapdoor closed and it would open downward. She must have hidden the sword in her office before the murder and taken it with her."

"Whoa!" Penny interrupted. "I've met this woman. Are you saying she chinned herself through a hole in the ceiling?"

"Or she set a stepladder on top of her desk and climbed up. Look at her." She gestured toward the forge.

Caroline labored with little apparent effort. She was dressed as a medieval man. Sweat had her linen shirt clinging to her arms and torso, at last revealing the well-toned muscles that, until then, Liss had only theorized she possessed.

"From her office, she got to the stage, and from the stage she went through the art gallery to the classroom without anyone being the wiser."

"Why a sword?" Penny asked, still playing devil's advocate. "Come to that, why kill him at all?"

"One of the oldest motives in the world—money. With Palsgrave out of the way, Caroline scooped the pot. She got grant money for her living history demonstrations. As for the sword, I suppose she thought of that as a kind of poetic justice. After all, it was a hand-and-a-half broadsword that was punched into that rock in Westford, Massachusetts, after Henry Sinclair lost one of his men."

"This is pretty convoluted reasoning," Gordon muttered, but to Liss's relief, he didn't dismiss it out of hand.

"Caroline must have been nearby when my father left Lincoln Hall. As soon as Palsgrave came back into his classroom, she killed him. Then she retreated through the art gallery, entered the theater, and went up the stairs to scenery storage loft number two, where she stashed the sword. She probably had extra clothes hidden there, so she could change into an outfit that wasn't stained with Palsgrave's blood."

Liss pictured Caroline in her mind. Almost every time she'd seen the professor, she'd been wearing a baggy tunic and slacks, both in neutral, unmemorable colors. She probably had a whole closetful of such interchangeable clothing. It would have been easy to substitute one nearly identical outfit for another.

"Leaving behind both the weapon and bloody clothes was a risk," Gordon said. "If Franklin had searched the entire building—"

"She was counting on the locked door to the art gallery to make him think only the classroom wing was in play. Did Detective Franklin even know that Palsgrave used that shortcut before I told him about it?"

"I don't think so. Someone screwed up," Gordon added. "The entire building should have been searched and cordoned off to keep people out, locked door or no." Then he sighed and ran a hand across the top of his short-cropped hair. "Damn budget cuts," he muttered.

"We need more manpower. And better lab facilities. And just about everything else."

"So," Penny said, picking up the story, "Caroline Halladay, in fresh clothing similar enough to what she had been wearing earlier that no one noticed the difference, returns to her office through the trapdoor and emerges from said office after the appropriate length of time for one of her regular half hour meditation sessions."

"Right. And that's just in time to send Willa Somener to look for Dr. Palsgrave," Liss agreed. "Then, once Caroline was certain that the police weren't watching the theater end of the building, she retrieved the sword and her clothes and headed for Moosetookalook. She could have put the sword into the trunk of my father's car at any time that night. He never remembers to lock it. I suppose she's long since destroyed the clothes."

"Even if Mac had locked his car, Caroline Halladay strikes me as the type who'd know how to jimmy open someone's trunk."

Liss sent Gordon a narrow-eyed look. "What am I missing?"

"Franklin had a feeling about her. Until now, though, we didn't have a clue how she might have managed to get out of her office to kill Palsgrave."

"Time to give Stan a call," Penny said, setting down her pen.

Franklin, Liss realized, had talked to Gordon, and Gordon had shared with Penny. Too bad no one had bothered to let her in on their thinking. She might have figured out what had really happened a whole lot sooner.

"What made Franklin suspicious?" she asked.

"The last call Leon Palsgrave received on his cell phone was from Caroline Halladay. She *said* she just contacted him to give him a heads-up that Mac was on his way to the classroom, but that made Franklin wonder why she thought such a warning was necessary."

Liss shook her head in wonderment. "If that's true, then it actually supports my father's story that no one was in the classroom when he arrived."

"A slip on her part. And, more importantly, it fills in a gap in the chain of events. I'll pass on this information to Stanley Franklin. He'll take it from here." Gordon swiveled around on the bench to give Liss a stern look. "And you, Liss MacCrimmon, about to be Liss Ruskin, are out of it. Go and get married."

"I had no intention of doing anything else!"

"Good."

He stood and Liss and Penny followed suit. They walked back toward the tents together.

Liss couldn't help glancing toward the blacksmith's shop. She gave a guilty start when she realized that Caroline Halladay was staring back at her. The other woman's eyes narrowed, then went wide.

"Oh, damn," Liss whispered.

Caroline flung the tongs she'd been using into the fire. Shoving her young apprentice aside, she fled the forge.

At Liss's side, Gordon stopped and stared. "We've been made. How?"

Penny looked up from stuffing the notes she'd taken into her fanny pack. "Shoot! She must have recognized me. Back when the games were going to be held at the fairgrounds, she met with me to talk about security for the conclave."

Neither Gordon nor Penny were in uniform, but that hadn't mattered. Caroline's guilty conscience had apparently been enough to make her jump to conclusions when she saw them with Liss. In this case, she'd been right to panic. They *were* on to her.

Gordon set off in pursuit. Penny followed a moment later. Liss stayed where she was. She'd done her part. She'd only be in the way if she tried to help.

A glance at her watch told her she'd better get a move on if she didn't want to be late for her own wedding. She sighted on the side entrance of the hotel and took the most direct route to get there . . . straight through the middle of the Medieval Scottish Conclave.

She could hear the glove maker's spiel as she passed the first tent. "Learn the mystery of a glover and whittawer," he urged a small audience gathered to watch him work. "We use softer white skins in contrast to tanners. Sheepskins, lambskins, and calfskins. We make gloves, purses, and other wares. Neat's leather is for shoes. Sheep's leather is for bridles. Horsehair makes bowstrings and we use calve's guts for fiddle strings. I make leather aprons, jerkins, and bottles. Cheveril or kid skin—that's from a goat, not a child—is soft and flexible and used for fine gloves."

Liss kept going, fixing her mind on the wedding gown waiting for her inside the hotel. She'd lost sight of Gordon and Penny. Caroline had long since disappeared. If she had a car parked nearby, she was already long gone.

They'd find her, Liss told herself. She'd be arrested and Detective Franklin would find proof she'd killed Lee Palsgrave. None of it was Liss's concern any longer.

The distinctive sounds of a sword fight in progress momentarily diverted her attention. She stopped to watch Kirby Redmond demonstrate the art of wielding a claymore. He held the huge bladed weapon generations of Scots had used in battle with an ease that belied its weight.

Liss was about to continue on when Caroline Halladay suddenly appeared. She popped out from behind a nearby tent and seized the claymore out of Kirby's hands.

Frozen to the spot, Liss watched the drama unfold before her. Gordon, unarmed, approached Caroline from her right. Penny, equally defenseless against the sword, came toward her from the opposite side.

Unaware of what was happening only a few feet away, the shoemaker began to lecture, increasing the unreality of the scene. "Black shoes are made of waxed calf. White shoes are made of tawed leather, prepared by soaking the raw skin in alum salts. Cream-colored or buff leather is made by tanning with fish oils. Red leather is from goat skin. It was called cordwain, and cordwainer was another name for a shoemaker."

"Back off," Caroline shouted.

Gordon and Penny kept coming.

Spectators were slow to realize the danger. Caroline was in medieval garb. At first glance, the standoff appeared to be part of a demonstration. Kirby, who did know that something was wrong, picked up a broadsword, but Caroline took no notice of him. Her head swiveled from side to side as she sought an escape route. Inevitably, her gaze fell on Liss.

"You!" she bellowed. "This is all your fault!"

Caroline Halladay charged toward Liss, the claymore raised to strike. Gordon's words flashed through her mind: *Palsgrave was hacked to death.*

Liss turned and ran.

Years of dance training gave Liss an advantage. She leapt over tent lines, swerved around a stack of handmade baskets, and sprinted toward the gazebo where her wedding was scheduled to be held in less than an hour. No guests had arrived yet. The only person in sight was Jake Murch.

Liss glanced over her shoulder. Caroline was hot on

her heels, the heavy sword swinging wildly as she pounded after her quarry. Behind her came Gordon and Penny, but they were too far back for Gordon to attempt a flying tackle. Nothing less seemed likely to bring Caroline down.

Liss took the three steps that led up into the gazebo in a single bound. Inside, she found exactly what she'd hoped to—proof that her mother had ignored her insistence that she did not want to add a handfasting ceremony to her wedding. All the necessary elements had been assembled: the broom, the anvil, the cords for tying her hands to Dan's . . . and the sword.

With a lunge, Liss grabbed the hilt of the weapon. It was a very nice reproduction broadsword, not unlike the one that had killed Professor Palsgrave. Her hands trembled, but she managed to lift the heavy weapon. She turned, praying she could hold Caroline off until Gordon caught up with them. He'd subdue Caroline, she told herself. He'd make an arrest. He would not allow his old friend Liss MacCrimmon to be stabbed, impaled, or hacked to death.

Sword awkwardly raised, she prepared to defend herself. She did *not* intend to die on her wedding day.

Caroline skidded to a halt at the foot of the stairs. She held her weapon in a menacing manner, as if she knew exactly how to use it. There was something not quite sane about the look in her eyes.

Liss did not dare take her gaze off Caroline to look for Gordon, but she listened hard, hoping for the sounds of imminent rescue. Instead, she heard Jake Murch's voice ring out, clear and cold: "Hold it right there, toots!"

Caroline whirled in his direction, claymore ready to strike down the newcomer. Murch, PI, stood a few feet away from her. The flap of the sporran he wore with his kilt was askew and he was holding the gun he had plainly been carrying inside. It was aimed straight at her heart.

Not Magnum, Liss thought, suddenly giddy with relief. Not Columbo. And not James Bond, either. Today, Murch was channeling Indiana Jones.

"I will shoot you," he said. "Without a qualm."

Liss believed him. So did Caroline. Slowly, she lowered the sword and placed it on the ground. All the fight seemed to have gone out of her by the time Gordon slapped handcuffs onto her wrists. Head bowed, shoulders slumped, she accompanied him toward the parking lot. In a low voice, he recited the Miranda warning as they went.

Murch and Penny followed them. Liss started to tag along . . . until she glanced at her watch and realized that she'd have to thank Jake Murch later.

Liss wore an assortment of summer flowers in her hair and carried multicolored orchids in a basket. Her gown fit like a dream. The skirt billowed out behind her—just a little—as she walked toward the friends and family standing in a circle around the gazebo. Her hand rested lightly on her father's arm.

Mac wore full Scottish dress. He was comfortable in it, which was more than could be said for the groom and his brother, waiting with the minister for the bride to arrive.

Liss had not told her parents everything that had happened earlier, but she had shared with them the news that there had been an arrest and that Mac was now completely cleared of suspicion in the murder of A. Leon Palsgrave. She'd had the pleasure of seeing her father's first genuine smile in weeks as he visibly relaxed.

While Liss had hurriedly dressed and combed the

tangles out of her hair, her mother had taken hastily written messages to Reverend Browne and to Dan and, a few minutes later, had brought back word that everyone would cooperate.

To Zara and Sherri, while they'd been dressing in the hotel room, Liss had given a whispered summary of the clues that had led to Caroline Halladay's downfall. She'd left out her own part in the final chase but gave Jake Murch full credit as the hero of the hour. Someday, after she returned from her honeymoon, she might tell them the whole story. Or not.

Right now all her attention was focused on Dan, waiting for her at the . . . anvil.

Parson Browne looked more resigned than disapproving. Liss concluded that he knew what had happened at the gazebo less than an hour earlier. Dan lifted quizzical eyebrows as she approached, then slanted his eyes toward the accoutrements of handfasting. She knew her note must have taken him by surprise, given how often she'd railed against the ancient ceremony, but the expression on his beloved face told her without words that he was willing to go along with whatever she wanted. When she joined him, he mouthed, "For you, anything."

They exchanged vows and rings just as they'd rehearsed, but afterward they shared a drink from the quaich, the traditional Scottish drinking cup. Then Vi came forward and loosely tied their hands together with silken cords. When she was done, the minister struck the anvil with a hammer to complete the handfasting. Only then did he go on to finish the regular wedding ceremony, pronouncing them man and wife and saying, "You may now kiss the bride."

Dan did so with enthusiasm, but he also took the opportunity to whisper in her ear, "Any more surprises?"

"Only one," she whispered back.

"I call for the *an sguab*," Vi said in a loud, clear voice as they turned, prepared to walk back to the hotel for the reception, "so that you may jump it and begin your life together."

Dan eyed the broom Vi held with some wariness. It was decorated with ribbons and flowers. He was even more taken aback when his new mother-in-law industriously began to sweep the steps of the gazebo and the ground in front of them. When she had completed this task to her satisfaction, she placed the broom on the grass.

In a more traditional handfasting, it would have been one of Liss's "handmaidens" wielding the broom, but somehow having her mother do the honors had seemed more appropriate. In some ceremonies, a groomsman placed a sword diagonally on top of the broom. Liss had remained adamant about omitting that part. She'd had quite enough of swords for one day. Besides, it was the broom that mattered most.

"You two are now one," Vi intoned in a solemn voice, although her face was wreathed in smiles, "for life and a day. Go forth together on your way. Jump the broom—the world's not so wide—hand in hand, and side by side."

"Uh, Liss—"

She lifted their bound hands until she could touch one finger to Dan's lips. "Too late, husband. The knot has been tied. You have no choice but to jump with me."

And so, he did.

Epilogue

"Well," Mac said, settling in on the sofa next to his wife. "That went well."

"It did. Our daughter made a beautiful bride."

Vi used the clicker to turn on the TV. Her husband took it away from her to channel surf. They'd already missed the eleven o'clock local news with its report on the capture of Caroline Halladay. Mac would have sailed right past the twenty-four-hour news channels had the words "body in baggage claim at Glasgow Airport" in the crawl not caught his attention. His expression grim, he backtracked, leaning forward to catch what few details were available.

"Oh, Lord! Is that where they're landing?" Vi was vibrating with tension.

"In Glasgow, yes, but not at Prestwick." He patted her hand reassuringly. "Liss and Dan are flying into Glasgow International."

Vi chuckled. "That's a relief. Although I don't know what I was worried about. Even if it had been the same airport, our newlyweds are still somewhere over the Atlantic. They couldn't possibly have found a way to get involved in another murder."

A Note from the Author

There really was a Henry Sinclair and he probably did explore the coast of Nova Scotia and New England about a hundred years before Columbus's famous 1492 "discovery" of America. For those who want to read more about it, I recommend *The Westford Knight and Henry Sinclair: Evidence of a 14th Century Scottish Voyage to North America,* by David Goudsward. Most of the theories Liss hears about concerning Sinclair and his reasons for coming to the New World are discussed in this book. Two—the story of a battle between Scots and Indians and the legend of a colony on an island off the coast of Maine—are figments of my imagination. All the characters and organizations Liss encounters are likewise my own inventions and do not represent any real persons or groups.

For readers who may wonder how July 25 managed to fall on a Saturday for Liss's wedding, the answer is simple. In Liss's world, time advances much more slowly than in real life. Her marriage takes place just two years after her return to Moosetookalook in *Kilt Dead*.

Liss MacCrimmon, newlywed and proud owner of Moosetookalok, Maine's Scottish Emporium, is thrilled to be organizing the rural town's Halloween fundraiser. And the abandoned Chadwick mansion will be the perfect *setting for a creepy old haunted house . . .*

A wee bit *too* perfect, perhaps. After all, the last owner was Blackie O'Hare, a notorious Boston hit man, so Liss knows those stories of buried victims and hidden loot may not be too far-fetched. And then there's the recent appearance of mysterious lights . . . and the unexplained moans and creaks . . . and, right where she left that fake skeleton, a very real-looking body with puncture-marks on the neck . . .

Gwen's cousin Ned? Who woulda kilt him, especially since he was supposed to be in prison? Was it really a vampire, recruiting another undead soul? Or maybe a more earthly being . . . like smarmy real estate agent Jason Graye, who gleefully spreads those haunted house stories so he can buy the once-bonny mansion for next-to-nothing? How about that out-of-town horror writer, who actually moved into the old mortuary?

Or . . . was Ned iced by one of his prison mates? Solving this creepy Halloween mystery is turning out to be harder than snapping a clear picture of Nessie. But Liss had better watch her back this time, because the killer—undead or not—is *much* closer than she thinks!

Please turn the page for an exciting sneak peek of the next Liss MacCrimmon Scottish Mystery VAMPIRES, BONES, AND TREACLE SCONES!

Chapter One

"**W**hat do you think?" Liss MacCrimmon Ruskin asked her husband. "Does that look like a haunted house or what?"

Standing beside her at the foot of a steep flight of concrete steps set into an overgrown terrace and flanked by a rusty iron railing, Dan stared up at the old Chadwick mansion with an assessing gaze. "High Victorian architecture. Peeling paint. Ivy run wild on one side of the building. Boarded-up windows. It has potential . . . *if* the structure is sound. The last thing you want is for someone to fall through rotting floorboards and end up with a broken neck."

Liss gave a theatrical shudder, although she was too much of an optimist to be seriously alarmed. The place would be perfect as part of Moosetookalook, Maine's Halloween festival and fundraiser. It already had the requisite unsavory reputation and its run-down appearance defined *spooky* to a T. Liss especially liked the round windows in the square tower. Lit from behind, they'd look like two glowing eyes.

"All our dead bodies will be department-store

manikins," she assured Dan. "That's why you're going
to go through the place today with a fine-tooth comb.
We'll have nearly a month and a half to repair any problems you find. If we can't fix something, we'll rope off
the problem area to keep the paying public out of danger."

"Uh-huh. As if that ever works. There's always some
bozo who takes a KEEP OUT sign as a challenge instead
of a warning."

Dan was unenthusiastic about his role as safety in-
spector. Liss couldn't blame him. He knew the "we" she
had designated to make repairs would consist of himself, aided and abetted by his brother Sam. If the house
didn't pass muster, the two of them would end up volun-
teering their labor, as well as donating building materials.
The Ruskins all had a strong sense of civic responsibility, and in this case, it was augmented by the fact that
Liss, Dan's bride of eight weeks and one day, had been
chosen by the Moosetookalook Small Business Associa-
tion to organize the festival.

"Let's go see how bad it is." Resigned to his fate, he
offered his hand and they started to climb.

By the time they mounted the porch steps, Liss was a
trifle out of breath. "Thank goodness this isn't the only
entrance to the house," she said with a laugh.

The driveway circled the mansion, leading to a small
parking area at the back. With the addition of a short
ramp, the kitchen door would also allow for handi-
capped access to the "haunted mansion."

Dan fitted the keys they'd been given into the locks.
The last owner had installed three, two of them dead-
bolts. "And we're in," he announced. The door creaked
ominously when he opened it.

Liss took that as a good sign. If all the other doors in

the place were as cooperative, she wouldn't need to use sound equipment to create the same effect. Eyes bright with anticipation, she stepped into the shadow-filled hallway.

There had not been electricity in the house for years. The only light came from the sun outside. It illuminated a rectangle of faded, flowered carpet runner and a swarm of dust motes.

Liss sneezed.

Dan reached into the pocket of his jeans and supplied her with a clean, white handkerchief before removing his backpack and using it to prop the door open. From the pack, he produced two heavy-duty flashlights and handed one to Liss. They turned them on, and she got her first good look at their immediate surroundings.

The hallway was long and narrow, ending in a closed door at the far end. *The kitchen*, she surmised. Two more closed doors flanked her. Before she could decide which one to open first, Dan's low whistle of appreciation distracted her. He had paused just inside the entrance to stare at a large, old-fashioned piece of furniture.

Liss had no idea what to call the object. *Coat rack* seemed inadequate to describe something that stood taller than Dan's six-foot-two. Maybe a hall tree? It had rows of three-inch pegs on either side of a three-quarter-length mirror and five drawers—two on each side and a single one at the center beneath the mirror.

"It's gorgeous," she said.

The streaked and dusty mirror reflected a dark and grainy image of the two of them. Dan's hair didn't show up as sand-colored, but rather a light gray. Her own dark brown locks looked muddy. Her eyes, which ranged from blue to green depending on what she was wearing, appeared in the glass to be murky brown. So did Dan's, although in reality they were the color of molasses. The illusion was nicely eerie, making it seem as if they'd aged several decades in the last few minutes.

"I think I'll keep this just the way it is," Liss murmured. "Being scared by your own reflection is a great way to start a haunted house tour."

Dan wasn't listening. He reached out to run one hand over the smooth wood. "A real craftsman built this."

"It takes one to know one," she said. In addition to his job at Ruskin Construction, Dan was a custom woodworker.

He glanced into the mirror, caught sight of something behind them, and turned to shine the beam of his flashlight on the staircase that curved gently upward from the first floor to the second. "And there's another work of art."

In places, the steps were coated in a layer of dirt thick enough to plant flowers in, but when Dan wiped off a small section on the lowest tread, Liss could make out the gleam of dark, glossy wood beneath the grime.

"Walnut," he said. "Expensive even way back when this place was built."

"To hear the old-timers tell it, the Chadwicks had more money than God. They could afford the best."

"Damned shame the house has been let go like this."

"The family died out." She shrugged. "And the last of them made the mistake of marrying Blackie O'Hare. But sad as it is, all that history makes this place ideal for our haunted house."

"Blackie" O'Hare, notorious gangster and hit man, had come into possession of the mansion through his wife, Alison Chadwick, the granddaughter and only heir of the last family members to actually live in the place year round. The old couple had died before Liss was born, so she'd never known them. Their childless granddaughter's death had followed not long after her marriage to Blackie, who might or might not have later used the mansion as a hideout when things got too hot for him in Boston. Many fanciful stories had sprung up over the years. One had Blackie burying treasure on the property. Another said it wasn't loot but rather dead bodies that he'd hidden in the wooded area surrounding the house. One rumor even claimed he'd murdered Alison and buried her in the basement.

What *was* certain was that Blackie's crimes had eventually caught up with him. He'd been arrested for murder, tried, convicted, and sentenced to life in prison in Massachusetts. During the investigation, a task force had been sent to Moosetookalook to search the mansion and its grounds. They'd hoped to turn up more evidence to use against him, but they'd found neither loot nor bodies. That hadn't stopped the locals from speculating. After all, those out-of-staters might well have missed something. Everyone in Maine knew folks from Massachusetts weren't too bright. Just look at the way they drove their cars!

Blackie had died in prison, stabbed to death by another prisoner. Afterward, no heirs having materialized, the town of Moosetookalook eventually seized the property for back taxes. The housing market being what it was, they'd been stuck with the place ever since.

It hadn't taken much effort on Liss's part to persuade the board of selectmen to let her use the Chadwick mansion for a municipal fundraising effort. Their only condition had been dictated by the liability insurance that covered the town—the house had to pass a safety inspection first.

With that in mind, Liss fished a lined five-by-seven tablet and felt-tip pen out of Dan's backpack. She'd come prepared to spend the next few hours trailing after him as he checked the place out, noting down everything that needed to be fixed. If there was one thing at which Liss excelled, it was making lists.

They started at the top of the house, climbing to the third floor and then up a steep flight of steps—more like a ladder than stairs—to reach the tower Liss had admired from below. The room at the top was smaller than she'd expected and unfurnished.

"Lights in the windows, yes," Dan said. "Anything else, no. Those stairs are too narrow for safety."

Liss took a moment to admire the view. The leaves had just begun to turn. Spots of brilliant orange, red, and yellow stood out in sharp contrast to the dark greens of balsam, pine, and spruce.

"Five heavily wooded acres," Dan said. "It's a nice piece of property. I'm surprised it hasn't sold."

The trees made an impressive barrier between the house and its neighbors. A long, winding driveway provided yet another layer of isolation. It led to a little-used rural road a quarter mile distant.

The Chadwicks had liked their privacy, and yet the mansion was not all that far from the center of town. From this vantage point, Liss could pick out the top of the memorial to the Civil War dead in the town square and the steeple of the Congregational church beyond. Those were, however, the only visible signs of civilization. If she'd been looking from her own front porch toward the mansion, she wouldn't have known the house was there at all.

The third floor would have been called an attic in most houses. In the Chadwick mansion it was broken up into three bedrooms. They were bare and cheerless with low, sloped ceilings and no heat. Servants' quarters, Liss supposed, back when people could afford live-in help.

The second story also contained three bedrooms, but

those were larger and crammed full of furniture. Upon entering each new room, Liss gave a cautious sniff. They all smelled musty—they'd been closed up for a long while—but she detected no hint of mold or mildew. Everywhere they walked, they left footprints in the dust and Liss had to duck more than one cobweb. While Dan did his safety checks, Liss poked around.

Drop cloths protected the contents in one room. In the others, the clutter had been left exposed. There seemed little rhyme or reason in the way items had been deposited. In the second room, two chairs with broken legs shared space with an exquisitely carved bedstead and highboy. Empty picture frames and an old steamer trunk were tucked into the third room between a four-poster and an old-fashioned standing wardrobe, but what instantly caught Liss's attention was the moth-eaten moose head mounted on one wall.

"Yuck," she muttered. "Imagine waking up to the sight of that monstrosity every morning!"

Liss didn't know much about antiques, but some of the furniture and a number of the decorative accessories looked old enough to be valuable. She picked up a lamp in the shape of an owl—brown glass fitted over a bulb. She supposed it was meant to be a night light. The words *art deco* floated through her mind, but she wasn't sure they applied to this piece. Still, it was certainly unusual and therefore collectible. She was surprised the town selectmen hadn't auctioned off the contents of the mansion to defray expenses.

"So far so good," Dan announced. "Ready to go back downstairs?"

"More than ready." She put the lamp back where she'd found it and wiped her fingers on the sides of her jeans to get rid of the grime it had left behind.

Back on the first floor, Dan suggested they start with

the kitchen and work their way forward to the front door. Liss half expected to find a nineteenth-century wood stove taking pride of place. Instead, she walked into a scene out of an old black-and-white TV sitcom. It would have been more tolerable *without* color. The cabinets were bright yellow. All the appliances were a sickly avocado green. The dinette set tucked into a corner had chrome legs, a laminate top on the table, and chair seats upholstered in yellow vinyl. The radio on the Formica countertop was big and clunky and made of the same hard black material as the rotary-dial telephone sitting next to it.

"I wonder what Blackie O'Hare thought of this," Liss murmured.

"Hey, this was ultra-modern back in the fifties! The Victorian décor in the rest of the house probably made him more uncomfortable. Assuming, of course, that he ever lived here." Dan crossed the room to examine the back door and the small porch beyond. "Shouldn't be too hard to build a ramp."

"Good."

Liss left him in the kitchen while she began to explore the adjoining formal dining room. Wallpaper had once covered the ceiling, but it had begun to peel away and hung in ragged swaths above a massive sideboard and an equally oversized table and chairs. Liss liked the effect and made a note on her to-do list. She was visualizing an ultra-spooky set piece for the room when Dan called out to her that he was going down cellar.

"Let me know if you find Blackie's cache of cash!" she called after him.

His voice was muffled as he descended the stairs to the basement. "If I find buried treasure, you'll be the first to know."

Liss barely registered his answer. Her flashlight beam

had come to rest on a painting that hung above the side-board. Although it was partially obscured by the tattered ceiling paper, she recognized the subject at once. It was a rather famous portrait in Scottish circles—a likeness of the piper of Clan Grant. She had always thought it was an ugly piece. It had been painted, if she remembered right, in the seventeenth or early eighteenth century by a rather mediocre artist. This was a reproduction, of course, but its presence hinted that the Chadwicks had Scottish ancestors. She resolved to find out more when she had the time. Her day job as proprietor of Moosetookalook Scottish Emporium made it good business to make connections to all things Scottish within the local community.

When Dan reappeared, cobwebs caught in his hair and a fresh smudge on one sleeve, they left the dining room by way of the door to the hall. "Back room or front room?"

"Back, then front," Liss decided. "Anything of interest in the cellar?"

"Damp and dirt. I don't recommend letting paying customers go down there."

The back room was a library, although books were outnumbered by knickknacks on the floor-to-ceiling shelves that took up the inner walls. "Hoard much?" Liss murmured.

"The Chadwicks appear to have collected more than their fair share of what the Victorians called curios."

The baubles were displayed on pedestals and tables as well as on the shelves. The walls between boarded-up windows were hung with dozens of framed pictures in all sizes and shapes, so many that the pattern on the flocked wallpaper behind them was all but obscured.

Closed pocket doors led into the front room. Liss supposed that would have been called the parlor back in the day. Another door, also closed, was located directly opposite the one that led to the hall.

"What do you suppose is in here?" Without waiting for Dan to answer, she reached for the doorknob and shone her flashlight into the gloomy interior, expecting more furniture or the ghostly effect of dust covers. Instead, dozens of pairs of eyes stared back at her. A sound embarrassingly like an "eek" escaped before she could stop it and she backed up at warp speed, slamming into Dan's chest.

He grunted and caught her.

A second later, she felt him freeze as he looked past her into the room and saw what she had seen.

"What the—?"

Nothing attacked. No sound issued from the darkness beyond the door. After a moment, common sense returned, and Dan's flashlight beam steadied to reveal that the eyes belonged to a flock of stuffed birds.

"Creepy," Liss muttered, disgusted with herself for having been frightened.

She ventured deeper into what she decided to call the conservatory. Represented were a variety of species. Some stood on pedestals while others were suspended from the ceiling. The room also contained a grand piano with a stuffed pheasant perched on top of it.

"Mr. Chadwick's little hobby, I presume," said Dan.

"Good. This is good." Liss heard the tremor in her voice and ignored it, just as she was ignoring the amused note that had come into Dan's. "Nice and scary. We won't change a thing."

She retreated with more haste than grace, opened the pocket doors, and entered the front room. It *was* a parlor. At least, it contained a parlor organ, together with a sofa and two chairs—one straight backed and one wing—and a couple of end tables. There was also considerable evidence that they were not the first visitors to this particular room. A layer of debris covered the floor, mostly fast food wrappers, empty beer cans, and cigarette butts.

"Teenagers?"

"That would be my guess," Dan agreed. "The house has been standing empty for a long time."

"Looks like they stuck to this one room."

A picture window would have looked out onto the porch if it hadn't been boarded over, but a few shafts of sunlight still managed to make their way in through knotholes and a long crack in a sheet of warped and weathered plywood. That was enough to reveal that one of the sofa cushions had a cigarette burn in its brocade upholstery.

"It's a miracle they didn't burn the place down."

Holding the notepad so he could see the words, Liss wrote *install new lock on back door.*

"That'll help," he agreed.

"So what's the verdict? Is this our haunted house?"

"The whole place is remarkably sound for having been shut up for so long. I didn't find anything that raised a red flag."

Liss pumped her hand in the air. "Yes!"

"But you've got your work cut out for you."

She followed his gaze to the litter on the floor. "This isn't so bad. A thorough sweeping will get rid of the mouse droppings and trash. Then we can pretty much leave the rest of this room as it is. I mean, just look at that chandelier." Suspended from the high ceiling, it was festooned with cobwebs. "Half my decorating is already done if I just keep the lighting fixtures and the peeling wallpaper the way they are."

"So the spiders get to live long and prosper, do they?" Dan slung an arm around her shoulders and joined her in regarding the elaborate glass chandelier above their heads.

Liss leaned back against him, redirecting her gaze from light fixture to husband. He was five inches taller than she, and years of construction work had left him with well-toned muscles and excellent upper body strength. She snuggled closer. At five-foot-nine she wasn't exactly tiny, but Dan was big enough to make her feel delicate and feminine.

"I've got you to protect me, right?" She batted her eyelashes at him and grinned.

He chuckled. "I'd like to see the spider you couldn't handle all by your lonesome."

Liss was about to thank him for the compliment when she heard a whisper of sound from directly above her head. She glanced up in time to catch sight of something that was *not* a cobweb. It was not a piece of twine, either. It twitched. Then it disappeared, only to be replaced by a pair of close-set, predatory eyes—eyes that were *not* made of glass.

She was not particularly fanciful, nor was she squeamish, but the sound of little clawed feet moving over glass pendants gave her the willies. She darted sideways, dragging Dan after her, just as fine particles of dust drifted down over the spot where they had been standing.

"I can handle spiders and mice, but *that* was a rat!"

Since they had already retreated as far as the door to the hallway, Liss kept going. She didn't stop until she was safely outside on the porch. Dan followed more slowly. If he was amused by her sudden panic, he was smart enough not to show it.

"I'll take care of the rodent problem," he promised as he locked the door.

Liss rewarded him with a quick but heartfelt kiss.

By the time they were back in Dan's truck and heading for home, Liss was already adding items to her to-do list. First and foremost, the other members on her committee needed to see the Chadwick mansion for themselves, and the sooner the better. They had a lot to accomplish in just a few weeks. The haunted house, for all that it would be the centerpiece of the event, was only one of the attractions planned for the Moosetookalook All Hallows Festival.